DEDICATION

In Loving Memory of Emily Rose. Born too soon, loved for a lifetime.

For my 'Gorgeous Girl' Megan

Words cannot express how much I love you. My 'miracle angel here on earth'

For my very own 'Cadog'

Thank you for all your love, support and belief in me

Special mention to my nephew, Jake Rees

Thank you for all your help, hard work and above all,

patience, in making the book cover and publishing

possible.

I would also like to dedicate this book to all 'Angel Parents' and their families. We walk this path together, in strength, hope and love.

CHAPTER ONE

If he drops one more bloody box! Mr. 'Strong man with a van' had actually turned into Mr. 'Coffin Dodger Nearly Dead' with a van that resembled a skip on wheels. But what could I do after finding out what really happens when the brown smelly stuff hits the fan at a rapid rate of knots. The man who I'd invested time, effort, love and above all, patience, had surpassed himself. Instead of his usual falling through open doors after a drunken Saturday night downing fifteen cans and acting like a twat, this time he'd fallen over as usual, unfortunately landing dick first into some trollop who resembled a cow's arse. That kind of carelessness went beyond the limits of even my patience and forgiveness and unsurprisingly, it was time to wise up. My only regret was smashing my favourite vase against the wall after narrowly missing his head. I was going to really miss that vase. One less thing for me to pack anyway. I needed to get as far away as possible. So, here I was, stuck with a doddery old fart who had delusions of grandeur when it came to advertising, alongside his sidekick who was quite frankly a drip that hadn't dropped, trying to save the rest of the battered remains of my life from being shoved, dropped and kicked through the front door of my newly rented home. To say I was relieved when he'd finally finished without dropping dead was an understatement. Now what was I going to do? Sitting on my sofa surrounded by chaos, it finally hit me like a smack on the head with a crow bar. Gut wrenching sobs rushed up from the pit of my stomach and before I could stop it, I was wailing like a possessed banshee. A tsunami of tears cascaded down my face, a torrent of water so strong, it would've appeared on thousands of Facebook newsfeeds within seconds of the news story hitting. I did wonder if a snotty selfie would've added weight but that was just pushing it. The explosion of emotion had been bubbling up all day, for weeks in fact. I may have put a brave face on things but deep down, I was hurting badly. Looking back, it may not have been the most loving of relationships but it had its moments, in between the drunken abuse, he had been quite charming. My sensitive little soldier ego had been stamped on the night he betrayed me and that's what I needed to remember now. It was time to put my pride in my pocket, dig that little bit deeper and embrace new beginnings. And that new beginning was going to start right now, in Mynydd Eira. So, who am I, I hear you ask? You joined my pity party, maybe even have been tempted to pass me a tissue.

My name is Rosie. I was born thirty something years ago, in a small village in the heart of rural Bedfordshire. The youngest child of an ordinary couple, living an ordinary life. I left home aged twenty, after marrying far too young. The marriage lasted longer than it should have. After a happy childhood, my life began to change once I hit my teens. My mother's attitude towards me changed. Nothing I ever seemed to do was good enough for her where my older brother was the apple of her eye and could do no wrong. I craved acceptance and affection from a mother I loved but never received and I always thought it was my fault, that I was useless and unlovable. Narcissism wasn't something I knew about then but the heartbreaking reality became clearer later. I had a close bond with my father, who I adored and I found normality in his company, he always had encouraging and supportive words and I was so much like him in personality. He was my safe haven. But I needed more. So, when, aged seventeen, I met an older man who at first showed me the love and affection I craved, I threw myself into a relationship. I was too young and stupid to see the warning signs. We married and moved away. The abuse started on our honeymoon. I'd left one narcissist for another but it wasn't just emotional abuse, it eventually turned into physical abuse. Having a

3

new ironing board thrown at me because I couldn't work out how to fold it up. Being slammed into walls because I looked at him the wrong way. Having him put his hands around my throat because I asked him for something. Then he started humiliating me in public, 'touting' my 'services' to strangers in pubs, telling any man who happened to be in ear shot that they could spend the night with me for money. Luckily no one took him seriously. My body and mind were being destroyed by cruelty and violence. I'd endured three traumatic miscarriages, each baby passing away within the first trimester. Each miscarriage caused by abuse. My family just told me that it was just nature's way but I knew the reasons why my beloved babies hadn't made it into the world. I tried telling my mother what was happening only to be told that it must've been something I was doing to deserve it. I'd tried to leave once before, only for my husband to manipulate my parents into thinking it was my fault, yet again. It didn't take much for my mother to believe him and my father believed what he was told to believe by my mother. My bond with my father was slowly being chipped away by a woman who was supposed to love me. I'd found refuge at a friend's house but my safety wasn't to last. My mother sent my father and brother to find me and said if I didn't return home to my husband, they would disown me. Being young and emotionally worn out, I allowed myself to be blackmailed into going home. The last year of my marriage was the worst as my parents had given my husband free rein to step up the abuse, although my mother always denied she knew what was going on. Finally, after a friend gave me a stark warning that I could either leave my husband by walking through the door or be carried out in a box, I summoned up all the courage I could and I left my marriage. I left with nothing, my mother disgusted at me for 'giving up on marriage'. It wasn't a marriage, it was a death sentence, one of which I'd finally found courage to escape. I was never good enough for her anyway so being the first divorcee in the family was just another string to my bow of being a disappointment. I ran as far away as I could.

I found myself over the Severn Bridge and settling in South Wales. I fell in love with the stunning landscapes and the locals seemed friendly. They didn't drop kick me back over the bridge so I must've been doing something right. Even after yet another disastrous relationship with yet another abusive idiot, I hadn't been tempted to go back to England, I just needed to drift to another mountain and another valley.

CHAPTER TWO

'd never heard of Mynyndd Eira before. In fact, ending up here had been purely accidental or pure luck, depending on how you look at it. After trawling through pages of houses for rent and wondering which body part I was going to have to sell to raise the bond and rent money, I suddenly saw, nestled in between the other adverts, a small five sentence advert for a two-bedroom cottage, in the small but picturesque village of Mynyndd Eira. The rent was in my budget, I'd googled the location but nothing of any consequence came up but what the hell. The strange thing about it was when I contacted the landlord, he sounded like he had been expecting my call. I mean of course he was expecting potential tenants to call but he sounded like he had been waiting for me in particular. My tenancy was provisionally agreed within minutes, he assured me it was the perfect place to settle down and start again and if I liked the cottage after seeing it, it was mine to move into immediately. He would even waiver the bond as he 'trusted' me to look after the place. Weird but I wasn't going to argue! So after packing up what was rightfully mine plus sneaking out a telly that hadn't been but he owed me something so bollocks to the nob, I was here. It was getting late but my tummy had started to remind me that all I'd eaten during the debacle of the move, was half a packet of chocolate Hobnobs that I'd swiped from the back of the cupboard on my way out. God knows how long they'd been there but after snaffling the spare telly, I didn't think he was going to miss them, it would probably take him six weeks to realise the telly was gone. It was time to venture out and find out what exactly was so lovely about Mynydd

Eira, although I'd be just grateful for a ham sandwich. Looking in the mirror, I shuddered at the first impressions I was going to make on any locals I encountered but as I was going to be here for a while, I doubt it would be the last time they see me looking like I'd been dragged through a hedge. Stepping out of the front door of a home I was going to be alone in felt daunting but strangely empowering for a second. In front of the house were open fields and I could see the two rather large horses who, after watching the entire farce of the day were probably glad that peace had been restored. They watched me with curiosity as I started to wander down the path towards civilization. Well, I say civilization, Mynydd Eira consisted of a Post Office, a small shop, which I seriously hoped was well stocked with chocolate otherwise I was going to be miffed. And then there was the jewel in the crown of the village. It was the oldest, most beautiful stone building I'd ever seen. Surrounded by a cobbled courtyard, trees and well-tended planters, my first encounter with 'The Snow Mountain Inn' had been a pleasant surprise. Because of previous experiences of public houses where all I'd done was try to stop a binge drinking boyfriend from peeing on the front steps, I wasn't really much for pubs. But this seemed different somehow and I couldn't think why. But my appreciation of historic architecture was going to have to wait a while as my tummy was still protesting and I really needed to stop it before the neighbours started complaining about the noise. Luckily, the village shop was still open, which surprised me. Obviously, no matter how small the village was, there was always going to be someone like myself who would sell their own granny for chocolate after teatime. My needs were slightly greater than a family sized bar of fruit and nut so I was really hoping that they had at least a pasty still in date in their fridge. As I pushed the door open, a tinkling of a bell heralded my arrival. I was suddenly transported back in time to days of my childhood, the inside reminded me of my home village shop, where sweets were stored in huge jars on shelves behind the counter and poured into large deep curved metal scales before being skillfully transferred into small paper bags and handed over to beaming children, happy that their good behaviour had been rewarded. The shop even smelt the same. A small elderly lady in a green pinafore looked up from where she was standing behind the counter and smiled.

' Oh, hello there! You must be the young lady who's just moved into Mr. Evans' cottage today. Welcome to Mynydd Eira, my name's Gwen'

Blimey, I must've been the cause of some excitement within the everyday sleepiness by the way she greeted me with such enthusiasm. It was a relief to be honest, I half expected to be viewed with some suspicion. Finding myself relaxing slightly after the trepidation of meeting my first inhabitant, I found myself extending my hand, which she shook with a firm friendly grip and we both stood there for a brief moment smiling at each other before we both pulled our hand gently away. She gestured to me to have a look around, offering any help if I didn't find what I was looking for. Sadly, it looked like my mission to find any kind of substantial sustenance was going to be a futile one. It did look like a varied selection of sandwiches and other tasty treats were for sale but only if you got up at sparrows fart to get them before they all went. The fridge shelves were empty. Seeing my shoulders drop from where she was standing, Gwen called me over to the counter.

' Oh my lovely, you must be starving after the day you've had. I'm so sorry but we do tend to sell out of fresh sandwiches by mid afternoon and we're not big enough to have a freezer in here as you can see.'

I smiled a weak smile and went to pick up a packet of crisps and a chocolate bar from the shelves behind me when she exclaimed

' Oh that will never do you til the morning!' then she gestured for me to stay where I was for a moment and went to use her phone. As quick as she had disappeared, she was back, looking rather pleased with herself.

' Right then, I've just spoken to Nick and Sue who own the pub next door. Lovely couple they are, been in the village for years. They are still serving food and they are keen to meet our newest neighbour so you get yourself over there and get yourself a decent meal. And don't worry about paying for it tonight, we're a trusting bunch and they're happy for you to pay when you're settled'

I stood there for moment, slightly overwhelmed by the kindness I'd been shown in only a few brief minutes. I hadn't been used to such behaviour in a long time and I'd forgotten how to react. Pulling myself together to remember my manners, I thanked Gwen for all her help and smiled as I turned to leave.

' It's good to have you here Rosie', she softly whispered as I walked through the door'

I don't remember even telling her my name....

CHAPTER THREE

Standing outside the pub, that familiar feeling in the pit of my stomach was starting again and it wasn't just the hunger. I should've felt a bit more relaxed after the friendly welcome and act of kindness that Gwen had shown me a few moments earlier but that didn't stop the nervous churning. This was the worst part of moving to a new place, the not knowing what was waiting for me behind each new door. Pulling myself up to my full height of four foot ten and giving my long dark cherry red hair a quick smooth over, I took a deep breath and pushed the heavy wooden door open and stepped over the threshold into the unknown.

It was like being transported back through time. I'd been in old pubs before but this was something else. The bar area was warm and cosy, thanks to the biggest open fire I'd ever seen in my life. The smell of burning logs filled the air and the gleaming brasses that adorned the walls twinkled in the glow of the crackling flames. Scented candles flickered on the shelf above the fireplace, mixing delicate aromas with the swirling smoke. I walked across the stone floor towards the bar, feeling slightly exposed as I did so, although there wasn't any customers there. It was deserted but I suppose it was early yet for any locals to be out for their evening pint, but late enough to wonder why no one was out. I guess things were different in a sleepy village, there was no need to be propping up the bar from opening to closing time, preferring to spend that transitional time from day to night with their families before having a quiet hour to themselves. Suddenly a door opened from behind the bar making me jump slightly and a couple, who I assumed to be the landlord and landlady appeared, both seemingly falling over themselves to be the first one to greet me.

' Hello there!' they both said in unison, ' you must be our newest neighbour that Gwen phoned us about! Welcome to our little pub, please make yourself at home', gesturing to the table by the fire.

Again, another warm and friendly welcome, making my brief colly wobble outside seem a bit silly. I pulled out the chair nearest to the fire, feeling its warmth flooding through me, making my cheeks flush, although I wasn't entirely sure it was just down to the fire. I still had the tendency to light up like a glow stick when meeting new people, that shyness from childhood that never really left me. Picking up the small menu that had been placed on each table, I perused the meals on offer, wondering if I should just skip the main meals and go straight for the pudding! It had been a day and a half and the thought of disappearing into a big slice of hot chocolate fudge cake was getting stronger. Just as my chocolate monster was beginning to win, the landlady came over and sat down across the table. Her short highlighted blonde bob framed her small face and although she was the wrong side of middle age, I could tell genetics had been very kind. Her skin was flawlessly smooth and even from behind her glasses, only a hint of fine lines were visible. Obviously village life suited her.

'Right then my lovely, first things first, I'm Sue' she smiled with her eyes as she extended her hand towards mine as I returned the pleasantries. 'You looked like a frightened little rabbit when you walked in, there's no need as we'll look after you! Anything you need, you just ask. Now, what can I get you to eat and drink?'

I didn't think going straight for the fudge cake would make a very good impression of my dietary habits so I ordered Scampi and chips and a diet coke and Sue left me alone again with my thoughts. The warmth of the fire was making me feel like curling up into a ball and falling asleep. God I was tired. I couldn't wait to get into my bed later. Luckily, I'd been organised for a change and it was all set up ready for me to fall into. Suddenly, out of the corner of my eye, I saw what looked like a shadow of a person sitting across the room. I blinked and looked again but obviously no one had come in. I was more tired than I thought and my eyes were playing tricks on me. My bed seemed more important than food suddenly but I couldn't be rude. Just as my eyes were closing, Sue came back holding a tray with a big plate of golden scampi, chips and peas and a tall glass of iced diet coke. Wow that smelt good! As she placed the plate, drink and cutlery on the table, I looked at her with a grateful smile and thanked her as I started eating. I couldn't remember when I last had a decent meal. Everything had been so up in the air; my appetite had been somewhat sporadic. It didn't take me long before I'd finished and I sat back in my chair with a contented sigh.

' Well it looked like you needed that!' exclaimed Sue, ' now, what do you fancy for dessert? We do a lovely warm chocolate fudge cake with thick cream if you fancy it?'

Dear God, this woman was a mind reader! Sue chuckled and nodded to herself as she cleared away the plates, as if someone had just said something funny. I guess everyone had their quirks. Within minutes she was back with the biggest slice of gorgeousness I'd seen in a long time. I was wondering if everyone had the same standard of service or whether I was being slightly spoiled as they had taken pity on me. I really didn't care as I dived practically head first into heaven. My chocolate monster was definitely going to be tamed after this. Well, for a while at least. Finally, my meal was over. I sat back in my chair, the buttons on my jeans were threatening to explode. Thankfully no one else was sitting across the room as they would probably have their eye taken out if that actually happened! Sue and Nick were talking together behind the bar. I hadn't really said much at all since arriving, I think I still felt a bit overwhelmed by everything. However, a full tummy, my aching muscles relaxed by the warmth of the fire, I got up and sat on the bar stool. They both stopped talking and smiled.

' I want thank you both for the lovely meal and for being so kind'

There, I said something finally, ice broken.

' Oh you are welcome my lovely! You don't look quite so frazzled as you did when you first came in' Sue chuckled, eyes smiling at me again. Crap, I must've looked rough if she said I looked better! I had planned to eat and run when I first arrived, partly due to being utterly exhausted by the day's events and mostly because I felt slightly uncomfortable being in a pub on my own. However, strangely enough, I hadn't felt on my own. Even though I had been the only customer in there at the time, I hadn't quite shaken the feeling of being watched. The ambience of the small cosy room, the friendliness of Sue and Nick had however calmed the nerves that were holding me back in the beginning and I had put the watched feeling down to just being completely and utterly drained. After spending another hour chatting and laughing, I decided that I really needed my bed. It had been an unplanned but enjoyable evening and my first impressions of Mynydd Eira had been boosted. Although the offer of paying another time was still there, I felt uneasy taking advantage of such generosity and kindness so I settled up and got down from the stool and walked towards the door. Suddenly, I felt a coldness go right through me, which was strange considering the fire was roaring in the hearth a few steps away. Nick and Sue looked over from across the bar with a sudden look of concern then their faces relaxed and they both smiled at me, bidding me goodnight. As I turned to say goodnight, I looked over towards the table where I'd been sitting and for a split second, I swear someone was sitting in my chair.

Where the hell was I? Oh yeah, my new house, stupid. The bedroom was bathed in bright sunlight, making me squint as my eyes adjusted. I was so tired last night, I'd forgotten to close the blinds. I picked up my mobile that I'd placed on the floor next to the bed and looked at the time. I had to look twice, nine thirty am, I had slept for a monumental twelve hours! I hadn't slept that long in years! I really didn't want to move but my bladder was telling me otherwise. I could leave it another five minutes but if I sneezed, it would be game over! I turned over and snuggled into the duvet, I could risk it for another five minutes surely, my pelvic floor wasn't that shot just yet. Oh bugger it, I had to move, I had far too much to do today and lying in bed, as tempting as it was, wasn't going to sort the chaos that was waiting for me downstairs. Looking around the bedroom, it wasn't exactly much better but it was going to have to wait. Pulling the duvet off, I felt a chill hit my bare legs. I was really going to have to find my pjs before tonight, looking at the piles of black bin bags dumped in the corner, containing all my clothes and probably other crap I'd shoved in there at the time. Pulling on my jeans, I grabbed the hoodie I was wearing last night and bolted to the bathroom before it really was too late. The neutrally tiled bathroom was small but clean and functional with a bath and a shower. The landlord had obviously taken pride in keeping his house up to rental standard and for that, I was grateful. I'd lived in some right dives after my marriage ended and there's nothing worse than trying to start over in a place you didn't want to be.

I padded down the beige carpeted stairs and headed for the kitchen. Standing in the doorway, I looked at the boxes piled up on the kitchen table and prayed that the kettle was there somewhere. I'd been lucky enough to find a place that white goods and a cooker had been included, which was just as well as I'd lost the battle with the ex over the washing machine and tumble dryer. That was the main reason I'd swiped the telly, he wasn't going to have it all his own way. Rummaging through the top box, my heart leapt as I found the kettle. Small things mattered in the first days of starting over. As well as the Hobnobs, I'd had the sense to grab basics out of the cupboards, small comforts that would keep me going until I had chance to stock up.

After making my first coffee, on the first morning in my new home, I walked into the living room and let out a big sigh. In the cold light of day, it looked more chaotic than it had last night. I sat on my sofa and looked around, mentally making plans of what needed to be done. I drained the final drops of coffee and started going through each box in turn. It's funny, you pack everything up and know what possessions you have yet when you move and look in the boxes you'd packed, it was like you'd never seen the stuff before. Two purple table lamps, an array of vases, a few pictures, some framed photos and a huge collection of fairy ornaments made up the majority of my worldly possessions, along with a mahogany veneered wall unit, a battered sofa that had seen better days but was extremely comfortable, a pine coffee table, a tv unit and of course, the stolen telly. Luckily, I had the old fart of a removal man manoeuvre the wall unit in place so all I needed to do was unwrap all the ornaments and put them away safe. I did unfortunately suffer from the occasional bouts of clumsytwatitis so the sooner I had them out of harm's way the better.

After an hour of unwrapping ornaments, the living room resembled Christmas morning but instead of brightly coloured paper, the paper mountain consisted of cheap and tacky tabloids. Luckily the landlord had left information on the black bin and recycling schedules so at least I didn't have the worry of feeling like an idiot asking neighbours when the bins went out. Again, it was the little things that made life easier in the early days. Now the wall unit was looking less forlorn and unloved, I made a start on the pictures and photos. I reached into a box and pulled out a pile of photo frames and just stared at them. Happier times stared back at me. I could feel a lump start to form in my throat as I stared into the face that betrayed me. Tears started to bite and I sat down on the sofa holding history in my hands. Suddenly, my mobile beeped, signally the arrival of a text message. Tapping on the screen, my heart stopped for a second. It was from ' him'.

' where's the telly from the bedroom!'

Bloody hell, he'd surprised me! I was half expecting a snotogram next week but not today! Now the dilemma, whether to text him back and risk the start of a text battle and stir up emotions that I didn't have the energy for or ignore him and block his number for good. As I was mulling it over, another text message beeped its arrival.

' Give it back bitch or I'll find you and get it back myself!'

Oh, you bloody think, so do you? I found my hackles rising and instead of the tears of missing happier times, my face started to flush in anger. Decision made! Blocking his number and deleting him out of my life for good was the best decision to take. If I had any chance of moving on, he had to go completely and the threat he'd made had brought me to my senses. Any lingering romantic longings had been squashed in one sentence. I really wanted to text back and give him one last rant but it wouldn't have achieved anything. I needed a break. Grabbing my keys, a walk around the village was in order to clear my head. It was getting towards lunchtime anyway so maybe popping into the shop to see Gwen and to see if any of those elusive sandwiches were still left was the best way of stopping the day from turning to shit.

The horses across the road came trotting over to the fence as I shut the front door. I wasn't really a 'horsey' person, they frightened me a bit with their sheer size and me being the height of an average ten-year-old didn't really help either. I'd been on a horse only once when I was younger and the whole experience had scared the living crap out of me. Wouldn't have been so bad if the damn thing hadn't moved! I walked over to the fence and they both came over. I plucked up courage, reached out and gave each one a gentle stroke before making my way towards the shop. Unsurprisingly, there were a few people about the village and as I walked past, they smiled and said hello. It wasn't just a one-off last night then, the locals did seem friendly and my over imaginative fears of being strung up at dawn for being an outsider were clearly unfounded. Pushing the shop door, Gwen was serving a gentleman and both stopped what they were doing as I walked over to the counter.

'Oh hello there Rosie, we were just talking about you!'

Oh really, I thought to myself, jungle drums were starting then.

' Hiya Gwen', I chimed as cheerfully as I could whilst wondering what they had been talking about me and nodding my hellos to the gentleman beside me. 'Just wanted to thank you for your help last night, I had a lovely meal.'

Gwen finished serving the gentleman, who said his goodbyes and then Gwen and I were in the same position as we were the previous evening.

' You're welcome my lovely. I did see Sue this morning and she said you enjoyed your meal. She was really happy to meet you. How was your first night?'

'Oh it was fine thank you', I replied as I made my way over to the fridge to see if the sandwich myth was really true. True to her word, there was a decent selection of freshly made sandwiches so I grabbed a couple and went back over to Gwen.

'Oh I'm glad you had a good first night, it's always daunting moving to a new village isn't it. I've been here all my life so I'm practically part of the furniture', she said chuckling to herself.

'Oh before I forget, if you didn't already know, there's a big supermarket about four miles from here. You've got a car haven't you, good, as the bus service is a bit hit and miss around here. As much as I'd love you to get your supplies from me, you probably won't want to all the time'

Looking at the prices of her sandwiches, I silently agreed with her!

Picking up some crisps and chocolate, I passed them over.

'Gwen, I was wondering, hope you don't mind me asking but how did you know my name last night?'

Gwen smiled and replied that she was related to my landlord and had helped him clean the house before he rented it to me.

Ohh so that's how she knew! I felt a bit daft thinking it was something a bit weird and spooky! Well...after seeing so many films where a thirty something female moves to a village in the middle of nowhere, only to get dragged into some witch crafty coven cult type shit, it's easy for the imagination to run riot! This was just a normal sleepy little village where nothing remotely weird was going to happen. I paid Gwen for my food and said my goodbyes when she suddenly remembered something else.

' Oh another thing I needed to tell you. I don't know what you do for a living but Sue mentioned to me this morning that she was going to look for a manager for the pub. She and Nick have decided they want some more time for themselves and they wondered if you were interested'

Hmm...now there's a thought. I thanked Gwen and left, stopping outside to see if the pub was open. After a career spanning twelve years as an admin officer in the civil service and doing the odd bit of bar work in between, I'd been temping mostly, here, there and everywhere and the uncertainty of work was getting me down. Now I was on my own, I really needed permanent wages as my savings weren't going to last long. Plus having a job where I could fall out of bed straight into work sounded perfect. It wouldn't hurt just to pop in and see what it entailed. I might not even be the person they were really looking for but if I didn't try, I would never know. I didn't feel very professional walking into a potential job interview in hoodie and jeans carrying a plastic bag with sandwiches in but I was right outside the pub and didn't want to run the risk of the job being taken. So here I was again, smoothing my hair down and that familiar churning in my stomach. Oh well, here goes nothing. Pushing the front door open, I noticed now it was daytime just how old and beautiful it was. It must've been at least a couple of hundred years old, with its little cracks and knots in the wood. There were a few people in the bar area this time having meals. The fire was lit as it was last night and even in the day, it hadn't lost its cosiness. Nick was behind the bar and as I approached, he called through to the back and Sue appeared.

' Hi Rosie, how are you my love, what can I get you?'

Trying to hide the bag of sandwiches on the floor by the bar stool, I sat down, or rather, mountain climbed up onto the stool and asked for a diet coke. Bar stools were always a tricky object for hobbits like myself to get on without the need for ropes and oxygen.

'Thanks again for last night both of you, I really appreciated everything you did'

A bit of good old-fashioned manners was always a good start to any potential job interview in my opinion.

' That's not a problem, we were glad to have you here. Have you seen Gwen today then? Did she mention anything to you? Nick looked at me with what seemed hopeful eyes, he was a quiet man, I don't think he had much choice to be honest, Sue was definitely the talker in the marriage.

Fabulous! Gwen was turning out to be a very useful person to get to know!

' Yes, she did actually', I replied taking a sip of my drink and trying to resist the urge to crunch on an ice cube. ' She said you might be looking for someone to work the bar, is that right?'

Nick and Sue grinned at each other and Nick looked rather relieved. He wasn't old by any means, probably late fifties I would've said but he did look a bit knackered. Running a pub is obviously hard work without help.

'Oh brilliant!' Sue exclaimed enthusiastically, 'tell you what, grab your drink and let's go over in the corner for a chat shall we, how about some chips to go with that drink eh, my treat'

Blimey! Free chips! This was turning into a bit of a result, if she threw in a slice of that fudge cake from last night, it would be near perfect but hey, how many people get free food at an interview. Sliding down off the stool trying to find the floor with my toes, I managed to half squash the sandwiches. Was this woman really going to trust me with her pub, I couldn't even get off a bar stool without half killing two slices of bread. I looked over at the customers sitting near me, hoping they hadn't seen but luckily, they were too engrossed in conversation and pudding.

By the time I'd faffed and farted about getting myself safely off the stool and situated on a much more hobbit friendly chair in the corner, Sue was back with a plate of crispy chunky chips and a cup of coffee for herself. She sat down across from me and placed the plate in the middle of the table and gestured me to dig in. In between mouthfuls, I told Sue my work history, thinking to myself that being an office jockey for so long didn't really qualify me for bar work but she didn't really seem bothered. She explained that she and Nick had been looking for someone for a while but previous people hadn't worked out for reasons she wouldn't go into. They would still be obviously running the pub on a daily basis, overseeing deliveries, the paperwork etc. but needed someone to work the bar so they could cut down their hours a bit. They had two other staff, a guy called Will, who did the cooking and a young girl called Lisa, who she brought in to waitress when they had larger bookings for meals. If I had the job, I'd be responsible for the bar and my time off would be covered by herself. She also mentioned that if things worked out, in time, she'd train me to do the paperwork and stock ordering. Sounded good to me! I felt a bit awkward as I wanted to broach the subject of money but didn't want her thinking that was all I was interested in but I had rent, bills and a life to pay for so it was kind of important. Luckily that was the next thing she covered. I was pretty happy with the starting wage, was more than I was on temping and I had managed to survive on that so any more was a bonus. Sue sat back in her chair, signaling the end of the most surreal interview I'd ever had.

' Well?', she asked with a hopeful look on her face ' do you fancy giving it a go?'

Sitting there with my mouth open, I couldn't get over my change in luck! In the space of twenty-four hours, I'd moved into a new home and bagged a job, with more money, practically next door.

' Are you sure?', I stammered. She must've sensed I was feeling slightly railroaded.

' Listen, we know you've only just moved in. We're happy for you to sort things out at home first, if you want to take a week or two to settle in first, we can agree a start date, no pressure. We liked you from the moment we met you last night which is why we mentioned the job to Gwen'.

Sitting up straight in my chair, I grinned at Sue.

' I'd love to work for you, thank you so much!'

Sue squealed with excitement, which took me by surprise a bit and jumped up out of her chair and gave me a hug, which surprised me even more!

' Oh that's fabulous Rosie! I was so hoping you would say yes! Welcome to our little team!'

I sat back in my chair, took a deep breath and hoped that I wouldn't let her or Nick down. It had been a while since I last pulled a pint. But nothing ventured, nothing gained. I glanced over at Nick who gave me a thumbs up. He seemed very pleased too. Taking a sip of my coke, I looked around the room, which last night had started off as my local and ended up today as my new place of employment. I had a feeling it wasn't going to be a pub full of excitement and rowdy nights but it was a job and I was grateful. Suddenly a chill went through me again, just like last night. Oh well, I could cope with a small draught problem.

CHAPTER FOUR

Over the next week, I spent a lot of time going between sorting the house out and Sue and Nick showing me the ropes at the pub. We decided between us that I'd do an hour here and there under their supervision before I started the job properly, just so I gained enough confidence to be there on my own. The pub was actually a lot bigger than I realised. It had a separate dining room through from the bar area which they used for larger bookings. Also upstairs were three bedrooms which could've been used for bed and breakfast accommodation but Sue had stopped that for now. I also learnt that the pub was older than I realised and was rumoured to have had a rather colourful history. Apparently, dating back to the early 15th century, it had been a coaching inn but there were rumours that it had, in fact, been used as a makeshift courthouse, trying people who had mostly stolen sheep. It wasn't exactly clear what punishments were dealt but back in those days, it wasn't unheard of that anyone caught stealing sheep were hung. Bit harsh by today's standards! I wasn't entirely convinced that any hangings had actually taken place, maybe it was the regulars just trying to wind me up as some sort of initiation. Going by their sense of humour, I was surprised they hadn't tried playing tricks on me to get me thinking the place was haunted. What a load of old nonsense. The only thing that was going to go bump in the night were the pipes. When I first arrived in the village, I felt quite alone and slightly bewildered, wondering what the future was going to hold for me. But as my second week fast approached, I'd managed to get the house looking cosy with the few things I'd managed to salvage from my previous life, I'd made a few friends and acquaintances and it looked like I'd taken to the job easier than I thought I would. It hadn't been all plain sailing however. Pulling my first pint after so many years had resulted in spraying both myself and Sue in Real Ale and having to spend the rest of the shift smelling like a couple of old soaks! And I'd almost landed poor Nick in hospital after forgetting to shut the cellar hatch! I found out that day that he did actually speak, quite a lot in fact and I even learnt some new expletives! Sue however, being the brave woman she was, was confident that I was now ready to go solo. I would be working split shifts which suited me. An old-fashioned pub with old fashioned hours, opening at 11.30am til 2.30pm then opening again from 6pm til 11pm. Least I could crack on with doing what I wanted in between. Part of me was excited about being left to my own devices but I was naturally nervous, even though I knew deep down I'd be absolutely fine. When Sue and Nick presented me with the spare keys, it felt like I was about to take charge of their child who they loved and nurtured and although they would be still around, I promised I would take care of everything. Laying in bed that night, my heart pounded slightly, knowing that come the morning, I would be responsible for the Snow Mountain Inn.

8am and after being blasted out of bed by the most annoying ringtone I could've chosen out of twenty equally annoying ones, I padded downstairs in my pjs and slippers, headed for the kitchen for my first coffee of the day. As I looked out the window, I watched as Mrs. Jones from two doors down was having her early morning moan fest at the postman, who had forgotten to shut her front gate again. A widow and retired school teacher in her early seventies, she'd sniffed at me the few times we'd passed going into our respective houses and she was probably the only one who viewed me with suspicion since I moved in. Mind you, I hadn't helped myself, when at a particularly stressful moment, having a fag in the garden, I had shouted over the fence at her pathetic excuse for a dog to shut the hell up with its constant yapping.

After growling at me for shouting at her rat of a dog, I then had to contain my giggles when she started baby talking to the bloody thing asking if ' the nasty lady had frightened her'. Poor old Shitty Woo or whatever the damn thing was called was obviously traumatized and would probably need copious amounts of doggy counselling and digestive biscuits if it was ever going to recover.

As much as I wanted to carry on watching the postman getting told off by a four foot nothing grey haired rottweiler in a pinny, I had a job to get ready for. Standing under the shower trying not to shampoo my eyes, nerves and excitement kicked in. What was I doing? I wasn't ready for this? This was mad, I'd only been here for two weeks and the local publicans were trusting a complete stranger with their business! I did wonder why no one else had worked out and why after only one evening of knowing me, they had concluded I would be ideal. It was a strange turn of events but I needed the money and I wasn't going to turn an opportunity down. Turning off the shower and wrapping myself in a fluffy purple bath sheet, I opened my wardrobe and started to panic. What the hell was I going to wear? Did I go for the casual jeans and t-shirt or posh it up a bit with smart black trousers and a blouse? What a stupid thing to get my knickers in a twist over! Speaking of knickers, I realised I hadn't had chance to do much washing over the past few days so I really hoped I actually had some still in my drawer. I was just glad that the village wasn't full of boy racers. I could just picture the doctors in the hospital telling any family, that luckily, after being run over, my injuries weren't life threatening and nothing he hadn't dealt with before but my fifty shades of grubby grey granny pants were beyond even his expertise.

To be honest, I'd had moments of complete brain fart over the past week, things seem to keep moving about but it was obviously me being a total numpty, like finding the tv remote in the microwave and the coffee jar in the fridge. Why on earth had I put them in there?! And my picture hanging skills needed some attention, I was getting fed up with straightening wonky frames every morning. Now was not the time to be losing the plot. Time was creeping on and I wanted to be there bang on 10am to make sure I hadn't forgotten to do everything before opening. Sue and Nick would still be going in early to clean each morning, which I was relieved about. Cleaning toilets at stupid o'clock hadn't appealed but I wouldn't have obviously minded if I'd had to.

Keys...where the bloody hell were my keys? I thought I'd left them in the door when I locked up last night. Oh this was getting ridiculous now! Checking the usual places, I'd previously found things, I still couldn't find them! Oh brilliant, just what I needed this morning! I was just about to throw a tantrum when I looked over at the front door. The keys were swinging in the lock! What the hell?! They definitely weren't there when I checked! I was beginning to worry about my sanity. I couldn't carry on like this. I made a promise to myself that if this carried on, I'd make an appointment at the doctors. Maybe I was just run down after all the stress of the break up, the move and the new job. Pulling myself together, I grabbed my jacket and bag and unlocked the door, taking a deep breath of clean crisp mountain air. It was a beautiful morning and I felt instantly better, forgetting all the strange things that had just happened. Everything was going to be fine. I walked across the road as usual to be greeted by my new equine friends. I'd started to look forward to each time I left the house and spending five minutes with them. They seemed to know how I was feeling somehow and they must've sensed I'd been a bit tense, as when I reached over to stroke them, they nuzzled into my arm. Why had I spent so many years being frightened of these amazing animals. Sadly, I didn't have more time to spend so I said goodbye and walked up the road towards the pub. Gwen was sweeping outside the front of the shop and smiled when she saw me approaching.

'Good morning Rosie, todays the day isn't it?'

It was more of a statement than a question, she was the oracle of the village after all.

' Morning Gwen, how are you?', I asked, hoping she wouldn't want to engage in a long conversation, I really did need to get to the pub.

' Oh I'm fine my lovely' chimed Gwen as she continued to sweep up, not that it was ever untidy outside her shop. I had my suspicions she did it just to be nosey half the time. But she was always nice to me and I would always be grateful to her for her help on my first night.

'So..today's the day' she repeated, suddenly seeming less chirpy than a few seconds ago. ' Can I give you some advice my lovely...just have an open mind, whatever happens. Everything will be fine, I promise you.'

What a strange thing to say, I thought to myself! I was just about to ask what she meant when she suddenly brightened again, gave me a huge smile, wished me luck then breezed back into her shop, leaving me standing open mouthed and confused on the pavement. Maybe she was just trying to encourage me to stick with whatever challenges were going to be thrown at me, after all, the others hadn't worked out so it was down to me to make a go of it. Well whatever she was on about, only time would tell.

Shrugging my shoulders, I walked the few steps towards the pub. Standing outside the ancient wooden door, I put the keys into the lock, and opened up for the first time as the newest employee.

Being alone in an empty pub was slightly unsettling. The atmosphere seemed different somehow. The fire was all laid ready to be lit so maybe once I'd done that, the place would become its cosy self again. I went behind the bar to start getting things ready. Sue had left me a note by the till telling me what had been done and reminding me of little things I might forget. She also wished me good luck and not to worry about anything. First things first, that fire needed to be lit, it was too dark and dismal in the bar and I really needed that cosy feeling I'd been so used to. I found the fire lighters on the shelf behind the til and went over to the fireplace, crouched down and struck a firelighter and carefully put it against a log. A whoosh filled the room as the logs and kindling caught, the flames crackled into life, dancing as they grew, a warm glow instantly spreading through me. As I stared into the flames, I suddenly heard a man's voice behind me

'now that's better isn't it'

I swung my head round so fast I almost gave myself whiplash, expecting to see Will or Nick laughing at me for almost crapping myself after their prank to scare me on my first morning alone. Except I was still alone, there was no one there. I got up off the floor and tentatively walked into the dining room. Empty. I made my way around and back through the door into the bar area, there was no one there, only me. Surely if someone had come in, I would've heard their footsteps on the stone floor but I hadn't heard anything. My imagination was running riot again and I seriously had to get a grip! Glancing up at the clock on the wall, time was getting on and I'd spent far too long chasing things that weren't there. I had to put my worries for my mental health aside and finish off. Any possible nervous breakdown was going to have to wait!

Luckily Will arrived a few minutes later so I had someone to take my mind off events. I was tempted to tell him what I'd heard but I still didn't know him that well and I really didn't want strange looks and whispers to Sue behind my back that employing me might've been a mistake. I was determined to prove to everyone I could do this job.

My first shift went really well. Being a weekday, lunchtime had been quiet but there had been a few customers come in for meals. I'd forgotten how much I'd enjoyed interacting with people in a social setting. Being stuck in an office with the same people bitching behind your back, feeling like a prison cell except with garish coloured walls and pot plants just wasn't me, this suited my personality. I'd put the strange events of earlier behind me, chalking it up to my vivid imagination and slight nerves. Will had been happy with the way I served the customers and my clear, concise order taking made his life easier in the kitchen. I think previous employees had faffed about too much and confused him. Maybe that was part of the reason they didn't work out. A happy chef made for a happy front of house so winning that battle on the first morning had been brownie points to me in a big way. Will had worked in the pub for six years, after moving to the village from Cardiff. A widower in his early fifties, he'd been a chef in bigger restaurants since being a young man but had left to look after his wife when she sadly became poorly with breast cancer. After she passed away, he'd moved to Mynydd Eira to start again and to live a quieter life. The village seemed to pull in those wanting to start again it seemed. A place for waifs and strays. His two grown up sons lived some way away so he didn't see them often so he only really had Sue and Nick and a few local friends. I wasn't entirely comfortable telling him my life story yet so I told him a few little snippets, leaving out the gruesome embarrassing details of failed relationships and estranged family, I was just an English girl who'd drifted into Wales and stayed. Well, I wasn't lying was I.

The only thing I needed to remember was to close the cash till drawer properly. For some reason, I couldn't have as a few times I'd turned around to do something, the drawer was open again. If a temperamental till drawer was the only thing that I hadn't mastered yet, things weren't going too badly.

Time was flying. I'd gone to bed on the first night of my new job and woken up two weeks later. Well that's what it was feeling like. I'd been in mynydd eira a month and it had felt like my feet hadn't touched the ground since that first eventful day of dropped boxes, elusive sandwiches and chocolate fudge cake by the fire. Everything was slotting into place nicely and it was beginning to feel like I'd always been here. The only thing that was overshadowing my new happier life was the weird unexplained events that seemed to be happening more and more frequently. I'd tried to shake it off but I was finding it hard to rationalise what on earth was going on. It wasn't just the finding of coffee jars in the fridge, or misplacing my keys every five minutes, I was beginning to hear voices, which of course is a definite fast track to the local mental health unit! Ranging from disembodied whispers in the bar to waking up at home just before my alarm by my name being called, far too often to be a dream. I was tempted to mention things to Sue, we'd grown quite close over the past weeks and she didn't seem the type to judge. I was just going to have to word it properly. I couldn't exactly ask her if she thought I was losing my marbles but that was what I needed to know. Before I had chance to pluck up the courage to text Sue to arrange a chat, my mobile whistled its merry tune heralding the arrival of a text message. Sue had in fact beaten me to it, it was from her asking, as tomorrow was my day off, would I be free for a coffee at the pub after she closed for the afternoon. Maybe it was a blessing in disguise, as knowing me, I would've bottled out texting her first. I text her back saying I'd be happy to, then started rehearsing my ' do you think I'm going mad' speech in my head. This was going to be a very strange conversation.

As I breezed into the pub, I could smell the freshly brewed coffee filling the bar area and a distinct whiff of nervousness emanating from me. I'd spent most of the night going over how I was going to explain everything and hoping that Sue wouldn't think my cheese had slid completely off my cracker. I could hear Sue finishing off in the back so I shouted my hellos then sat myself down in my favourite spot by the fire. As I sat staring into the dancing flames, Sue came through carrying a tray with coffee and cake and placed it on the table before sitting herself down across from me.

' Hiya my lovely, you ok?', she asked as she passed me my coffee and a plate of Victoria sponge. We chatted about nothing in particular for a few minutes and I noticed that she was looking a bit tired. I was hoping that after I'd taken on the job, she would've had more chance of taking a break but obviously she was still as busy as before. She also seemed a bit nervous about something. Oh god I hope she wasn't going to let me go. After previous employees not working out, I was hoping the same wasn't going to happen to me! I thought I was doing a reasonable job keeping the bar running and hadn't had many problems, apart from thinking I was going mad.

'I'm glad we've got this chance to catch up Rosie', she said taking a sip from her cup. 'Firstly', she continued, ' I want to tell you what a fantastic job you're doing! We're so happy with everything you're doing. The customers love you and Will and Lisa think you're brilliant to work with.'

Phew! This didn't sound like an impending sacking so that was one less worry.

' It's been a month now and you've fitted right in and I just wanted to ask you how you think things are going and to tell me if anything is bothering you that I could help with?'

Oh where to bloody start, I thought!

I sat back in my chair, feeling the warmth of the fire beginning to burn the right side of my body.

'There is something Sue' I mumbled, taking a nervous sip of my cooling coffee, trying not to let it catch in the back of my throat as I swallowed. I started to fidget, picking up a bar mat and twiddling it around in my fingers, then feeling a bit of an idiot as I dropped it on the floor.

'You're gonna think I'm daft honestly you are!', I blurted, feeling tears beginning to prickle my eyes.

Sue leant forward and placed her hand over mine, looked at me with kind eyes.

' Try me...', she said gently

That was it! The floodgates opened and my mouth went into overdrive, words flooding out at a hundred miles an hour of how I thought I was losing my mind, the voices, finding things in the most stupid of places and wondering if I was having some kind of post-traumatic stress meltdown. I'm surprised cups and cake didn't go flying as my arms flayed wildly in dramatic animation. Finally I stopped, exhausted. Slumping back in my chair, cheeks burning and nose feeling distinctly snotty after crying all over the place. Sue had just let me rattle on, apparently not batting an eyelid at anything I had just said. I scanned her face for any kind of indication that she thought I was one sandwich short of a picnic but there was nothing like that. In fact, she was the one beginning to shuffle uncomfortably in her chair, a kind of guilty look spreading across her face. She got up from her chair, walked behind the bar, took two glasses and put two double brandies into each from the optic. She came back and placed a glass in front of me.

' Rosie, there's been something I haven't exactly been honest about. I couldn't tell you when we were talking about you working here as I wasn't sure you'd take the job if you knew.'

She downed her brandy in one gulp which took me by surprise, I'd never seen her drink much before. ' I think you're gonna need that', she said, gesturing me to do the same. I just took a sip as I wasn't really into slugging back the booze.

' Rosie, can I ask you something, do you have an open mind?'

I sat there looking at Sue looking back at me when I suddenly remembered, that was what Gwen had said the very first day I started working here. Coincidence or something more ominous, I was about to find out.

I nodded, taking a bigger sip of my brandy, feeling its warmth at the back of my throat.

Sue sat forward in her chair. ' I'm sorry you've been feeling like you have. I feel awful now, I shouldn't have let it go on this long before telling you'.

I wish she'd just bloody get on with it!

Suddenly she jumped and shouted 'Alright, alright!'

And there was me worrying that it was my cheese that was sliding off my cracker!!

Sue composed herself, cleared her throat but before she could speak, a cold whoosh of air went straight through me.

Sue suddenly shouted ' No!! Not yet, she's not ready!!!'

I sat there, my eyes widening, my heart thumping in my chest! What the hell was wrong with my friend!? What wasn't I ready for? I looked around the empty room, wondering who the hell she was shouting at and still shivering from the blast of unexplained cold air. The atmosphere in the room had changed from the usual light cosiness to oppressive and I was beginning to feel a bit scared.

'Of course she's bloody ready woman!' boomed a male voice from nowhere, making me jump, almost falling into the fire

'Oh do be quiet Owain and stop being so bossy!' a female voice shouted from the opposite side of the room.

' Will you two just stop it, can't you see you're scaring the poor girl!', shouted another male voice, right by my ear.

I jumped up out of my chair, leaping towards a bar stool which I clung to as if for protection.

'WILL YOU JUST TELL ME WHAT THE FUCK IS GOING ON!!!'

I screamed at Sue, who was visibly shaking at this point.

Just as Sue was beginning to open her mouth, tables and chairs started to shake all over the room! Lights started flashing on and off and the brandy glasses went flying off the table, smashing all over the floor.

I bolted for the door but it wouldn't budge as I pulled frantically for it to open. I ran behind the bar and crawled into a ball on the floor. Suddenly as it started, it all went quiet. From my safe haven on the floor, I could hear Sue and other voices having a rather heated discussion.

' Owain, for crying out loud, why couldn't you have just waited a minute, I was gonna tell her gently!' hissed Sue

' Yes Owain, you're a very silly man, look what you've done now, she's frightened to death behind there! Oh will you tell him too, Deri ' joined in a female

'Well butt, looks like another one's not gonna come back thanks to you. I liked her I did too! Everything always has to be over the top with you, doesn't it!'

I could hear a mumbled grumpy groan emanating from far end of the room.

' Well...' said the unknown female, ' anyone going to check she's alright behind there?'

I heard footsteps coming towards me so I curled up tighter into a ball, thinking if I made myself smaller, I'd be safe. Sue walked slowly towards me then sat down on the floor next to me. She looked ashen and shell shocked. She gently took my hands in hers.

' Rosie I'm so sorry! I wanted to break this to you as gently as I could but bloody Owain as usual decided to do his poltergeist impression and frighten the shit out of you in the process!'

I looked at Sue, who did genuinely look extremely sorry.

' Who.the...fuck.are...they?!' I stammered, words catching in my throat

'Why don't you come out and meet them and we can explain everything' Sue asked, holding my hand tighter.

I shook my head manically and curled up tighter, like a frightened child during a thunderstorm.

' No, no Rosie, its ok ' soothed Sue ' they aren't going to hurt you, I promise you! They really are friendly, even Owain, believe it or not, although he's just a grumpy old bugger at times, truth be told.'

' What...are...they Sue?!'

I looked at her with wild frightened eyes which made her squeeze my hand even harder, doing her best to reassure me.

' I think you know what they are Rosie. You can do this, I know you can. That's why we chose you, they chose you! 'she whispered gently, her eyes pleading into mine. ' Come out please, give us a chance to explain'

I sat there staring at the floor and fidgeting with my fingers, feeling five years old again, deciding whether or not to come out of hiding in the corner.

Sue squeezed my hand again, playfully bumped my shoulder with hers.

'C'mon, what do you say eh...give them a go?'

I looked at her again, let out a big sigh and summoning all my courage from deep within, nodded.

Sue got up first then pulled me up from the floor and held my hand as she led me from behind the bar and back into the room.

Chairs were all over the place and I could see smashed glass twinkling on the floor. The room was empty, I began to wonder whether I was actually dreaming and any minute I'd wake up safe and warm in my bed. Sue sat me down in my favourite chair by the fire then went to get another brandy to replace the one that had gone flying across the room. She came back, handed me my drink which I promptly downed in one then pulled up a chair close to me.

'Are you ready now?', she asked.

What a bloody question to ask! I reluctantly nodded.

' Ok you three', she said loudly, ' you can come back now'

Cold air filled the room followed by a quiet whoosh as three figures materialized in front of us, standing in a row. I gasped as I saw them, grabbing Sue's hand.

' it's ok!', she whispered, giving it a squeeze.

The female stepped forward first. Dressed in a long pale blue dress with a high laced neckline, long puffed sleeves, a white pinny and mop cap, her long blonde hair tied loosely, the ponytail draped over one shoulder. She looked in her late teens, a pale but pretty girl with a kind face. She dipped down in a quick curtsey.

' My name is Bronwen Price, I'm very pleased to meet you Miss. she said in a soft valleys accent, before stepping back into line.

Next to her stood a man, who appeared to be in his thirties. He was dressed like an old-fashioned farmhand, heavy dark brown trousers tucked into laced up black boots, an off-white shirt with one button undone at the neck, black braces and belt. He had a peaked cap; his brown hair framed a face with a hint of stubble. He stepped forward, removed his cap and gave a little nod.

' Hello Miss, terribly sorry about all that nonsense' he said, giving the man standing next to him a bit of a dirty look. 'my name is Deri Jones and I'm very honoured to finally meet you properly'. His voice was also a soft valleys. Then it was the last one's turn. He just stood there, a grumpy look on his unshaven face. He was older than the other two, maybe late forties. He was dressed similar to Deri but had a dark but dusty overcoat. His dark black hair was longer and unkempt, he had a wild look about him. Deri suddenly jabbed him in the ribs with his elbow. ' Go on then you grumpy bastard, it's your turn and make sure you're nice!'

The older man growled at Deri before he was pushed forward towards me. I could tell he was reluctant to speak but he didn't seem to have any choice by the looks of things.

' My name's Owain' he growled, before stepping back

Deri hit him on the arm. ' And...!!!' he shouted at Owain, before pushing him forward again.

Owain looked at the floor before looking up towards me, trying very hard not to make eye contact.

' My name's Owain Thomas. And I suppose I have to say sorry but dunno why I should have to, to be honest but there you are', his gruff voice getting louder with each word. He stepped back and both Deri and Bronwen looked at him in disgust, Deri shaking his head and Bronwen tutting under her breath.

Well this wasn't what I'd been expecting when I came in! What started out as coffee and cake had turned into Tales from the Crypt and I seriously considered smacking my head against the table to make sure I was still awake.

'You ok?' Sue asked, as I remained sitting there, shocked and numb. I gave her my best Paddington Bear stare before looking back at the trio of whoever and whatever the bloody hell they were.

'You must have so many questions Rosie, just take your time', Sue continued.

That was it, I let rip!

' Oh you fuckin think so do you!? Jesus fuckin Christ what are you people on!?

I jumped out of my seat and started to pace around the room, waving my arms frantically, expletives littering manic ramblings about the whole world had gone mad!

Bronwen tried to calm me by reaching out but I stopped and pointed at her, shouting ' Back the fuck off!'

Then I stopped and stared at her. Her face had fallen and I could see tears prickling her eyes. I suddenly felt guilty for shouting at her and for one second, our eyes connected. She looked as lost as I had felt when I'd first moved to the village. I felt myself relax slightly, my hot temper fueled by shock and fear beginning to wane. They might not have been alive in the true sense of the word but it suddenly became apparent that they had the same emotions as anyone.

I steadied myself against a chair, took a deep breath in then let it out slowly before walking back to where I'd been sitting. Sue touched my arm as I sat down and I smiled at her weakly. I felt like I'd been run over by a truck.

' Right then...', I said quietly and calmly, ' could someone please explain to me everything.'. It was more a demand than a question.

Owain grumbled, rolled his eyes and muttered under his breath but Deri whispered something to him and he went quiet. Then Bronwen and Deri moved closer to the table but thought better of it as I immediately tensed up. I wasn't ready for them to be that close. They went to a neighbouring table and sat down, looking at Sue to start the conversation. Owain looked at the other two, rolled his eyes then disappeared, only to reappear again sat on the windowsill at the opposite side of the room. Sue shuffled in her chair before clearing her throat.

' Well, it's like this', she started ' Nick and I bought this place twenty years ago. We'd felt drawn to the place and fell in love with it as soon as we saw it. There had been stories obviously about how it was haunted but with a building as old as this, there was bound to be. The owner was retiring and was looking for buyers who would keep the place long term. He didn't want anyone who would be passing through after a couple of years. We found out the first week that we had unexpected lodgers'

Bronwen and Deri chuckled to themselves and they looked at Sue. She smiled back at them with what seemed genuine affection.

' Like you, we were shocked and a bit scared but we never felt threatened by them. Owain tried his best to push us but even he tolerated us eventually. It was us that were the outsiders really, after all, Bronwen, Deri and Owain had been here for over hundreds of years. I'll let them tell you about themselves in your own time, if you want them to. The reason why you've experienced things in your house is Bronwen used to live there. '

I looked over at Bronwen who looked back at me slightly nervously. I smiled weakly at her, still feeling guilty about shouting at her a few minutes earlier.

' It's been me Miss, moving things and saying your name. I wanted you to find out about me being there but didn't know how. I just wanted to be friends. I'm sorry if I've caused you distress Miss, honest I am'

Bronwen looked like she was going to cry again and Deri put his arm around her. She was so young, she seemed so innocent and sweet, I had the feeling that she had been a good person whilst alive, maybe too good, too trusting. I knew how that felt.

' That's ok Bronwen', I said quietly, ' I'm sorry for shouting at you. I'm in your house am I? Well I promise to look after it.'

Bronwen instantly brightened, her smile lighting up her small pretty face.

Sue looked at me and nodded, smiling, as if she'd seen a tiny breakthrough in the start of a possible friendship. She continued.

' We've been extremely happy here. We've had moments when people have come to see if the stories were true, you know, paranormal people but we've been reluctant to let them do their investigations. We've become very protective of them you see, they've become family.'

Suddenly there was a snort coming from the window. I'd forgotten Owain was there! He was chuckling, shaking his head and mumbling to himself.

'Oh shut up', Sue laughed, looking over at him ' you can carry on with your grumpy nonsense all you like but I know you Owain Thomas, you're not as tough and miserable as you pretend to be'

' Be quiet woman!' he snorted, looking slightly embarrassed at being chastised. He looked at me with suspicious eyes.

'So...', I said, jumping into the conversation as Sue was about to carry on. ' The time I lit the fire, on my first day, who spoke then?'

Deri sat up straight and put his hand up. ' That'll be me Miss!', he said cheerily. ' I forgot myself that day so I am sorry for that but you really looked like you love that old fireplace, the way you went straight for it and it really does make the place all homely doesn't it!'

Deri seemed a cheery soul, completely the opposite to his miserable friend over on the windowsill, who was still grumbling to himself in between giving me what seemed like dirty looks.

'Rosie, there's something else I need to tell you.' Sue continued

' The reason why we needed someone to help with the pub.' I could see a shadow fall across Sue's face, her eyes dimming. ' Nick's not been feeling well these past few months. The doctor told him he needed to slow down so we decided to try and find someone to take the pressure off him. It wasn't just finding the right person for the business but also someone who would accept these three. The reason why the others didn't work out was that they freaked out when these three made contact. Owain did his theatrics which didn't help. One girl literally dropped what she was holding and ran, we never saw her again, she only lasted three days!'

I wasn't entirely surprised by that, about half hour ago I was trying to do the same thing! I wasn't sure how I felt about anything. The main thing was I'd calmed down. After Sue had finally told me about Nick's health, I could hardly turn my back on them now, any of them. Sue and Nick had been so good to me. As for the small issue of dead people however, now that would take some time. But as Sue said, they came with the pub and it was me that was the newcomer, not them.

Sue, Bronwen and Deri all looked at me with hopeful eyes. The miserable old sod on the windowsill however still looked like he couldn't care less. Against my better judgement, I nodded.

'Ok then, you win, I'll give it a go.'

Sue jumped up and hugged me tight. As she did so, I looked over at Bronwen and Deri, who were both smiling. Deri mouthed a thank you and I nodded acknowledgement. Owain jumped off the windowsill, grunted something which I couldn't quite catch then promptly disappeared. At least I knew I wasn't going mad, well not in the way I had feared anyway! As for being mad for sticking around, no one would be able to answer that one!

CHAPTER FIVE

Unlocking my front door after the most mind-blowing day in the history of my life so far, I felt completely exhausted. Sue had kindly given me an extra day off as she knew I wouldn't be sleeping much that night, no matter how tired I was. As I turned on the living room light, I saw flowers laying on my coffee table. A present from Bronwen no doubt, a sweet gesture that would've had me phoning the on-call psychiatrist a few hours earlier but seemed perfectly rational now. I picked them up to smell them before walking into the kitchen to hunt down a vase. On my kitchen worktop, there was a mug with a teabag in, a plate with a sandwich on it and I noticed there was steam coming from the kettle, as if it had just that minute boiled. I found myself smiling and saying thank you under my breath. Bronwen was obviously trying to make the end of a traumatic day into a pleasant one and this time, I really didn't mind her doing things. I really wish I hadn't shouted at her the way I did but I hoped she understood it was only because I was scared. I boiled the kettle again and made my tea then arranged my beautiful flowers in the vase. After I'd eaten my sandwich and drunk my tea, I really needed to try and sleep so an extremely early night it was going to be. I wearily climbed the stairs and went into my bedroom. On my bed, my pj's were laid out, my duvet had been turned down and my pillows had been plumped up. Oh bless her heart. I undressed, put on my pj's and climbed into my bed. I sat up in bed and listened. I could hear a faint noise from the doorway.

'Bronwen, is that you?' I asked gently

Suddenly, an imprint appeared on the edge of the bed, as if someone had just sat down.

'It's ok Bronwen, you can talk to me if you want to'

Bronwen slowly appeared before me, her pretty eyes looking into mine.

'Hello Bronwen' I said smiling at her, 'thank you for doing all this for me, it was very kind of you'

' You're welcome Miss. It was the least I could do after the fright we gave you today. I'm really sorry again Miss, I am, honest'. She was so sincere.

' Oh Bronwen it's me who should say sorry again for the way I treated you. I was extremely rude swearing at you like that, I hope you'll forgive me'

'Of course, I do Miss! You did shock me though, I'm not used to hearing that word come from a lady, if you don't mind me saying', she said, looking serious in her innocence.

I chuckled, reminding myself she had lived in another time, where ladies were supposed to be gentle souls, not exactly how I'd been earlier!

' You must be tired Miss, I'll leave you to get some rest', she said, smoothing her dress as she got up from the bed.

' No, no, please stay' I urged, suddenly feeling more awake and not wanting to be alone just yet. Bronwen slowly sat back down and we just sat in silence for a few moments, both of thinking what to say next.

Finally, I broke the silence.

'So, Bronwen, tell me about yourself. Sue said this used to be your house?'

Bronwen's eyes lit up, apart from Sue, Nick and her companions, she probably didn't have anyone else to talk to and to be asked about herself was a big thing for her.

' Oh yes Miss! I was born in this house, in the year of our Lord 1765.

Wow! When Sue said they'd been around for hundreds of years, she wasn't kidding!

' There was me, my mam and dad and my younger brothers and sisters. I was the oldest out of seven children. It was a bit of a squash but we managed somehow. I shared a bedroom with my three sisters My brothers shared the other bedroom and my mam and dad slept downstairs'. Blimey, I thought, nine people lived in this house! Hard to imagine how they all managed to live, the house was hardly huge.

'Mam stayed home looking after us kids, she was a seamstress so she used to do that to earn extra money. Dad worked as a farmhand at the Big House in the next village. We never had much but we all had each other. When I was old enough, I went to work at the Big House too, as a scullery maid, I must've been about twelve when I was sent there. But I was lucky, I could come home every day, I loved my family'.

She looked both happy and a little wistful talking about her past life. Must've been a tough life but the love I felt from her was immense.

I wondered how it all ended for her so young but part of me didn't want to ask. But she looked at me as if she could read my mind.

' I was 17 Miss', she said as a veil of sadness descending over her. I became poorly. My mam looked after me the best she could but by the time my parents had enough money for the doctor, I was bedridden, coughing up blood. The doctor said it was consumption. All I remember is fighting for breath then everything just faded into darkness. When I woke up, my mammy, daddy, brothers and sisters were all gone'.

Bronwen's eyes filled with tears and I felt awful for wanting to know, for her to have to recall the moment she died and the moment she found herself alone.

That was enough for one night, I decided. I didn't want to put her through anymore and I'd made her cry twice in the short time I'd known her! I'd be beating myself up over this for months to come.

Bronwen sniffed loudly and shuffled about on the edge of the bed.

' That must've been rough', I murmured, then thinking how ridiculous that sounded, how much more rough could it have been! Talk about a tragic double whammy! Time obviously hadn't made things easier.

' Thank you for telling me, Bronwen and I'm really sorry for everything you went through'.

Bronwen looked at me and weakly smiled as she nodded.

'Right then!', I half shouted, patting the duvet with both hands, breaking the sombre moment, ' I think I'd better get some sleep. I'll see you tomorrow shall I?' smiling at Bronwen, who was looking a little brighter.

' Yes Miss, I'll be around if you need me. Goodnight Miss, sleep well'. With that, Bronwen faded, leaving just a dent in the duvet where she'd

been sitting. I touched the place where she'd been, it was cold. Hardly surprising but I drew back my hand quickly.

As I snuggled down, I still couldn't quite believe what had happened. But what I did know was that life was going to be a little more interesting to say the least.

I sat bolt upright, gasping for breath and drenched in sweat. My night had been filled with dreams of swirling mist, glass smashing all over the floor and disembodied voices calling my name as the room started spinning and I had felt like I was falling into a deep black chasm. It was still early, dawn had just started to break and I could hear the beginning of the birds starting their chorus. I breathed in deeply then let it out in one swift sigh as my head fell down against my pillow again. As I lay there looking at the ceiling, I still couldn't quite grasp yesterday's events. Although it had answered some questions, one being that I wasn't actually having a nervous breakdown, it had caused a heck of a load more unanswered ones. I'd managed to get Bronwen's story but what about the other two? I was curious to find out and why were they still here? And why had they 'chosen' me to ' look after' them? I wasn't a sceptic by any means but I was hardly used to seeing dead people on a daily basis. I'd always been told I was a sensitive Piscean but I always took that as the reason why I felt like crying after seeing fluffy bunnies squished on the road. Soft sod that I was. Just as I began to nod off again, I made a mental note to use my day off to find out more.

It was my mobile phone ringing that woke me up. I fumbled around the bedside table to find it then groggily answered.

'Rosie? Its Sue, my lovely, just ringing to see how you are'.

I quickly checked the screen for the time, nine forty-five am. Good job I had the day off!

' Yeah hi Sue', I croaked, still half asleep and not entirely with it.

' Oh I haven't woken you up have I? Sorry!' apologised Sue, who sounded remarkably chipper for someone who had revealed a huge secret the day before.

I propped myself up on my elbows, trying not to drop the phone as I did so.

'Nah, you're ok Sue. Yeah I'm good thanks, are you alright after yesterday?'

I looked over and caught a glimpse of myself in my wardrobe mirror. Bloody hell, I looked the dead one this morning, white as a sheet with wild cherry bed hair. Thank god I hadn't embraced video chat technology!

' Yes I'm fine thank you' replied Sue, ' I hope you managed to sleep last night, I'm sure it was a lot to take in. Listen, if you're up to it later, do you fancy popping in after lunch for a coffee, I promise there won't be a repeat performance of yesterday!'

Oh did I really want to just now? Maybe a day away from the pub would do me good but I'd only go stir crazy staying in all day.

' Yeah ok, no problem' I agreed, ' be round at 2.30pm'

Sue said her goodbyes then hung up, leaving me to try and get the energy to haul my half dead carcass out of bed. I'd half expected Bronwen to appear but maybe she had decided I needed my privacy, which was quite a relief. I was feeling slightly strange knowing I was living in her former home, like I was squatting somehow but I guess after over a century since she'd lived here, that was a daft notion to have. I wonder if any of the other former occupants had felt her presence around the place? Maybe that was the reason it had been empty for a while and that the landlord had agreed the tenancy as quickly as he did and waived the bond so easily. So many questions and not so many answers as yet but I planned to find out. Suddenly, I had an idea! A miracle in itself considering I was half asleep still but one that had me leaping out of bed and diving into the shower. I needed to get this out of the way before going to the pub. Showered and dressed in half an hour, I quickly swallowed down a cup of coffee before pulling on my boots. I was going to need good footwear for where I intended to be going. I grabbed my coat and keys and headed out. My horse acquaintances nodded their hellos over the fence but I had no time to go over to see them. I was on a mission. I could feel their eyes staring at me as I walked down the path, probably wondering why I was going in the opposite direction to normal. Two minutes later, I stood at the gates of St Mary's church, wondering where on earth to start. If Bronwen, Deri and Owain were still here in spirit, especially with Bronwen living here all those years ago, chances of them being buried here would be quite high surely? Even if I didn't find Deri and Owain, finding Bronwen's grave would be a start. Left or right side of the churchyard? I needed to formulate a systematic approach. Take the left and walk round. There was no point in hanging around too long where the headstones looked in reasonable condition, Bronwen died in 1782 so her headstone would be ravaged by weather and time. That's if she was here at all. Crows squawked in the trees making me jump. Bloody crows, why do they only hang around graveyards?! As I stumbled around the uneven ground in amongst the graves, I was beginning to wonder what I was doing hanging around to be honest. I began to feel like a spook stalker, the chances of finding anyone in this coffin in a haystack place was zero to...

'Oh shit that hurt!', I shouted as I twisted my ankle in a hidden dip in the ground, before feeling a tad guilty for swearing in church grounds. Any minute now, I was expecting a bolt of lightning to hit me, leaving a smoking pile of ash. Oh well, least I would be environmentally friendly. I steadied myself by leaning on a moss encrusted headstone, my ankle throbbing through my boot. I glanced at it for a second. The words were worn away but I could just about make them out. No! Really? Someone was having a laugh! I pulled a rather old but clean tissue out of my pocket and started to clean away the mossy grime that was obscuring some of the letters but there was no doubt.

Bronwen Angharad Price. Born 22nd July 1765, Died 13th November 1782. Beloved Daughter.

What were the chances of that? Hang about, yeah what WERE the chances of that? I suddenly heard a faint giggle by my ear.

' Thought you may have needed some help Miss', the voice whispered.

Oh cheers Bronwen, you could've just said where you were and not make me almost break something, silently grumbling to myself! Composing myself, I suddenly realised that she had been real. She had lived, sadly only a short life but a life all the same. She had been loved then mourned. A parent's nightmare, to bury their child. I knelt down and started pulling out the weeds that were growing up the stone. I stared at her name as tears suddenly started streaming down my face.

'Oh Bronwen, I'm so sorry this happened to you', I whispered, realising I'd used my one and only tissue to wipe the moss away. Using the back of my hand to wipe my nose, I sniffed loudly as I got up, still staring at her name. I promised myself I would come back and clean her stone properly and lay flowers. There had been no one to tend her grave for so long, I suddenly felt it was my sense of duty to take on the role. I was living in her house after all.

' Whoah, get a grip now girl', I told myself, still feeling emotional. I'd found Bronwen, now to find Deri and Owain.

' Over there Miss, by the hedgerow.' whispered Bronwen. I looked around, wondering where by the hedgerow she meant. I then felt myself being guided by unseen hands to a corner, away from all the other graves, through a gap in the hedge, seemingly outside the graveyard. There were no headstones, just wooden sticks in the ground. Names had been crudely engraved into the wood, which had turned green and brown over time. I crouched down, having to get close to read them, time had ravaged the wood but it was just visible.

D. Jones and Thomas. I'd found them but why were they here, outside the graveyard with no headstone with full names, dates or sentiments?

'You need to ask them Miss, it's not my place to tell you', I heard Bronwen say gently. Emotion had been replaced by curiosity. Buried outside church grounds. They either hadn't been religious or...no, that wouldn't happen, would it? Maybe they had been denied a Christian burial for some reason. But why?? Lack of money for a funeral perhaps? But Bronwen's family hadn't been that well off and she was in the graveyard. My brain ticked over for an answer but I had no idea. After the emotion of finding Bronwen's grave, I felt a surge of pity and sadness for Deri and Owain. Bronwen had said that I would need to ask them for the reasons but it wasn't exactly something you pop into a conversation, especially with Owain! I could just imagine his face, the rolling off his eyes as he either decided to blow up a lightbulb or smash me round the head with a chair. After yesterday's introduction, I was actually a little scared of him. I pulled out my mobile from my jacket pocket. I'd been in the graveyard for over an hour. It was time to leave, I'd found what I'd been looking for. I just needed to find out more about the lives of the deceased who were going to share my home and workplace. As I walked slowly back towards home, ankle still throbbing from my minor mishap, I thought how nuts that sounded and wondered if I was really doing the right thing. But how could I let down Sue and Nick, especially as he was poorly. I'd also started to feel a strange kind of loyalty towards Bronwen now that I'd discovered how she died. Whether it was slightly maternal given her age, so young at the point of death yet centuries older than me! Mixed emotions were always my problem, sensitive little soldier that I was. Deri and Owain would take some time but maybe once I had some answers, then I could possibly feel some affinity towards them. It was still extremely early days in my little mixed up world.

As I approached my house, I saw my friendly horses waiting for me by the fence. I went over to them and they nuzzled into my hand affectionately, seemingly relieved that I hadn't forgotten them after all. ' What do you think I should do eh?', I whispered. They looked deep into my eyes, our chocolate brown eyes staring into each other's before rubbing their noses against my cheek. How I wished they were the ones who could talk.

After I'd tidied myself up and dug out a grubby looking elasticated bandage for my still throbbing ankle, I made my way to meet Sue. I saw Gwen sweeping the front of her shop, not entirely coincidental I thought, chuckling to myself. I hadn't talked to her in days as I'd been so busy. She waved as she saw me approaching, in between sweeping the part she'd been sweeping for the past two minutes.

'Hello my lovely! How are you?', she chirped, looking towards my feet. 'You're hobbling, what have you been up to then eh?'

Oh nothing much, just falling into potholes whilst looking for dead people, as you do....

'Oh its nothing Gwen', I replied, I just went over on it this morning, it's fine.'

Gwen looked at me as if she knew I'd just withheld the reason behind my little mishap but I wasn't going to tell her. I could just imagine the looks I'd get from the locals once the jungle drums had done their job.

'How are you getting on working at the pub my lovely, any problems?'

Oh what was she fishing for?

' No, no problems at all' I found myself saying, shuffling about, both my ankle and the whole direction this conversation was going in, making me feel uncomfortable. I needed to make my excuses to leave and quickly.

'I'm sorry Gwen, I've got to get to the pub. Maybe we can catch up another time?'

Gwen smiled and nodded. I turned to walk to the pub when she suddenly shouted after me.

' I think it's a wonderful thing you're doing for them Rosie, ALL of them'

My mouth opened but no sound came out. Was this her way of telling me she knew? I nodded then turned towards the pub, feeling as confused as I had the first day. It wasn't just dead people I needed to find out about, Gwen was starting to worry me too.

I tentatively opened the door into the bar and took a quick look in. A table of customers were just finishing their drinks and getting up to leave but apart from them, it was quiet. Sue was behind the bar and her face lit up when she saw me, beckoning me to come in. I held the door open for the customers to leave, they looked happy and relaxed and had clearly enjoyed their time in the pub. Obviously no activity had spooked them which was just as well as they probably wouldn't come back. I was wondering what the hell I was doing coming back in all honesty, visions of me cowering in the corner behind the bar flashed in my brain. I was here now so there was no bottling out. I had some pride left so I wanted to retain it.

Instinctively, I cleared up the table of dirty glasses and took them behind the bar for washing. I glanced over towards the window and suddenly there was Owain, sitting on the windowsill as he had been the day before.

' Came back then I see', he grunted, fiddling with something that looked like a pipe.

I stood looking at him, determined not to let him intimidate me.

'Why, did you think I wouldn't then?', I asked, as bravely as I could muster.

'Dunno, to be honest. Never saw the others back. Maybe there's more to you than them.' he said, looking me up and down.

Was that his way of a compliment?

'Yeah well...I don't run away from things easily Owain'. I'd started feeling a little braver.

'So I noticed', he replied, jumping down off the windowsill and walking towards me.

Oh hang about, that's close enough sunshine, I thought to myself as I backed off a bit.

Sue came through from the back and looked at the both of us with a concerned face.

'Everything ok here?', she enquired quickly.

I looked straight at Owain, holding his gaze. 'Yes Sue, everything's fine. Owain was just saying hello'. They both seemed to look surprised before Sue broke the uncomfortable silence.

'Right then, coffee or something stronger Rosie?' she asked

'Coffee would be great, thank you Sue'.

I limped back round towards my favourite table and sat down.

Owain stared at me as I did so.

'Been looking for things have you?'

I wasn't sure whether that was a question or an accusation.

My ankle throbbed. I really hoped I hadn't done anything serious to it.

'I just needed to satisfy my curiosity', I replied, knowing full well he knew what I'd been doing that morning.

'And have you?', he grunted

'No, not really Owain, maybe you could enlighten me sometime' I replied. Maybe that was a little too brave!

Owain grunted again then disappeared. Obviously, he wasn't exactly thrilled by my new-found confidence. I was just relieved he hadn't decided to rearrange the room again.

Sue came back with coffee and cake. Deja vu. Sitting herself down, she smiled at me whilst placing them in front of me.

' I was worried about you yesterday', she said, putting sugar in her own cup. She was worried about me?! I was worried about me! I started to feel a bit embarrassed about hiding like a five-year-old and having to be coaxed out by my employer! Thank god I'd kept control of my bodily functions!

' Owain was alright with you, just wasn't he?', she asked with concern.

' Oh yeah honestly, he was fine. Bit surprised that I'd come back though', I mumbled, mid mouthful of Victoria sponge.

'I know this is a daft question Rosie but how do you feel about all this? Please be honest'

Crap, talk about being put on the spot, especially as I hadn't completely worked that out yet.

'Well I can't say I understand any of all this. It's a bit bonkers really isn't it!'

Sue nodded her head, a wry smile forming, probably remembering the first time she encountered her three unexpected inhabitants.

'I did find out about Bronwen last night though. She was really sweet when I got home, she got me flowers, made me a sandwich and even put my PJs on the bed'.

'Oh Bronwen, Bronwen ', sighed Sue, ' she's a sweet one that girl. Always eager to please, never one to take advantage. I think she's been so lonely, confused too. She did ask me once why she hadn't gone to heaven, worried she'd done something wrong whilst alive'.

Oh, bless her heart.

'She told me how she died last night, about her family. I found her today'. Sue suddenly sat up straight.

'Found her?' she asked

'Yeah, I went to the church and walked around trying to see if any of them were buried there.'

'Did you really!' exclaimed Sue, surprise mixed with a hint of happiness.

'Well that's lovely! I do know where they are but none of them wanted me to keep going there. Goes to show she trusts you already'

' She helped me, well I literally stumbled on her, truth be told', lifting my aching ankle to emphasise the point.

' I hope you don't think I didn't care enough to tend her grave. She didn't want me to', she said, sadly.

Maybe she wouldn't want me to tend her grave then, I thought. I'd have to ask her.

Sue then looked at me again, a veil of seriousness etched on her face.

'And what about Deri and Owain? Did you find them?'

Oh yes...

' Well there's the thing' I replied, ' I did find them, with Bronwen's help. I wouldn't have otherwise. They were outside the church grounds with only a stick with their name on. Curious don't you think?'

An open question if any there was one. I searched her eyes for any clues. She had to know the reason, surely?

'Well...at least you found them'. Sue was skirting the question. Now what? Push her for more information or just leave it for now?

We sat in silence for a moment, both picking up our coffee cups and taking a sip at the same time, looking everywhere apart from each other.

I was the one to break the awkward moment.

' So, did you talk to them after I left yesterday?'

' What? Sorry...talk to who?'.

I wasn't sure where Sue had been for the past minute but it wasn't here.

' Bronwen, Deri and Owain. Did you talk to them about me?'. I thought I had some sort of right to know.

' Well kind of. Bronwen and Deri were quite hopeful about you staying. Owain...well Owain was Owain.'

' Have you decided to stay or will you be leaving us? I know you said you would give it a go yesterday but you've had time to think about it now haven't you'. Sue looked slightly dejected as if she was expecting a negative response.

What choice did I really have?

'Listen Sue, when I said yesterday I would give it a go, I meant it.'

Yeah right Rosie, liar, liar pants on fire....

' But you've got to understand it's going to take time for me to get used to this. I don't really know what any of you want from me.'

Sue sat forward and looked me in the eye.

'All I ask is that you carry on doing a brilliant job of looking after this place so I can concentrate on looking after Nick and also, make friends with Bronwen, Deri and even Owain. They've had it tough, they need someone to protect them from those who make it their business to expose them to the world. If you can do that, believe me, they will return that friendship and loyalty, even if they aren't 'real', in the true sense of the word.'

Loyalty and friendship. Not something I'd had in abundance throughout my adult life so far, I admit. That was the trouble with being stabbed in the back time after time, trust had oozed out the wounds, unable to be replaced. However, Sue seemed sincere. She'd obviously had twenty years of sharing her life with them. They wouldn't have stayed at the pub that long if they hadn't been able to endure it.

As I looked around the pub, I imagined what it would be like to move on, to leave a place I'd felt settled in at last. I suddenly realised that it wasn't a pleasant thought.

' Ok Sue, I'll stay and I do mean that'

Sue looked relieved.

Pants on fire extinguished.

' But tell me something, does Gwen know about all this?' I enquired

'Oh, you could say that', replied Sue, ' she's related to Deri'.

CHAPTER SIX

Just as I thought it couldn't get any more complicated, Sue had to throw that little addition into the bag of mixed up nuts.

'How do you know that?!', I stuttered

'Well...', replied Sue, looking a bit unsure whether she should've said anything at all but it was a bit late for that now.

'When I found out about them in the beginning, I was like you, a bit freaked out and wondering what on earth we'd let ourselves in for'.

Wonder if she'd hid behind the bar trying not to crap herself, I thought to myself. I found myself stifling a giggle thinking about it, highly inappropriate after such an important revelation.

'Gwen's family had always had the shop apparently, passed down through the generations, so I thought I'd ask her about the history of Mynydd Eira. Well....' Sue shuffled into her chair, getting comfortable for the long haul by the looks of things.

' It so happened that the landlord who'd sold us the pub was related to Gwen somehow too'.

Hmm...small village, I thought, everyone related to each other, someone possibly marrying their sister inadvertently along the way...

'In fact, your landlord is the grandson of the former landlord of the pub so he's related to Gwen too', she continued.

Why had banjos suddenly started playing in my head! Get a grip girl and try to keep up!

'So, I asked Gwen if she had heard anything strange going on at the pub and then it all kind of came tumbling out about Deri, Bronwen and Owain. I thought Gwen would think I was as mad as a box of frogs but she never battered an eyelid. She then went on to tell me that way back in the 17th century, Deri had been married with a family but something happened which was so serious, it was deemed a family secret and not something outsiders were meant to know but she and the pub landlord were direct decedents of Deri Jones'

I sat up straight in my chair after having a lightbulb moment!

'So she'd know why Deri was buried outside church grounds then!' I shouted, a bit too enthusiastically.

Sue suddenly looked worried.

' Yes, probably but please don't just go charging in there asking her!', she exclaimed.

Suddenly, Deri appeared standing behind Sue. He'd obviously been listening to the whole conversation and didn't look happy. Sue turned around and he shot her a look that confirmed that she'd maybe gone a bit too far disclosing information. I sank into my chair, preparing myself for any fallout that could come but Deri's face changed as he looked at me.

'You deserve to know the truth Rosie, doesn't she Owain'

Owain appeared at the other side of the room. He seemed unusually sheepish, until he caught my eye.

'Yes, she does and I think we need to tell her now before she starts asking more questions, she's beginning to vex me.', he said abruptly.

Oh and he's back in the room...

Sue looked at the time.

'Listen I need to start getting things ready for evening opening. Why don't you use one of the upstairs rooms? This isn't a conversation to be had in here.'

Sue went and got the key to one of the bedrooms and I was surprised when she handed me a large rum and coke to go with it.

'You're going to need that.,', she whispered.

All these revelations were apparently going to drive me to drink and eat into the pub profits at the same time considering the amount of booze Sue had given me for free!

Drink and keys in hand, I made my way through the small room at the back and through the door leading to the stairs. As I slowly walked up the ancient staircase, it creaked with each step I took. Each stair had been worn away in the middle, I wondered how many feet had been on them during the course of time. I reached the landing and looked through the cracks in the old floorboards, the lights of the room below shining through. I was all for original features being left intact of old buildings but it was slightly unnerving being able to see downstairs through the floor! I definitely wasn't tempted to jump up and down to test the condition of the floorboards that's for sure! I put the key in the lock of the dark wooden door, which looked the same age and in the same condition as the boards. I entered the bedroom and looked around. The large airy room was dominated by a huge old four poster bed with a burgundy bedspread. The other side of the room had been made into a sitting area with a small sofa, a coffee table and against the wall was a tv unit. Sue had also put a large wall unit against the opposite wall with an array of ornaments and jugs. It obviously hadn't been used recently as there was a thin layer of dust on the surfaces. I wandered through another door which led to a few steps leading down into a functional, if a little dated, bathroom. I made a mental note to talk to Sue, if the other rooms were like this but not used to their full potential, the pub could be missing out on regular Bed and Breakfast income.

I settled myself on the sofa and waited. I had absolutely no idea what was going to be revealed but it was obviously serious. Even Owain seemed adamant that I was told now and not leave it any longer. I felt goosebumps on my arms as the temperature suddenly dropped by several degrees then saw Deri and Owain appear by the bed. I felt slightly nervous. This was the first time I'd knowingly been in a room on my own with them and my heart was thumping against my chest. Deri must've sensed how I was feeling as he approached me in a way that a person would approach a frightened animal, gently.

'There's no need to be frightened Miss. We aren't going to hurt you, please always remember that'

I shot a glance over at Owain who was sitting on the bed, he was looking as nervous as I was feeling which was surprising.

'Don't worry about him either, I'm afraid he's not made a very good first impression but I'm hoping what we tell you will help you understand what kind of men we are, or were'. I couldn't believe I was in a room beginning a full-blown conversation with two people who weren't actually alive.

Deri settled himself on the edge of the coffee table then looked over at Owain. He nodded at Deri.

'Rosie, we're going to tell you the full story of who we were. You're welcome to ask us any questions but I would like you to hear everything first. Is that acceptable to yourself?' he asked politely.

I nodded.

' It's not a pleasant tale I'm afraid but we believe you're a strong enough young lady to be able to endure it'

I gestured to Deri to carry on.

'I was born in Mynydd Eira in the year of our Lord 1645. Owain was seven years older than I. Our families were friends, our fathers worked together as farmhands, our mothers helped each other raise us and our siblings and Owain and I, despite the difference in ages, became like brothers. When Owain was fourteen, he went to work alongside our fathers at The Big House. That's what we called the house and farm owned by the local landowner. Idris Evans was the Master, the house and land had been in his family for generations and was the main employer for the area. When I became of age, I went to work there too. We were happy, I helped look after the sheep and the land and Owain worked his way up to Gamekeeper, he had the ear of the Master and was in a very responsible position. Mr. Evans was a firm but fair man. Years went by, we both married local girls and had families of our own. The Master, alongside our fathers, sadly passed on and his son, Glyn, inherited everything. He was a harsh man, we remembered him as a child, growing up with us, a spoilt, nasty boy who used to bully and belittle us, out of the earshot of his father. He was worse an an adult, using the local girls, then throwing them aside when they became with child and sacking hardworking men for no reason, just because he could. Our lives turned from happy to harsh but there was nothing we could do. We had families to provide for. When I was thirty-eight years of age, I had an accident at work. I was helping to shear the sheep but the one I was shearing got away from me, I fell and the shears cut into my leg. It was a deep wound but one that would heal in time. However, the Master wouldn't give me time. He said because I couldn't work, he'd give my job to someone who could.'

Deri stopped for a moment, the memory of that time was obviously still vivid and painful. Owain then looked at me.

'As I was Head Gamekeeper and Deri's friend, I begged Mr. Evans for Deri's job. But he was having none of it. I tried so hard I honestly did', Owain looked visibly upset.

Deri looked at Owain with understanding eyes.

Deri continued the story.

'After I was laid off, things were hard. I tried getting another job but as Evans was the main employer around here, there wasn't much else. My wife tried to get a job in the Big House but they weren't taking anyone on, or rather wouldn't take her on due to her being married to me. We began to starve. Owain tried helping the best he could, bringing us food when he had spare but he had his own family. I told him to be careful in case Evans found out and let him go to. It killed me seeing my family suffer, all because I was careless that day shearing them bloody sheep. One night, after my family had gone to bed hungry again, I snapped. I left my family asleep and went up to the fields where the sheep were. I grabbed one and slit its throat and was dragging it back when I heard a shout. I turned and saw a man with a flaming torch run towards me. I still couldn't run tidy as my leg was still bad at times. I thought that was it for me but then I realised it was Owain, he was checking the fields for poachers, men like me desperate for anything to keep our families fed. When he realised it was me, he had words I admit but he told me get home. He'd hide the sheep then get it to me once he knew it hadn't been missed the next day. But unknown to us, the Master had been out in the field with one of his latest girls and had seen the torch light. He came over and saw Owain standing by me, the dead sheep on the ground. He obviously thought Owain had caught me poaching and was taking me in. It was too late for me. Owain was trying to get him to see reason but the man was a tyrant and had no pity for me, even though it was him that had made me so desperate to begin with. Owain was just about to knock him to the ground to let me escape but I shouted at him no. There was no point in both of us being dragged away. I was taken to the courthouse. Do you know where that was?'

Deri looked at me for a second. Courthouse? Where had I heard that before? Then the penny dropped.

'Oh my god! ' I gasped as Deri started nodding.

'The holding cell was through there, down those steps', he said, nodding towards the bathroom.

'The next morning, I was taken downstairs by court wardens to where the main room is now. The Judge was there, his name was Jeffries'

Oh this was getting worse by the second! I'd always been one for History and the name Judge Jeffries rang a godawful bell in my head, was that really here??

'I can tell you're familiar with that name', said Owain, prompting me for an answer.

I looked at my feet, feeling all the blood draining into them. I looked up at the both of them, clearing my throat.

'The Hanging Judge', I whispered. I felt sick.

Deri and Owain looked at each other before Deri carried on.

' It was over in minutes. Evans spoke his piece. Owain then explained what had happened but tried to defend me until he was cut short by Jeffries on the insistence of Evans. I had no chance to speak in my defence, no chance to tell him why I went out and killed that sheep. Jeffries found me guilty and condemned me to death by hanging. I was dragged back upstairs to the top of the landing. Just outside the door to this room. They threw a rope over the beam then tied the noose round my neck'.

'STOP!!!', I shouted, grabbing my drink and taking a huge gulp. I jumped up and started pacing around the back of the sofa then I stopped and bent over the back of it, resting my head in my hands. I suddenly felt a coldness on my shoulder and when I looked up, Owain was standing next to me, his hand on it.

'Are you alright for us to carry on Miss?', he whispered, genuine concern in his voice. I stood up, composed myself and nodded before walking back round the sofa to sit down.

Deri looked at Owain. There was obviously more to this story but Deri's had finished for now, for blatantly brutal and obvious reasons.

Owain looked at the floor before looking at me.

'After Deri had died, I was overcome with guilt and grief. My anger was building and my hatred towards Evans was becoming known to the whole village. A week after Deri was hung, Evans came up to me in the farm courtyard. He was vile, saying Deri deserved to swing. He went too far by saying Deri's wife could save her family from starvation if she....'

Owain stopped and looked at Deri. Although visibly upset, Deri urged Owain to carry on.

'Evans said Deri's wife could save her family if she...gave herself to him. In return, Evans said he would give her money to feed her family. It took four farmhands to hold me back. I shouted at him, I know I shouldn't have, he was my Master. But the man was an animal, he deserved no respect. I thought he would sack me but he didn't. He said he would let me keep my job but would make my life a misery. All because Deri had been my friend. I stormed off before I did something I'd regret and I didn't see him for the remainder of the day. I went home to my family that night, I didn't even bother doing my nightly rounds of the sheep. The next morning, must've been dawn as the light was just coming through the window, I heard banging at my door. I opened it to find men from the Big House and from the courthouse standing there with muskets. They grabbed me before I had chance to ask what was going on. I didn't even get the chance to say goodbye to my family. They dragged me to the courthouse and threw me in the holding cell. I don't know how long I was in there for, seemed like an eternity. I banged on the door a few times demanding to know what was going on but no one came. It wasn't until a warden opened the door to give me bread and water. I demanded to know. He said I knew why but of course I didn't. As he was about to slam the door, he just said MURDER'

I took another gulp of my drink as I stared wide eyed at Owain. I could see the hurt and pain in both men's eyes. My heart was pounding against my chest as I tried to take in what was being said.

' I spent what seemed eternity in that cell', Owain continued, after composing himself. ' Eventually, the door was opened and two wardens dragged me off the floor and out of the cell. I was taken down the stairs to the court room and then tied to a chair. As I looked around, I saw farmhands from the Big House, some local men who I'd known all my life and others who I'd never seen before but they were well dressed, so I assumed they were gentlemen of the law. Suddenly Judge Jeffries appeared and sat at the table in front of me. I won't lie to you, I was frightened, really frightened. I had no idea what I was supposed to have done! The warden had said murder but I hadn't hurt anyone! Jeffries then asked for the charges to be read out. Mr. Glyn Evans had been found dead two days previously, in the grounds of the Estate. He had been brutally slain, with wounds to his head and neck. They said he'd had his throat cut. They said it had happened a few hours after we'd had words in the courtyard. One of the farmhands, a young lad, said he'd heard me say to Evans during the fight that I would 'get him for what he'd done to Deri' but I never said anything like that, I know I didn't! Whoever had done away with Evans, it definitely wasn't me! I looked at the boy, all confused as to why he'd said such a thing but he looked scared and wouldn't look at me. I suddenly realised what was happening. Someone had killed Evans for whatever reason and they needed someone to blame and I was the last one seen fighting with him. The boy had obviously been threatened into lying. I begged for someone to listen to me but a warden hit me hard and shouted at me to be silent. My fate had been sealed. Judge Jeffries passed sentence then I was dragged back up the stairs and to where the hanging rope was. I cried out for my wife and children, for someone to listen to me but no one would'.

He didn't need to tell me anymore. Two men had been sent to their deaths, one for a crime he was driven to commit by a tyrant but was judged harshly, another for a crime he was innocent of but was made a scapegoat due to circumstance. I felt like I'd been run over. The brutality of the time was hard to imagine, the unfairness of it all was heartbreaking. I looked at Deri and Owain, tears prickling my eyes. They had been good men, ripped from the world by the evil of others. They hadn't deserved this.

'So...', I finally said, after downing the last of my drink. ' The reason why you were buried outside church grounds was...'

'Because we were convicted criminals', Owain said, finishing my sentence. 'We couldn't be laid to rest in consecrated ground'.

'I'm so sorry', I whispered, ' it's so unfair! Neither of you did anything to warrant what happened to you!'

All three, Bronwen, Deri and Owain had died tragically and my heart ached for them. I could understand why Owain had come across the way he did. I'd be extremely bitter if that had happened to me! He'd had double to deal with, the death of Deri on his conscious and the injustice of his own.

'Do you have any questions Miss?' asked Deri after a few moments of reflective silence.

I sat for a moment thinking of diplomatic ways of asking things without sounding heartless. I was curious about so many aspects of what I'd just been told but wording questions was going to be hard!

'When did you come back, had a lot of time passed?'

Deri spoke first.

'I awoke in this room. I obviously thought at first that it had all been a terrible nightmare but then I realised everything had changed. It had become a bed chamber, similar to this. I was confused, I didn't realise I was actually dead at first. My death had been so swift. I'm not sure how long had passed but the building was no longer a courthouse but a tavern. I drifted through from room to room, seeing people but they didn't see me. It was the strangest, loneliest feeling, trying to get them to hear me but of course, they couldn't. I tried to leave, to go outside but something was holding me back. I didn't know where my family were and I was desperate to find them but I wasn't able to, not at first anyway. After a while, I tried again to go outside. I found myself being able to go wherever I chose. Looking back now, it was because I was finding energy to be able to transport myself. I had no physical body to speak of but my soul was growing again, like a child I suppose. But by the time I was able to search for my family, they had gone. Time had passed and my wife and children had naturally passed on. I was alone in a place I recognised but no longer knew. But just when I felt all was lost, Owain appeared to me. He was feeling equally confused, not realising at first that he too was dead. We mourned together the loss of our families, the loss of the lives we could've lived.

I used to have faith in our Lord but we both felt forsaken. We always believed that when we died, we would take our place in Heaven. We thought it was because of what happened that we were denied eternal rest. We became bitter but in time, we found Bronwen and her gentle nature helped us. We'd all died through no fault of our own and although we didn't know why we were still here, we accepted it'.

The room was getting dark. The afternoon had turned into evening and I realised I'd been listening to their heartbreak for hours. I got up and put the table lamp on then curled back into my place on the sofa. I didn't want to leave them after hearing their stories. Not just by going home, I didn't want to leave them at all. My mind was made up.

'Do you have any other questions for us Miss?' asked Deri.

'Yes I do but the rest can wait for now. I need another big drink before I go home! And I'd better have an early night, I've got work in the morning....'

As I winked at them both, Deri and Owain smiled back. As for me, I'd just made friends with three ghosts. Now that warranted another drink!

CHAPTER SEVEN

Life went on pretty normally after that. I actually started to look forward to seeing my ghostly companions on a daily basis. We developed a mutual respect for each other, although Owain was still a grumpy old sod from time to time and we did have the occasional heated discussions. I still had questions floating around in my head which I was determined to find answers to. If Owain didn't murder Glyn Evans, then who did? Finding that out would probably be impossible, no records would exist now, if any had been made at the time. There was also the subject of Gwen's ancestral link to Deri. Surely with some digging around on family tree websites, I could find out for definite. I couldn't say anything to anyone though, not until I had facts. I had time, it wasn't as if anyone was going anywhere. After the dramatic start to life in Mynydd Eira, everything was settling down into a busy but happy routine. My new world was beginning to overtake the shadows of the past and I hardly ever thought about my previous life. I was a world away from the mire I'd been dropped into and I counted myself extremely blessed to have been given another chance to restart living. My circle of friends may have been unconventional but a mixture of the living and the dead worked rather well considering. Sue continued to watch over me from afar whilst looking after Nick, who was sadly becoming increasingly poorly. Numerous medical appointments had failed to discover the cause so he was now being referred to the hospital. It was a worry and deep down, we all feared the same although we didn't speak of it and never to each other. Individual sleepless nights, secret Google symptom searches and the nagging knot in the pit of individual stomachs, we quietly got on with daily life, hoping that hospital tests proved our secret self-diagnosis wrong. Days weren't always marred by worry however. I provided, inadvertently, many comedial moments, mainly due to my stubbornness to trying to do everything myself. I've never been one for heights. In fact, it was a phobia that had me breaking into a sweat standing on a chair. Probably why mother nature only made me four foot ten tall. Changing ceiling lightbulbs was a job that Nick usually did but I wasn't having him going up and down ladders in his condition. So, when the lightbulbs needed replacing in the main bar, I, somewhat hastily, volunteered to do them. With an audience of my ghostly friends, I turned off the mains power then set up the ladder and proceeded to gingerly climb up, box of lightbulbs in one hand, holding onto the ladder for dear life with the other, mentally writing my will with each step.

'Oh do be careful up there Miss', urged Bronwen

'Do you really think this is wise'? questioned Deri, seeing my face change from a determined look to one of sheer terror when I reached the third step.

'Oh just get a grip woman!' hissed Owain who was having one of his days.

'Look, I'm doing the best I can here guys!', I shouted, trying not to freak out when the ladder wobbled.

'Would it actually kill any of you to hold this damn ladder?!'

I suddenly realised what I'd said. I looked down to see three bemused faces looking up at me. Stoney silence. Oh me and my big mouth!

'Bit late for that Miss, remember?', Deri smirked finally. Bronwen tried to stifle a giggle and Owain just glared at me. Trying not to drop myself in it any further, I managed to suck up my fears and reached the top of the ladder. I carefully unscrewed each old lightbulb of the four fittings and replaced with a new one, before carefully descending the ladder. I sighed with huge relief but then realised I had another eight lightbulbs to replace. Why on earth have so many on one ceiling! It wasn't as if it was a huge room! I made a mental note to suggest to Sue that a couple of brass standard lamps might just look better, saving me my sanity and safety! After fitting the last ones, I felt like kissing the floor but that would just be unhygienic. Sighing with relief, I turned the mains power back on and prepared to turn the light switches. It felt like the grand turning on of the Christmas lights.

'Right then guys, are we ready?', I shouted breezily before flicking the switches.

BANG!!!

'Bugger, bollocks arseholes and shit!', I cried, jumping about ten feet in the air as lightbulbs exploded, fusing most of the downstairs in the process!

' Oh Miss, that wasn't very ladylike!', cried an expletive sensitive Bronwen

'Oh dear, I don't think you screwed them things in tidy', said Deri, stating the obvious.

Owain just stood shaking his head and rolling his eyes, muttering something under his breath. Sue, who had just come in, came running through from the back.

'I just heard a huge bang, what the hell happened?!' she cried, looking at lightbulb carnage.

Owain looked at me then looked at Sue.

'That stupid wench, that's what's happened that is! ' he shouted, nodding in my direction. 'Dunno why you just didn't use bloody candles! We never blew up our houses in my day!'

I looked sheepishly at Sue, my bottom lip beginning to quiver before I blurted out

'Took me bloody ages fitting them bastard lightbulbs and another thing, I hate heights and that ladder is lethal! Can we just get bloody standard lamps instead!?'

Sue looked at me, then looked at the carnage before looking back at me again before calmly and quietly replying,

'Think it might be safer to be honest, don't think my insurance covers my bar manager trying to blow up the premises...cuppa tea?'

Good job it wasn't in the cellar, that really would've been Lock, Stock and several smoking barrels!

Apart from almost blowing up my place of employment, I did redeem myself. After having our afternoon of revelations in the bedroom, Sue and I finally discussed renovating the three rooms with a view of providing Bed and Breakfast again. They had obviously been used as such in the past but it had dwindled until it just stopped, which to me was a shame. What the rooms had been also used for back in Deri and Owain's day hadn't been lost on me but sentiment had no place in business and it was an emotion I needed to suck up. Nick was feeling a bit better and being included in plans for the pub seemed to cheer him up, although he did go rather pale again whilst budgets were discussed. We agreed between us that the decor in each room be changed. Soft neutral colours were probably going to be better, although I was a bit disappointed when my suggestion of a purple bedroom was turned down. The four poster beds were definitely going to stay. After doing research on several businesses claiming to be 'olde worlde with four poster beds', their room rates were slightly higher but always fully booked. Also, after speaking to Deri, he was sure the beds had been there for decades. After closer inspection of the ornate wooden carvings of the headboards and posts, I concluded that he was possibly right. The original open fireplaces in each room would definitely stay, even if they were just purely for decoration. The main renovations would be the bathrooms. They'd been stuck in an avocado time warp and they seriously had to go! If we could modernise but still keep as many of the original features as possible, maybe we could be onto something. I spent my free time slowly losing the will to live gathering quotes, looking into each business's reputation and previous work done, trawling countless testimonials from happy smiley customers who seemed overjoyed with their new all singing all dancing self-flushing toilets. How did that work then? Did it detect when a bottom had plonked itself on the seat then give it five minutes? Budgets didn't allow for such a luxurious item which was just as well. If I heard shocked screams from guests, I wouldn't know whether it was Owain up to his tricks or they'd been taken unawares in mid sitting by an over enthusiastic flushing system. We all decided to play it safe, three bathroom suites from a local company, Pugh's Plumbing and Bathrooms, comprising of a normal toilet which hopefully wouldn't shoot water up the unsuspecting guests' backsides, a white bath with shower and a pedestal basin. Boringly neutral and functional but twenty first century finally and hopefully, with a bit of eyelash fluttering from Sue, a bit of discount for bulk buying and fitting. Leaving the pub in the capable hands of Nick and Will for the lunchtime shift, Sue and I headed off, with Sue guarding the business credit card like it was the Holy Grail. I had a feeling it didn't get a pounding that often apart from the usual stock payments. The bathroom shop wasn't exactly the biggest, I don't know what I was expecting, it was hardly going to be warehouse size where roller-skates and a Sat Nav would come in useful whilst losing the will to live trying to find staff that actually knew their nuts from their u-bends. As we walked in and started to look around, I could see a casually dressed man in his forties looking over at us from a desk in the far corner. He acknowledged our presence and indicated he'd be with us in a moment, giving me time to just have a quick play with the self-closing toilet seats. I really did need to get out more if this was amusing me. Sue looked at me grinning and shaking her head and wandered off to look at taps, probably trying to pretend she wasn't with me.

'Hello there can I help you', a voice behind me, making me jump as I was still engrossed in the apparently fascinating technology of loo seats. I swung round to be faced with piercing blue eyes and a friendly smile and I found myself blushing slightly.

'Oh yeah, ahem, sorry, fabulous loo seats you got' I replied.

What the hell was that? Fabulous loo seats you've got?? Oh for crying out loud Rosie, you bloody numpty. Just bloody glad I wasn't looking at stopcocks!

He chuckled as he saw my embarrassment. 'Are you looking for anything in particular?' he asked.

Yeah, the ground to open up and swallow me would be nice just about now. .

'Um, yeah, we need bathrooms' I stuttered. No shit Sherlock, in a bathroom shop, well done again you stupid bint!

He laughed, 'Well as you can see, we stock quite a few of those'

Thankfully, Sue had noticed my beetroot face from way over the other side of the shop and came striding over to rescue me from myself.

'Hello!' she said, rather too enthusiastically, putting on her posh business voice whilst extending her hand towards the seller of fabulous toilet seats.

As she engaged him in conversation about what we wanted, I noticed he kept looking at me smiling. He was probably thinking I was a bit simple and was being kind as I was having a day out. I smiled back politely, trying not to look like a deranged meerkat pretending to look around whilst avoiding as much eye contact as I could. Sue suddenly jabbed me in the ribs as he walked away to show us a display.

' He fancies you he does', she whispered as we followed him.

'Shh!', I hissed through gritted teeth, thumping her on the arm. I was looking for bathrooms and definitely not anything else! I suddenly felt very vulnerable. The thought of getting into another relationship so soon scared me but at the same time, I'd been feeling pangs of loneliness or maybe they were just the pangs of something else that had been lacking for a very long time! In any case, it would take someone extremely special to make me give my heart away again.

'What about this one Rosie?' Sue asked, snapping me out of my dilemma daydream

Oh yes, back to choosing toilets. Quite apt after briefly thinking about the heap of shit from my past. I looked at the rather unremarkable plain white bathroom suite on display and shrugged my shoulders.

'Looks alright to me, will do the job I suppose.' I replied, suddenly not in the mood for anything and feeling desperate to go back to the safety of home. The seller of the fabulous self-closing toilets showed Sue the final price for three suites and after a little haggling, managed to get a few quid off. She hadn't really needed me and I'd been a useless bumbling buffoon the entire time anyway. Sue must've sensed my unease and whilst Mr. toilet seat seller went to sort the order out, she stood beside me, both of us looking at a particularly shiny pair of taps.

'You alright my lovely? You've gone ever so quiet. I haven't said anything have I?'

I nudged her playfully. 'Nah, you're ok, just me being daft. I just felt a bit uneasy that's all when you joked about him fancying me, it's nothing.'

She looked at me sympathetically. ' He really hurt you didn't he, your ex. Don't let him ruin the rest of your life though eh, they aren't all like that you know. You're a very pretty girl, remember that, you are going to have admirers from time to time!'.

She was right of course, that is, about not letting my ex ruin my future. The guy only smiled at me, it wasn't as if he'd proclaimed his undying devotion after a few seconds of me walking into the shop. I put my arm around Sue in a silent thank you. Mr. toilet seat seller came back from the office with paperwork for Sue to sign for the fitting and receipt for the deposit and balance to be paid on completion. He explained that a team would be assigned and each bathroom would take approximately three days to a week to complete, depending on whether any pipes would need moving. So, that was that. Operation Bathroom successfully underway. He smiled at me again as we shook hands, a grip that was firmer than I would've liked but I wasn't going to make an issue out of it.

'My name's Stephen Pugh by the way, thank you for your order' he said as we drew our hands away. I nodded acknowledgement then hastily retreated outside before my face spontaneously combusted. When we got back to the pub, I started feeling a bit better and a little stupid at overreacting to a situation that didn't warrant it. I'd gotten so used to my safe haven with people I had grown to trust, I'd forgotten how to interact with strangers and viewed anyone I didn't know as potential predators who would rip me apart with an innocent, friendly smile. As Sue quite rightly pointed out, not everyone was the same and I needed to remember that, if I had any chance of having a happier and full life. I felt slightly angry that I was still allowing the past to hold me back. Putting my embarrassment behind me, I concentrated on more important things. I was quite excited at our plans to revamp the bedrooms. It would be good for the pub to add another string to its bow. It had too much potential and appeal to just be a country pub which offered meals, plus it made business sense to expand what it had to offer. No one needed to know the history and I wasn't going to exploit the tragedy behind it just to get paying customers, who were into the macabre and paranormal, to stay and Sue and Nick agreed. They had spent twenty years preventing any paranormal buffs from poking around after all and I had no intention of changing that. My loyalty towards Bronwen, Deri and Owain was growing and they needed to remain a secret. Obviously they had to take some responsibility too by not scaring guests half to death during their stay, particularly Owain, who, despite softening towards me slightly since telling me how he'd died, was and probably always would be, moody, hotheaded and bordering on the overdramatic.

After a week of waiting, our bathroom suites were ready to be installed. A team of three plumbers arrived bright and early bang on nine am, as arranged, which was a good start. One thing that always bugged me was having to get up early for workmen who never turn up on time. I'd been always slightly OCD about timekeeping, some would've said borderline obsessive, always having to have a rock iron time schedule if I needed to be anywhere for a certain time and if that deviated for any reason, it would send me into a panic that any normal person would just not worry about. Before they arrived, I made sure that my three ghostly companions understood that they were, under no uncertain terms, to not frighten the living shit out of them! Owain particularly got the benefit of my 'Paddington Bear stare', a facial expression inherited from my mother and it had come in extremely handy over the years. It was enough to send Owain off with his usual grunt and rolling of the eyes but I knew he understood how important the renovations were to me so it was just his usual dramatics.

Luckily, access to the upstairs accommodation was via the backdoor so none of the work was going to impact the daily running of the pub. The three plumbers got out of their van, which they'd been able to park in the rear carpark, out of the way of any customers wishing to use it. Two were in their late twenties and the third, to my surprise, was Mr.

Seller of the fabulous toilet seats. He smiled at me as I let them in, looking a little amused at my surprised reaction to him being there.

'I didn't realise you were going to be fitting them', I blurted as I showed them up the ancient staircase to the rooms.

'Full of surprises I am see' he replied with a chuckle, 'bloody hell, this landing's a bit dodgy isn't it!', he added, with the same look of concern that I had the first time I'd stood looking through the gaps in the ancient floorboards.

'Oh you'll be fine but I wouldn't go jumping up and down on it if I were you, just in case, you wouldn't want to end up in a heap down there would you', I replied, joking. He looked at me with wide eyes, before looking at the floorboards with a slightly scared expression, probably beginning to regret taking the job on until he realised that I wasn't actually serious.

'Oh very funny you almost had me there', he laughed, with a hint of sarcasm and embarrassment.

'Full of surprises I am see...', I replied, bringing the banter to a draw.

I showed the team into the first bedroom to be done, the same one that Deri and Owain had revealed their tragic story. Suddenly the temperature dropped and sitting on the bed were Bronwen, Deri and Owain! Oh for God's sake, do they not listen to anything I ask them!

' Don't panic Miss, we just wanted to see what was going on', Deri said, seeing the look of horror and annoyance on my face.

'We'll be good Miss, promise', assured Bronwen, who I could never really be angry with, sweet, innocent child that she was.

Owain just grunted as usual. I looked at the plumbers, who were going into the bathroom, hoping they hadn't seen or heard anything when walking past but thankfully they seemed oblivious to who and what was sitting on the bed!

'Will you three just bugger off!!', I hissed through gritted teeth, waving my hand at them to leave! They were worse than children!

Mr. seller of fabulous toilet seats turned around, catching me waving at nothing.

'Everything alright?', he asked

My face flushed and I had to think fast on my feet.

'Oh fine' I replied quickly, ' Cobwebs...room hasn't been used for a while, walked straight into it...'

'Right....' he said, looking at me as if I wasn't quite right in the head.

Looking over at the bed again, all three looked back with grins on their faces, even Owain looked amused! I gave them my best 'Paddington Bear stare' and with a chuckle from Deri, they disappeared to probably cause mischief elsewhere. I didn't care as long as they didn't scare the plumbers away. The last thing I wanted to do was look online for an idiot guide on how to install three new bathroom suites single handedly! After making sure the plumbers were happy, leaving them with a kettle and enough teabags, sugar and milk to prevent them from bothering me every five minutes, I left them to start the carnage of knocking the bathroom apart. I decided to put a polite notice on the front door apologising to customers for any noise disruption and to inform them that we wouldn't be serving food until the work was done, due to intermittent water supplies. I just hoped everything would run smoothly but I always had a really bad habit of speaking too soon.

Just as I was locking the front door for the afternoon, I heard a voice calling from the door leading to the stairs. Mr. seller of toilets came through into the bar looking a bit flustered.

'Everything alright?' I asked. He looked at me as if he was reluctant to say anything at first.

'Erm, I hope you don't think I'm being funny' he stuttered ' but have you ever noticed anything a bit weird going on with your electrics?'

I smiled to myself, remembering the time I'd almost blown up the place changing lightbulbs.

'No, can't say I have, why do you ask?' I replied

He looked at me, slightly exasperated.

'We've had nothing but bother with everything this morning. Lights kept going on and off, our tools drained of power then wouldn't charge, really don't know what's going on to be honest'.

Oh for crying out loud! I knew exactly what was wrong and it was going to stop!

' Oh yes sorry, we've had some intermittent power outages this morning, I think the whole village has had them. I'm sure it won't last and things will be sorted soon'.

He nodded then went back upstairs. I waited until I was sure he was out of earshot.

'Right you three, get in here NOW!', I shouted.

One by one, Bronwen, Deri and Owain appeared. Bronwen looked like she was going to cry, Deri looked sheepish and Owain just looked like he usually did.

'Oh Miss, please don't be angry, we had good reason!' wailed Bronwen.

'Yes Miss we did', agreed Deri, putting his arm around a distressed Bronwen.

'Oh really! Would someone care to explain exactly why, when you promised you wouldn't do anything!', I replied, folding my arms and trying my best to look as angry as possible.

'They said things about you', grumbled Owain, perching himself in his usual place on the windowsill.

'What things?'

Bronwen suddenly blushed, I'd never seen her do that before.

'Oh Miss, they were rude Miss, they said things about your....', she stopped herself and looked at the floor. Deri gave her a supportive squeeze.

'Aright then boys, are you able to tell me then?'

I looked at Deri, who'd also started to look embarrassed and refused to say anything so I shot my gaze over to Owain to see if I'd get anything out of him instead. He shuffled about on the windowsill, looking slightly uncomfortable.

'Well??' I demanded

'We were curious as to what they were doing. The young ones started it. They started talking about you so we stayed to listen. They made comments about the size of your...' Owain clammed up suddenly too.

'Comments about the size of my what Owain?!' This was like pulling teeth!

'For God's sake woman, breasts! They were talking about your breasts!'

Oh shit, really?! No wonder poor innocent and sensitive Bronwen looked like she was just about to faint. My anger subsided, how could I stay angry at them. In their own way, they had been looking out for me, although it had set back work being done. I looked at them, all three looking rather dejected and a little hurt. I relaxed my tensed-up body and smiled at them, feeling appreciative of their growing loyalty towards me.

' Alright, I'm not angry with you anymore. You were only doing what you thought was right and I thank you for that. Just do me a favour, if you do hear anything else though, can you please tell me first before you decide to take things into your own hands. We really need this work to be done. I've got underpants older than those boys and I think I can handle a few comments.'

Bronwen looked relieved, her sensitive nature probably couldn't take me losing my temper too many times. Owain and Deri nodded their acknowledgement to my request.

'Oh just one other thing...', I added...'Did they say I had nice ones then?'

With that, Bronwen swooned and promptly vanished. I concluded that I probably wouldn't have anyone to talk to at home for a while.

Days went by and true to their word, my three ghostly friends left the plumbers to their work and the first bathroom was coming along nicely. Bronwen, however, still wasn't really talking to me after I'd sent her over the edge about my boobs but I knew she wouldn't stay mad for long. Deri and Owain reported a few comments had been made by the young plumbers but nothing really bad and they seemed to be reprimanded by Mr. Seller of toilet seats who, despite being the boss of the company, seemed to take great interest in our renovations and do a lot of the work himself. Maybe he just wanted to get out of his shop and do the job he had obviously been trained for years ago.

Although I hadn't really had much to do with him during the course of the first week, he'd occasionally wandered into the bar on his break, sitting quietly in the corner of the room, reading his newspaper and drinking coffee. I hadn't disturbed him during his breaks but as it was getting towards the end of the first week, I wanted to check on progress and also to make sure there hadn't been anymore electrical mishaps caused by 'unexplained' occurrences. Walking over to where he was sitting, with a jug of freshly brewed filter coffee in my hand, he looked up at me and smiled, folding up his paper as he did so.

'More coffee Mr....?' I asked

'Call me Steve please' he replied as he nodded, gesturing another cup would be welcomed.

'Do you have a minute to talk about progress?' I asked as I filled up his cup.

He nodded and I sat down across the table. I suddenly felt slightly shy. I hadn't been sat across a table with a man in a one to one conversation in what felt like a lifetime. We hadn't really spoken at length before, I'd just shown him the rooms and let him and his team get on with their work, only really speaking when there had been that electrical problem caused by my increasingly overprotective ghosts.

'Well, Miss...' he started

'Call me Rosie', I interrupted before he could carry on. I could feel my face beginning to flush in Chenoble proportions and I started to fidget nervously in my chair. Oh for crying out loud, how old was I! I'd been dealing with men on a daily basis ever since I'd moved to Mynydd Eira so why was I feeling so awkward talking to him!

'Ok...Rosie....' he continued, looking me straight in the eye as he smiled, making my face furnace burn down my neck and onto my chest.

I seriously hoped it wasn't glowing as red as it felt!

'We're about a day behind for the first bathroom I'm afraid due to that problem we had, if you remember, but things are going well. Hopefully, without any more mishaps, we should be complete on all three bathrooms in three weeks maximum. There're no changes to the location of the plumbing, just to replace worn parts so it's just a case of ripping out the old and installing the new. Hope that timescale's ok with you?'

I just nodded like a car dashboard bobblehead. What the hell was wrong with me?! It wasn't as if he was some LA, tanned, six packed, chiseled jawed stud wannabe actor, who was between jobs replacing knackered toilets, he was just a normal bloke. Maybe it was just me, waking up from my nun like hibernation and realising that maybe all I needed was a damn good seeing to. WOW, I'm glad I hadn't said that out loud!!

'So, you're happy so far then yeah?' Steve asked, looking slightly concerned that if I didn't stop nodding, my head would possibly fall off.

I snapped out of my bobblehead bonanza and my sudden, silent revelation to myself that my bits and bobs had started to bite and bob again.

'Yep, yep...fab...I mean..yes, I'm happy...aha...' I stammered, making a conscious effort to keep my head still as my neck was beginning to get a bit sore.

'That's good, thanks for the coffee. Can you add that to my tab please?'

Steve stood up, smiling at me. As he made his way towards the back stairs to start work again, he turned back towards me.

'Oh just one other thing...on your night off, do you fancy going for a drink with me?'

What...the...fu...did he just ask me out???

'Let me know yeah?' he asked before making a swift getaway upstairs.

Suddenly I felt a familiar whoosh of cold air and one by one, my ghostly friends appeared.

'Well Miss', grunted Owain, ' looks like it's not just the young ones you've charmed with your...'

'Owain, don't be so disgusting!' shouted Bronwen before sitting next to me, grabbing my hands into hers.

'Well I don't think you should get familiar with him, I don't like him', snorted Owain.

'You don't bloody like anyone Owain, to be fair!' I retorted, giving him my best Paddington.

Bronwen and Deri chuckled before Owain did his usual grunt and eye roll. He was still getting used to me giving as good as I got and he didn't like it one little bit.

'So, what do you think I should do? Should I say yes?' I asked, looking at Deri as he was the most level headed of the three, although in fairness to Bronwen, her tender youth and inexperience of life, despite being hundreds of years old in death, wasn't much help in the girlie advice department.

'I don't trust him Miss Rosie, I don't think you should' snorted Owain

'Yes, thank you Owain, I'd gathered that', I snapped

Deri sighed and sat beside me.

' Miss, you're a grown woman. If you don't mind me saying, I believe that you're lonely and in need of company of someone closer to your own age. If you decide to step out with this gentleman, then that is obviously up to you but I will say, please be cautious. You have a tender heart Miss Rosie and we would hate to see you being taken advantage of'

I nodded gratefully for his honest advice. I think deep down, that's what Owain was trying to say too but as usual, his way with words wasn't as diplomatic as Deri's.

Deri was right though. I was lonely. I thought living on my own was the best way to be after being hurt but I was starting to crave affection and attention again. I wasn't sure if I was ready for a full-blown relationship but a bit of fun surely couldn't hurt. I sat back in my chair and sighed. Bronwen was still squeezing my hands, bless her, making them colder with each passing minute but I didn't want to make her feel bad about that. I smiled at her and squeezed back then tactfully broke contact by gently moving my hands from hers.

'Alright then', I sighed

'Let's get this over with then'. I stood up and made my way up the back stairs, leaving my three ghostly protectors wondering what my decision was going to be. I found Steve with a sealant gun in his hand, putting the finishing touches to the bath. He stopped what he was doing and looked at me curiously.

'Are you serious about that drink?' I asked, looking around the bathroom as if to check out the work, to try and conceal my awkwardness.

'Of course I am, wouldn't have asked otherwise', he replied, as a blob of sealant dripped onto the newly tiled flooring, making him swear under his breath as he grabbed a cloth.

'Ok then, I'm off tomorrow night if you're free'.

That was it, no backing out now, I'd said it.

Oh shit.

Steve's face seemed to light up. I wasn't sure if it was because he'd managed to clean the blob off the floor or me accepting his invitation.

'Oh, that's great, yeah I'm free tomorrow night. Pick you up around Seven pm?'

I smiled and nodded then swiftly exited the bathroom as quickly as I could before my face burnt to a crisp.

I then suddenly realised that I had only twenty-four hours to rectify months of singledom slobbery.

This was going to be like 'Mission Impossible'. I'd spent best part of an hour trying to find hedge clippers, more commonly known as my epilator, which I found shoved in a drawer under my best pants. No wonder I hadn't seen it for a while. I'd been making a half-arsed effort with a disposable razor for so long but this needed just that little bit extra. As I sat on my bed in my underwear and started defuzzing my legs, I realised I'd forgotten the time-consuming high maintenance pain of possibly getting up close and personal with someone again. Finally, after twenty minutes of getting into every undignified position to make sure I hadn't missed anywhere and dealing with the excruciating cramp that came with it, the battle with my legs was finally won and as I smothered each one in body lotion, I suddenly stopped. A horrible realisation hit me! I stood up, walked over to the mirror and pushed my underwear down an inch.

'Oh you've got to be fucking kidding me!' I sighed. I was gonna need a bloody epidural for this one!

I was still sore when I went into work the next morning! I honestly didn't know why I'd even attempted to make myself 'Beach Ready' when A: I wasn't going anywhere near a sodding beach and B: I had no intention of dropping my newly rediscovered best pants on a first date! Even if I had been that kind of girl, the affected area wasn't in a fit state to be seen, let alone anything else! As I filled the ice bucket, other uses for the cubes sprang to mind! Sue wandered into the bar and looked at me with a bemused look on her face, as I gingerly walked over to give the tables a quick wipe over,

'A little birdy tells me you've got a date with Mr. Bathroom...'

'Aha...'I replied, wincing as discreetly as I could, as I moved bar mats on the table from one side to the other.

'Where's he taking you then?' Sue continued. I could feel her eyes burning into the back of me as I continued to hobble around the room.

'Er...dunno, he hasn't said....'

'Rosie, if you don't mind me asking...why are you hobbling about with a face like a slapped behind when you've got a big date coming up'

I stopped what I was doing, looked at her with a half Paddington and whispered...

'You really don't want to know.....'

As I carried on finishing cleaning the tables, Sue stood as if in thought then said

' I always swore by Aloe Vera myself, back in the day...takes the heat out of it I found'. She then made a very hasty retreat.

Throwing the cleaning cloth across the table, I let out a loud sigh and looked up towards the heavens. Between my burning bits and now burning face, I was beginning to wonder what the hell I was thinking, going out with a man I barely knew. I was just about to go upstairs to tell Steve that I wasn't going to be able to make our date when he breezily walked into the bar, making me jump. I straightened my back and tried not to show my lingering discomfort and recent embarrassment and forced a smile.

'Good morning Rosie, how are you? I'm really looking forward to tonight!'.

Damn! That was my get out of jail free card screwed then. How could I let down someone who seemed as enthusiastic as a playful puppy? I hadn't had anyone wanting to spend time with me for so long. I still hadn't quite worked out what I wanted to lift this mood. Was I in need of a damn good seeing to or just a shit load of Jaffa cakes. Both equally nice to have, although considering my past relationship track record, Jaffa cakes would probably last longer. Did I really need another car crash?

'So...', continued Steve, snapping me out of my Jaffa cake or jump dilemma. ' I was wondering, shall I meet you here at seven pm? Maybe have a drink before heading off into town?'

His eyes, which had been wide with childlike excitement suddenly looked at me with concern.

'Are you alright?' he asked, looking a little dejected at my obvious lack of enthusiasm. I needed to get a grip. This was just a drink with someone of the opposite sex. I wasn't about to marry the man! Tarring someone with the same shitty brush wasn't fair and my insecurities weren't his fault. Seven pm here would be great', I said finally, trying to sound as positive as I could. Steve's face relaxed again as he nodded with a smile.

'Brilliant!' he half shouted before heading back upstairs. I could hear him whistling to himself as he reached the bedrooms. Maybe this evening was just what I needed. An ego boost as well as an opportunity to expand my social circle to people who were actually alive. I also didn't have any Jaffa cakes.

Standing in front of the mirror, I cast a critical eye over two hours of exfoliation, moisturisation and cosmetic transformation. My long dark cherry red hair glistened after being deep conditioned, blow dried then curled by an ancient curling tong that was hotter than Chernobyl. If I did have too much to drink later and fell on my head, my brain would at least be protected by the rock-hard hairspray that was still choking me. I had to make do with what makeup I had lurking in my rather grubby makeup bag but as long as I didn't think too much about the possible germ fest that was now on my face, my smoky eyes and full raspberry lips looked quite hot. It had been a while since I'd done 'The Works'. It felt good, heavy as hell but good all the same. My entire wardrobe was now all over the floor and bed, mostly due to a spectacular toddler tantrum and cursing myself for not going shopping sooner for new clothes for those 'just in case I got a life' moments. I'd settled finally for a plain black skater skirt, a black and white patterned cold shoulder top. My waist was pulled in within an inch of its slightly flabby life by a black cincher belt with silver buckle. Not one to get my stumpy legs out often, I'd played safe with black opaque tights and my trusty but slightly sexy black calf length boots. Turning in every direction possible, even bending over to make sure my tights covered what it needed to cover under a skirt that was slightly too short, I suddenly wondered if it made my bum look big. It wasn't the skirt that made my bum look big, it was my bum that made my bum look big. Too late to lose weight off my weeble behind now, I only had half an hour before I was meeting him. Nerves suddenly kicked in and I seriously wished I'd bought a bottle of wine earlier. Just as I was about to have a confidence crisis, I felt a chill in the air before hearing a soft knock in the doorway. Turning around, I saw Bronwen standing there, smiling. She clapped her hands, rather too enthusiastically in my opinion but that was just Bronwen being an excitable 'teenager'.

'Oh my word Miss, you look beautiful!'

'Do you really think so?', I asked, pulling at my top to try to cover my voluptuous bottom.

'Yes, indeed I do Miss. I don't believe I have ever seen you looking so ladylike, if you don't mind me saying so'.

Was that Bronwen's sweet way of telling me that I normally looked like a crock of crap? I smiled gratefully for her compliment then turned back for a final peruse. She glided beside me and I felt a cold but not unpleasant touch on my arm.

'Believe in yourself Miss. All we ask is that you stay safe and well.'

It wasn't the first time that my three spirit companions had expressed concern for my wellbeing. A bond was forming between us, slowly but surely.

'Thank you', I whispered as Bronwen gently faded away. Resisting the urge to brush my hair for the hundredth time, I slipped on my cropped black leather jacket and headed downstairs, determined, that whatever happened tonight, I would enjoy a few precious hours outside my life.

I hadn't been so apprehensive about walking into the pub since that very first day that I'd arrived in Mynydd Eira. It was a home from home now but for a split second, it felt strange and unfamiliar again. I pushed the door open and walked as confidently as I could into the bar. My insides were churning. I hadn't been on a date for so many years. I'd forgotten what it was like. Steve was already there, sitting by the bar, chatting to Sue. They both looked up and I could see Sue's eyes widen.

'Wow!!" she mouthed silently, giving me a wink. As I walked up to them, as ladylike as I could in my heeled boots, Steve broke into the biggest grin I'd seen on his face since I met him.

'Hiya guys, you ok?' I said, as breezily as I could muster without my nerves betraying me.

'Wow Rosie, you look stunning!' exclaimed Steve. He got off his stool and gave me a peck on the cheek, which took me by surprise. Slightly forward of him but I let it be what it was, a gentlemanly gesture.

'Why thank you kind sir', secretly high fiving myself on two hours well spent. Sue handed me my drink then gestured to Steve that this one was on the house. I took a sip then nearly choked at its strength. Sue winked at me again. She had learnt to read me like a book over the past months and I gave her a wry smile as I raised my glass to her. She knew, that although on the outside, I seemed alright, on the inside however, I was fighting demons.

We spent the next half an hour chatting between us. Having Sue behind the bar helped me relax slightly. Steve told me he'd booked a table at the Chinese restaurant in town so I knew that my Sue shaped comfort blanket was going to be temporary. I was a grown woman however, I couldn't hide behind my friend all night. Then the time came for us to leave. Steve excused himself to use the gents, leaving Sue and I in the bar alone. I heard a cough from the direction of the window and looked round to see Owain in his usual place.

'You mind yourself tonight Miss Rosie' he said, his usually stern face softer than I'd seen before.

We looked at each other for what seemed forever, a silent understanding was forming and I nodded, grateful for his concern. The door to the gents opened as Steve came back into the bar and Owain quickly faded.

'It's definitely getting chillier at nights now, have you noticed? Its freezing in that toilet'

Sue and I exchanged amused looks, both of us realising where Deri had been whilst Owain was giving me the pep talk.

'Ready to go then Rosie?' asked Steve as he put on his jacket. He did scrub up rather well, I had to admit, as I caught a whiff of his aftershave. Yves Saint Laurent if I wasn't mistaken. The same one as the cheating twat of an ex. What were the chances of that! He looked more muscular than I'd noticed before in his straight legged, stone washed jeans and white open collared shirt. I tried to resist the urge to check out his backside but it was only going to be a matter of time before my eyes wandered. No harm in looking. I wasn't entirely sure but he even looked like he'd had a haircut. We said our goodbyes and as Steve held the door open for me, I looked back round for reassurance. Owain, Deri, Bronwen and Sue stood there and I gave them a final weak smile before going outside into the unknown world of 'Date land'. I was, in all honesty, scared to death. Steve unlocked his Audi and opened the passenger door for me to get in. Posh car and manners. Maybe this wasn't going to be as bad as I thought. As he got into the driver's seat, he looked at me with a grin.

'Well I hope you're hungry. You do eat Chinese, don't you? Oh I should've asked, shouldn't I!'

I chuckled and told him not to panic. Chinese was my favourite and the look of relief on his face was clear to see. The thought of having something a bit more exciting than the rather tasteless microwaveable frozen meals for the sad and single definitely appealed. It was only a ten-minute drive into town, enough time to soak up the posh car smell mingling with Yves Saint Laurent and a car vent air freshener. Obviously business was doing well for him. I was in the wrong job. How many toilets did he have to sell to afford one of these I wondered.

We parked in the restaurant car park and I was halfway out of the car before he'd gotten to my door. I think he was going to open it again for me but I didn't like to presume, plus I wasn't used to having doors opened for me anyway. We were welcomed by a smartly dressed young man who showed us to our table. An intimate table for two in a quiet corner by the biggest fish tank I'd ever seen. At least if Steve turned out to be the most boring conversationalist on earth, I'd be able to amuse myself by trying to find Nemo. After ordering drinks, we spent the next five minutes with our heads in our respective menus. Another first date dilemma reared its head, did I opt for the cheapest thing on the menu in order to keep down my side of the bill or to take advantage of an Audi owning businessman who might be paying for the lot.

' Choose what you want Rosie, this is my treat', he said, hiding behind his leather-bound menu.

Problem solved!

I ordered the crispy shredded beef with special fried rice. A dodgy option, considering my grubby habit of getting my dinner down my top but anything spicier was reserved for those alone moments. Nothing worse than having to squeeze one's bum cheeks for hours on end. Then the dreaded question came.

'So Rosie, tell me about yourself? I can't believe a lovely girl like you is single!'

Oh god, why the hell do I begin? Should I tell him everything? Being rejected by my mother for not being good enough. Being used as a walking, talking punchbag for years by a borderline alcoholic husband then being dumped by another binge drinker fiancé who clumsily fell into another woman's pants. Oh and not forgetting that my best friends just so happened to have been dead for a couple of hundred years. It would be nice to actually make it past the starter at least so playing safe, I just said I hadn't met the right person.

'So, what about you then?' I asked, quickly deflecting the conversation away from me and back onto him.

'Well', he said ' I'm divorced, have been for a while now. We were childhood sweethearts, got married way too young then drifted apart. We haven't got any kids. We did think about it but by the time I'd finished my plumbing apprenticeship then started the business, we didn't have time for anything else. I think that's why we drifted apart, we just had the business in common in the end'.

I was surprised by his honesty, considering he didn't really know me. That boded well, at least he felt comfortable sharing his personal life even if I didn't feel the same way. As the waiter brought our food and placed it onto the table, our conversation went to lighter subjects such as taste in music, film and television. Although we did share the same taste in rock music, when I mentioned that I was a horror film fan, his face screwed up a bit and he went a bit white. I tried stifling a chuckle. If only he'd known that ever since he'd been working in the pub, he'd been sharing it with three very dead people. Also, if he'd known he'd been standing next to Deri in the toilet, I'm sure his stone washed jeans wouldn't be in the same pristine condition.

'What are you smirking at?' he enquired with a bemused look, as I tried hard not to choke on my special fried rice.

'Oh nothing, sorry. Just thought of something that happened earlier that made me laugh. Nothing to do with you being a complete bloody wuss at all'. He started laughing. The ice was beginning to break. For the rest of the night, we didn't stop talking and laughing. Nemo stayed unfound and my life started to spark.

As he stopped the car outside the pub, we sat in silence for a moment before he broke it.

'Can I see you again?' he asked quietly. The yellow light from the lamppost softly lit his face.

'Course you can, I'm back in work tomorrow afternoon remember!', I said, nervously making light of his question.

'You know what I bloody mean!', he chuckled. ' Well? Can I?'

I sat there for what seemed an eternity.

'I'd like that', I whispered finally, looking at him through my fringe.

He smiled gently then leaned over and softly kissed me.

'I'll see you tomorrow', he said, releasing my seatbelt. I opened the car door and got out. I put my head back into the car to give him a final smile.

'Yep, you certainly will. Thanks for tonight. Night then'

He nodded then I shut the door and watched him drive away. As I walked the short way home, my heart was banging in my chest. What had I started?

CHAPTER EIGHT

It turned out that my need for Jaffa cakes was very quickly squashed after our first date, we began to see a lot more of each other after that. A lot more. At all sorts of different angles. I was surprised how devious he became in order to spend time with me. Our liaisons tended to be during afternoon closing. He sent his boys to get parts from suppliers which were much further away than they needed to be. As I was technically one of the people employing his services, I didn't mind too much that he had an hour or so off during the afternoon. The bathroom renovations were slipping behind a little but I didn't care anymore. It meant I saw him on a regular basis as well as improving the pub's potential. What did strike me as odd however was his reluctance to stay the night at mine or indeed invite me to stay the occasional night at his. In fact, I still didn't know where he lived. I was always guilty of overthinking things so maybe it was just far too soon to be leaving a spare toothbrush in our respective houses. It was what it was. Before we knew it, four weeks had flown by. Four weeks of what could be described in some romantic novels as ' a torrid affair'. I just called it being shagged bandy. I was living in my very own porn film and apart from finding it difficult to walk up the stairs sometimes due to suspected hip displacement, I was enjoying every second. The renovations were completed and it was time to let my lover move onto another job. I was sad to see him go, our afternoons had made the days an absolute delight. However, I was sure that we would still see each other after work and let our relationship flourish into something more. It was going to unfold very differently to how I'd hoped.

After Steve had finished our renovations, any contact we had become sporadic to say the least. The odd text message here and there, a two-minute phone conversation in between. There had been no more date nights and definitely no more horizontal gymnastics. At first, I tried being understanding. He had a business to run after all. My patience and understanding came to an abrupt halt at six fifteen on a blustery morning, three weeks after he'd left.

'Oh my fucking god, just kill me now!' I begged to the universe as my guts suddenly ended up down the toilet. That's all I needed, a stomach bug on top of everything else. By seven am, I was still in a heap on the floor of my bathroom, dry heaving and knackered. I finally managed to crawl back into my bed and lay there, wanting the world to end. I couldn't be ill, I didn't have time to be ill. Now all the bedrooms had new bathrooms and been revamped with new bedding and soft furnishings, we were due to start advertising our pub as a Bed and Breakfast and I had to be there to help Sue get it off the ground. I'd taken advantage over the past weeks and felt I needed to give something back. The only thing I wanted to give back at this moment in time was my right to live. I fumbled for my phone and text Sue.

'I'm dyin' I wrote, rather melodramatically. ' can I come in later please?'

My phone rang two minutes later.

' What's up lovely, are you alright??' Sue questioned, concern in her voice. Luckily I wasn't a sickly person normally so for me to ask for time off sick meant I must've been poorly.

'Oh god Sue I'm bloody dying here, I'm so sorry. Just been throwing my insides down the toilet for the past hour'. I felt like crying. I tended to regress to my inner five-year-old when not very well. A comfort dippy egg and soldiers however wasn't appealing to this little girl just now.

'Aww poor love. Listen, take the day off, we'll manage. If you're being sick you can't come into work anyway, health and hygiene rules and all that. See how you feel tomorrow, alright my lovely. I'll text you later. Oh by the way, Deri sends his best wishes, he's just popped up to tell me he felt you weren't well. I never knew they could feel that, that's a new one eh! Get some sleep. Bye my love'.

Just as I was about to snuggle back under my cosy duvet, my stomach had other ideas. I narrowly made it to the bathroom before my conversation with the man upstairs continued. I could feel Bronwen's presence. As she stroked my hair, I began to wonder how long it would be before I joined her.

I managed to drag myself into work the following morning. Sue was stocking the fridges.

'Bloody hell Rosie have you seen yourself!', she exclaimed, almost dropping a mixer on the floor.

'Oh cheers! Morning to you too!', I pouted, dragging myself onto a bar stool and resting my head on the bar.

'Well in all honesty my love, I have seen you looking more radiant. I don't think you should be here again today. Go home!'

I lifted my head up and caught sight of myself in the bar mirror. She had a point. Dark circles and bags the size of suitcases under my eyes stared back. Suddenly a voice from behind made me jump.

'From your pallor, I believe even we look more alive'

With all my effort, I turned my head to see Owain sitting on the windowsill. I really didn't have the energy for his sarcastic bullshit today

'May I suggest you see a physician', he added.

'And may I suggest Owain that you just fuck off', I groaned, as my stomach started to churn again.

Oh that was a bit harsh.

'I'm sorry Owain, that was uncalled for. I apologise'.

He jumped down, strided over and stood beside me, looking me up and down.

'Considering your state of health, I won't take offence at your response. I am however offering my advice, consult your physician. You really do not look well' he grunted.

I nodded weakly then Owain faded away. Suddenly my stomach lurched and I leapt off the bar stool and ran like a gazelle to the Ladies, narrowly avoiding decorating the bar floor with what little stomach contents I had left. As I sat on the floor, I took my phone out of my pocket to call the surgery. I noticed the date on the screen. A wave of confusion suddenly hit me. In all of the dizzy haze of lust filled days followed by the crashing low of being possibly dumped, I hadn't noticed that a certain monthly event hadn't happened. I tapped on the calendar and started to count backwards. I didn't need a doctor, I needed a chemist and quickly. I heaved myself off the floor, told Sue that I was going to go home if that was still alright. As I drove the short distance to the chemist, I started praying that my suspicions were wrong.

'Why the bloody hell can't they make these things longer!', I cursed to myself as my dignity went out of the window. Not only do women have the feelings of excitement/dread when doing a pregnancy test, weeing all over one's hand didn't sodding help the situation. The soft and fluffy television adverts never showed a woman having to wash wee off herself after peeing on a stick. I replaced the cap over the end of the pregnancy test and put it on the bathroom shelf. Three minutes it said. The longest three minutes anyone would ever spend! I didn't want to look at it. I paced up and down the landing. I walked into the bedroom then walked straight back out. I could see the tester on the shelf, like a ticking time bomb. Had my wee done its thing or was it still making its mind up. The three minutes were definitely up. I picked up the stick, closed my eyes, took a deep breath then opened them. Well the scores on the doors were in. My plumbing had been well and truly plumbed by the now absent plumber.

'Oh shit!'

There was no doubting the result. The glaringly obvious happy smiling face and the phrase ' you stupid fucking mare ' disguised in the word 'pregnant' left no confusion. That was that then. How could I have been so stupid!! Part of me tried to justify the situation. I'd become pregnant three times during my marriage. Three times I'd miscarried due to his abuse. Three times my heart broke until telling myself it was for the best. Then years passed without falling pregnant again even though I'd been in a relationship where safe sex just meant he'd passed out drunk before the money shot. I resigned myself to the fact that I wasn't able to conceive after the miscarriages, I thought it would never happen.

'You know what thought did Rosie. You thought it was just a fart and it wasn't and look at the fucking shit you're in now!'

'You're wh..what?' stammered Sue, as she almost dropped her coffee cup. I felt like a stupid teenager telling her mum that she'd gotten herself into trouble after a quick bunk up behind the bike shed.

'Pregnant, up the duff, bun in the oven, fucking screwed..whatever you'd like to call it, I'm it!' I cried, trying my best not to burst into tears.

Sue slumped back in her chair, let out a big sigh then straightened herself again.

'And you're definitely sure?' she asked

I looked at her with frightened eyes.

'Well, the happy smiley face on the pee stick kind of gave it away a bit' I sighed, picking up my coffee cup then putting it back down again when my stomach lurched at the smell.

'Does Mr. Bathroom know?' she enquired, leaning back just in case it was a question I didn't particularly like. Pushing the coffee cup away from me before I upchucked all over the table, I grumbled to myself, swearing under my breath.

'I take that as a No then' Sue said gently

Tears prickled my eyes then started to roll down my cheeks.

'Oh Sue, I dunno what the hell's going on there! I haven't heard from him really since he finished the job! I thought we were getting on. I've text him but replies have been few and far between. It's like he's just disappeared off the planet'.

She looked at me sympathetically. I could tell what she was thinking. It was the same horrible realisation I'd tried very hard not to reach. He'd used me.

'Have you thought about maybe going to the shop? He's bound to be there at some point. Even if things are over between you, it would be closure at least. You don't have to tell him about the baby but he does have a right to know'.

I sat back in my chair and stared up at the ceiling. I could just imagine the confrontation in the middle of the bathroom displays. Oh yeah hi Steve, remember me? I'm the one you shagged while plumbing in my new toilets and by the way, you've plumbed my pipes as well.

Oh what a bloody mess!

Maybe she did have a point. Instead of driving myself mad wondering what had gone wrong, finding out for definite was the only way forward.

'Whatever happens Rosie, you're not on your own', Sue continued. 'You're family to us now. If you decide to have this baby, Nick and I will be behind you all the way, you have no worries there!'

I blew my nose, pulled myself together then got up and gave Sue a hug. She'd become like a mum to me and I knew whatever life was to throw at me, she would be there. Something I wasn't used to.

Suddenly, the room chilled and one by one, Bronwen, Deri and Owain appeared. Obviously, conversations weren't private anymore.

'Oh Miss!' cried Bronwen, ' you won't get sent away will you to one of those horrible places! That's what happens doesn't it, to those unwed and with child! Oh I couldn't bear it if you were sent away!'

Oh, poor sweet innocent Bronwen! I reassured her that being sent away didn't happen anymore and she seemed to brighten up.

Deri looked unusually sombre. I hoped he wasn't disappointed in me. But as he put his hand on my shoulder and gave it a gentle squeeze, I knew he wasn't going to judge me. Then it was Owain's turn. He stood with shoulders back and looked me straight in the eye.

'I did warn you Miss. I told you I didn't trust him!' he said abruptly

'Now you hang on there Owain!' Sue leapt to my defence as my face started to crumple again. Suddenly Owain raised his hand and the room darkened for a second.

'BUT!' he shouted ' But...I may not show it but I have grown fon..'he stopped mid-sentence, cleared his throat then carried on.

'I have grown to tolerate you and I am sorry to see you in this situation. Therefore, you can count on us also to help, as limited as that can be.'

I wiped my nose with the back of my hand as my tissue was battered beyond any further use. Looking at them all standing there, I suddenly felt more wanted than I'd ever had before.

' Thank you', I whispered before looking directly at Owain, 'all of you'.

My stomach finally lurched beyond saving and on this occasion, I didn't quite make it to the toilet. I looked at them all staring at the mess and I just wanted to die even more than before.

'I'll get the mop then' Sue said finally. 'I think maybe some sick bags in your pocket might be an idea next time eh?'

The woman was a saint!

Sue gave me time off. I think she wanted to protect the pub from my head spinning, projectile vomiting episodes. She also wanted me to get my mind settled, well as settled as anyone could be facing impending single motherhood. I had my pregnancy confirmed by the doctor and I was roughly six to seven weeks gone. Nothing could be taken for granted however considering my previous miscarriages so I was going to take each day as it came. I did decide however to find out where I stood with the plumber. He didn't have to know about the baby yet but I needed to know why he'd suddenly gone cold. I picked my moment carefully. The last thing I wanted was to throw up in the middle of a bathroom showroom whilst possibly being officially dumped.

I stood on the pavement outside the shop with my heart in my mouth. We'd shared ourselves intimately with each other but it felt like I was confronting a stranger. He was, in all honesty. I didn't know much about him, we never got that far. Grabbing courage from the pit of my stomach, I pushed the door open and walked in. I still remembered the very first time I'd been there. The first time I'd seen him, the first time he'd made me blush. There was a woman sitting at the desk, writing paperwork. She smiled then rose to walk to greet me. I noticed she had a baby bump underneath her smart charcoal grey tunic. I resisted the urge to blurt out that I was in the club too.

'Hello there, can I help you?' she enquired putting a protective hand on her bump.

'Erm, yeah, well, I was actually looking for Steve to be honest. He did a job for us in Mynydd Eira, the pub renovation'

I looked at her whilst she thought for a moment then her face seemed to register.

'Oh yes I remember! You must be Rosie, right? He's told me about you and the pub. He said the renovation was quite a job! It overran if I remember rightly'

I nodded, wondering what else he'd told her about me.

' Is there a problem I can help with? He's not here at the moment but I'm expecting him back any time now. We're shutting early today, I'm off for a scan'.

She patted her tummy excitedly. I smiled at her and felt her obvious joy at becoming a mother.

'How long have you got left?' I asked, hoping it wasn't too personal.

'Eight weeks and counting! It's been pretty eventful to be honest, I haven't been well at all. I've been in and out of hospital which has been so tough, especially on my husband. We've been trying for so long to have a baby, we thought it was never going to happen!'

Just as she was about to carry on telling me her life story, a door opened from the back storeroom and in walked the absent plumber. The woman's back was to him so she didn't see his face go ashen white as he saw me. He quickly composed himself and forced a smile as he walked towards us both. My heart skipped a beat before slamming against my chest.

'Oh you're back, brilliant! Rosie here from the Mynydd Eira renovation is here to talk to you Steve. I've told her we're closing early but we've got time before we need to leave'. Steve nodded and she turned to me.

'I'll leave you again in the capable hands of my husband. It was nice to meet you'.

I smiled weakly, unable to speak.

Husband?!

What...the...fu...

As she disappeared into the storeroom, Steve rushed up to me.

'What are you doing here?!' he whispered, with a mixture of desperation, shock and anger.

What was I doing there? I felt like smashing his head against the 'Athena' bathroom suite with gold waterfall taps and whirlpool jets.

'Listen Rosie', he whispered, trying not be too loud or remotely animated. 'I'm sorry I lied alright. Things have been so stressful, what with the business and the baby on the way...'

Make that 'babies', arsehole

'What we had was fun, wasn't it? I thought you knew that's all it was. We never spoke about anything more than what it was!'

He sounded even more desperate and just a little scared. Scared that I would blow a hole in his nice cosy marriage to his not so ex-wife with a baby nice and cosy inside her.

I looked him up and down. My animal instincts were telling me to punch him in the head. My pride however, was more reserved.

I went right up to him and fixed him with the most vicious Paddington I'd ever given. He backed off slightly, fear emanated from his eyes. I whispered as loudly as I dare.

'You are the most pathetic, lying, cheating twat I've ever had the misfortune to meet!'

Since the last pathetic, lying, cheating twat that is.

You don't deserve to have a nice wife, let alone a baby on the way! Do yourself a favour, next time you feel the urge to cheat on your wife and use someone to boost your grubby little fantasies, have a wank instead!'

I spun on my toes and walked through the showroom, with my head as high as I could muster then slammed the door behind me for effect. As soon as I was in my car, I sat and broke my heart all over the steering wheel.

Sitting by the fire in the bar, I stared as the flames did their dance in the hearth to a soft crackling tune. I didn't want to be alone. The seasons were changing outside and so was my life. Again. The dangling carrot of happiness always seemed to be snatched away from me just as I was about to grab it. All my life it seemed, people had used me and lied to me, taken advantage of my trusting, loving nature then when it suited them, thrown me away with the rubbish. How the hell was I going to do this when all I knew were lies and deceit. I wrapped myself up in my waterfall cardigan like a comfort blanket and carried on watching the little fairies in the flames. I only had a few brief hours to sit here before opening time again. I tried to forget how I'd spent my afternoons upstairs, just a short time ago. The air chilled and I looked up and saw Owain standing by the window. He walked over and stood by the table.

'May I sit?' he asked

I nodded without taking my eyes off the flames.

We sat in silence for a while. He didn't talk and I didn't really want to listen but I don't think he was actually there for conversation. Not at first anyway.

'I've seen my fair share of people stare into that fire over the years' he eventually said. 'Truth be told, I felt quite envious. I still miss the warmth of a good fire'. We both stared into the flames.

'When my wife told me she was with child, I was pleased of course but I was also very afraid. I didn't know if I was the kind of man to be a good father. I lay awake at nights worrying how I would be able to provide for my child. I lay awake worrying I wasn't a good enough man to teach my child how to live a righteous and good life. When my son was born and he was placed into my arms for the first time, when his eyes looked into mine, it didn't matter anymore. I knew that he would love me whether I could give him everything or not. From that day on, instead of worrying if I was good enough to be a father, I knew I was a good father. Because I felt love. It doesn't matter how this child has come about, Rosie. This child will love you because of who you are'

Owain rose from the table then gently touched my shoulder before fading. I hadn't taken my eyes off the flames. Tears dripped onto my cardigan. I put my hands onto my stomach and held them there. My child.

CHAPTER NINE

Life carried on as normal. I'd put my humiliation behind me and the plumber out of my mind. He wasn't worth any of my thoughts and no one else mentioned him again either. Instead we threw ourselves into getting the bed and breakfast side of the pub off the ground. It took a while to get all the advertising organised. We were the blind leading the blind with regards to getting a website up and running. Owain was back to his usual grumpy self. He did a spectacular rant whilst looking over our shoulders as we tried to construct a half decent site using Sue's antiquated laptop. After nearly losing the will to live uploading photographs of the bedrooms and pub itself, Sue and I looked at each other in amusement as Owain paced around the bar, waving his arms so much I thought he was going to take off. He was ranting that we were in league with the Devil. We both almost lost control of our respective pelvic floors during his finale. Apparently, we were all going to be murdered in our beds when the Devil and his Disciples found their way through the 'box of evil' and we only had ourselves to blame when we woke up dead. I couldn't hear what he said after that as Sue was shrieking and half crying in my ear. It probably wasn't very nice so doubt I missed much. To be fair, he probably wasn't the only one who thought that. There were plenty of technophobes. Ones who even still had a pulse. He obviously realised that we weren't going to 'heed his warning', especially when I got the hiccups through laughing so much. He stood glaring at me, pointing his finger. The final straw came when I accidentally broke wind after a rather violent hiccup and Sue ended up in a hysterical heap on the floor. He then stamped his foot in frustration and disappeared in a spectacular strop which sent a chair sliding across the floor. It was hard to believe that only a relatively short time ago, this kind of behaviour had me hiding on the floor behind the bar like a frightened little child. I couldn't imagine my life without him in it now, any of them.

The bed and breakfast business soon started to grow and me alongside it. It wasn't long before the buttons on my jeans were popping open but I was still refusing to surrender to maternity wear just yet. My exorcist style vomit fest began to subside and I had reached the 'safe' first milestone of my pregnancy. Sue accompanied me to my first scan and as we saw the grainy images on the screen, I realised that I was in love with my baby. Owain was right. It didn't matter how this happened. It didn't matter that it hadn't been planned. The fact of the matter was that it had happened. I'd been given another chance at motherhood and this baby was going to change my life for the better. No matter what challenges faced me. It wasn't long before the village jungle drums had started and by the time I was showing, most of the village knew my condition. I hadn't seen Gwen for a long time. It felt like a lifetime ago that I'd first set foot in the shop on the hunt for sandwiches. Cravings were beginning to hit. Mine were a strange ensemble comprising of corned beef, salt and vinegar crisps and chocolate, all between two slices of white bread! Part of me was beginning to wonder how much of my belly was actually baby! I was spending a small fortune too! Not only was I buying for my own cupboards but I was replacing everything I was 'borrowing' from Sue's too! Even Will had banned me from the kitchen before I ate my way through the pub's entire menu. I'd always laughed in disbelief when hearing of pregnant women sending their partners on a midnight trek to an all-night shop to feed their overwhelming cravings. I wasn't laughing now! It was uncontrollable! When they hit, I would turn into a screaming banshee until they had been fed and put back to sleep. A far cry from those gut-wrenching hours spent on the bathroom floor. As I pushed the door open to the shop, the familiar ding of the bell rang out. Gwen popped her head out from behind a shelf of baked beans and broke into a huge smile.

'Well I never! Hello stranger, how are you?' she exclaimed.

She obviously hadn't minded me shopping at the local supermarket for months by her warm reaction. She came up to me and embraced me, like a prodigal daughter returning to the fold.

'How is the little one?' she asked, putting her hand lightly on my bump. Suddenly, I felt a kick! My very first one! Gwen obviously felt it too as she drew her hand away in surprise.

'You've got a feisty little one in there haven't you!' she chuckled as I put my hand onto my belly, hoping to feel it again.

'Now then, my lovely girl, what can I get you today?'

I grabbed as many tins of corned beef as I deemed polite, several multipacks of salt and vinegar crisps, five family sized bars of chocolate and two loaves of medium sliced bread. Gwen smiled to herself as one by one, I piled them up on the counter.

'Cravings?' she enquired with a chuckle. I nodded, feeling my face begin to flush. She walked over to another shelf then put a large jar of chocolate spread alongside my stash.

'A little gift', she said as she rang up the total. I noticed she didn't charge me for all of it either, as she placed my goods into two plastic bags.

'Thank you', I said gratefully.

'You're welcome my lovely. It's so nice to have a new member of our community on the way'.

I picked up the bags, groaning under my breath.

'Can you manage?' Gwen went to help but after acknowledging that I was fine, she opened the door instead. As we said our goodbyes, she looked at me, a sudden veil of sadness on her face.

'How's Deri?' she whispered

Well that was a bolt out the blue. I put my bags down and put my hand on her shoulder.

'He's fine' I reassured, 'in fact they all are'. Relief spread across her face. 'I know you'll look after them', she whispered, taking my hand. I nodded. We all had our secrets to keep, sharing them only with those involved. I had a responsibility to keep the spirits of Mynydd Eira safe from those who would share them with the world. In return, I knew they would keep me safe from whatever the world threw at me next.

As the weeks flew by, the pub started to bustle with more life and excitement than I'd seen in a long time. We started getting more and more guests staying, thanks to the website. We were getting good reviews for our hospitality as well as the pub food. Will began experimenting with more varied menus and our reputation was beginning to reach far and wide. My three ghostly friends behaved themselves, only making themselves known when the pub closed for the afternoon. Bronwen still kept me company when I was at home. Deri and Owain were also working on gaining energy to be able to leave the pub and appear elsewhere. They knew the importance of keeping themselves a secret. It would've been so easy to exploit them in order to make more money. To advertise ourselves as one of the most haunted pubs in Wales would've attracted visitors by the thousands in a space of a year but I wasn't prepared to have them become a side show. My love for them had grown and although they never said it in so many words, I knew that the feeling was mutual. My pregnancy was progressing as it should. The cravings subsided, thankfully, as I was beginning to resemble the size of a small country.

It was around two fifteen on a bright afternoon that I had the biggest shock since finding out about the baby. Our staying guests were all out for the day and our bar customers had all eaten their fill and left happily. I was enjoying some peace, sitting behind the bar folding napkins when I heard the door open. I looked up, hoping it wasn't anyone wanting food as the kitchen had closed for the afternoon and I hated letting people down. But it wasn't anyone wanting food, it was someone wanting something else.

'Hello Rosie', he said sheepishly, as he walked slowly towards me.

Stephen Pugh had dared to darken my door again, after everything he'd done! The look of shock on his face when I heaved myself off the bar stool, revealing my extremely pregnant self was something to behold.

'Fuck, you're...you're...' he stammered.

'Think the word you're looking for, Steve, is pregnant' I spat, trying to contain my bubbling anger at his cheek for even coming back to Mynydd Eira.

'It's not mine, is it?'

'Well it's not fucking Father Christmas' you twat!' I shouted. 'What the hell do you want Steve?'

The blood had left his face, leaving him a horrible grey colour and he steadied himself against a stool. He just stared at me, open mouthed and quite frankly, dopey looking. He finally got a grip and cleared his throat.

'I've been feeling really bad about how I treated you. I've been wanting to apologise for months. That day you came into the shop, did you know you were pregnant then?'

I was really digging deep at this point to contain my anger.

'How's the wife then Steve? You must be up to your neck in nappies now eh. What did you have then, boy or girl?'

I went back to folding napkins. I had to give my hands something else to do other than putting them round his throat.

He shuffled about where he stood, looking around the bar instead of looking at me. He was uncomfortable. Good.

'Erm, it was a boy' he mumbled

'Aha', I replied, emotionless as possible.

'Listen, I was only with my wife for the baby. We hadn't been happy for ages but never got around to doing anything about it. I wanted a divorce but she wanted to try and make a go of things. Then she got pregnant and I couldn't leave her then! Then I met you and, well, I really liked you!'

That was the flame that lit the fuse!

' You gutless pathetic little man!' I yelled. 'The only thing that comes out of your mouth is lies! You used me because your poor wife was pregnant and couldn't indulge your grubby little fantasies so you hit on someone else! I said all I wanted to say in the shop, this conversation is over. You'd better leave now please and I never want to see you again!'

I stared at him, my face beginning to contort with anger and increasing venom.

' What about this baby then Rosie?' He started to raise his voice. ' If it's mine, like you say it is, I've got every right to be involved!'

'You've got no right Steve! This is MY baby! You lost any right to being in my life the day you left this pub and stopped contacting me. You may be the father of my child but you'll never be it's dad, EVER!'

Steve suddenly started to kick the stool and he hammered the top of the bar with his fist. His true nature finally exploding to the surface!

'You can't stop me seeing my baby you bitch!' he yelled as he tried to get to me behind the bar.

That was his final mistake.

The temperature in the room chilled. I could see my breath blowing into the air.

'I think you'd better go Steve, now!' I warned. He looked at me with angry eyes.

'Oh I'm not going anywhere until we sort this out!' he spat as I frantically tried to lock the bar hatch.

Although it was bright outside, the room darkened. There was a storm coming.

'Steve, I'm warning you one last time, you'd better leave right now, I'm being serious!' I pleaded. Owain, Deri and Bronwen appeared, standing together at the far side of the room. Their collective energies were growing and I could see their faces changing from the ones I loved. In their place were three terrifying nightmares. Their faces were almost skeletal, their eyes sunken, black as coal and their lips had rolled back revealing rotting teeth. Bronwen's dress was flying around her and her hair was white and wild. Steve lunged towards me in fury, too wrapped up in his own anger to notice the hell that was behind him. Suddenly the door flew open!

'GET OUT!'

Swirling wind sent chairs flying and glasses started to smash behind the bar. Steve screamed in terror as he stopped his attack on me. The spirits surrounded him. Deri and Bronwen grabbed him by the arms, dragging him away from where I was standing as Owain put his hideous face against Steve's terrified one.

'GET OUT!!!' he boomed.

The air was filled with putrid filth as their decomposed remains dripped with centuries of death. Maggots fell from their eye sockets, their clothes had become dirt covered rags, hanging off their skeletal frames. Steve couldn't control his fear and I saw as bodily fluids dripped from the legs of his jeans onto the floor.

They threw him out the door, which slammed shut behind him. The room started to calm and Owain, Deri and Bronwen's forms changed back into the ones I knew. Tears were streaming down my face as I steadied myself against the bar. I put my hands onto my stomach and felt the reassuring kicks of my baby. Bronwen rushed over and pulled me into her arms. She felt cold but I felt her protective love surround me. She led me from behind the bar and sat me down by the fire.

'Are you well Miss?' enquired a worried looking Deri as he joined Bronwen by my side. Owain was peering through the window, making sure that Steve had actually gone. I don't think there was any danger of him returning. Not after that! Owain then left his lookout and joined the others by me.

'Where the hell did that come from?' I exclaimed, not quite believing what I'd seen

'You were being threatened Miss' stated Owain, pulling an upturned chair off the floor and pushing it back under a table.

' He was lucky to still have his life. We are and always will be, your protectors. I'm sorry you had to witness us in our withered forms. I hope that will never be necessary again'.

I stared at each one in turn. There were no remaining hints of the terrifying skeletal wrath that had just swept through the pub. They were back to their gentle selves. Their energies were growing. It was like they finally had a purpose after so long in the shadows and they were growing stronger, individually and collectively. But I now feared for them. They'd made themselves vulnerable thanks to an abusive idiot causing trouble. If Steve made his experience known publicly, I would have to think of something to cover it up. They said they were my protectors and I was theirs. We had made the final bond.

Luckily, nothing happened over the passing days. Steve was probably a babbling wreck still and hopefully questioning his sanity. If he knew what was good for him, he wouldn't set foot anywhere near the pub again. The guests that had stayed that night were none the wiser. We'd cleaned up the mess before they arrived back from their excursions and my three spirits had gone dormant but were protectively watching over me. I didn't tell Sue what had happened. There was no point in worrying her. There were more important things to concentrate on. My pregnancy was advancing and before I knew it, I was 23 weeks and two days. Sue was there as usual, holding my hand as we looked in awe at my baby during my detailed scan. As the technician checked every aspect of my baby's growth, we cried as we saw my beloved bundle suck their thumb and laugh as they began to hiccup. My baby was perfect. The technician asked if I wanted to know the sex but I resisted the temptation, wanting to wait until the birth to find out. After the scan, I showed the photos to Deri, Owain and Bronwen. They looked at the grainy images with confusion.

'I don't understand Miss', Bronwen exclaimed ' how did they get into your belly to see your baby?'

'It's witchcraft if you ask me!' grumbled Owain as Deri nodded to himself. I smiled to myself, feeling lucky to be a part of something so unusual but extremely special. We were a family, of sorts. I couldn't wait to bring my baby into the world to be a part of it.

CHAPTER TEN

Six Forty-Three in the morning. I'd been used to being woken up early due to baby bladder but this was really uncomfortable. None of the baby books could prepare someone for the unrelenting battering of the internal organs. I heaved my gargantuan carcass out of my warm bed and waddled to the bathroom. My bowels had packed up now and nothing I was being given by the doctor was shifting things. The pressure was getting really sore. I finally gave up and went back to bed. As I lay on my side, pain in my stomach gripped me, making me groan. Oh I seriously needed the toilet. Again, nothing. The pain was coming in waves. As I walked back to the bedroom, I suddenly doubled over. This wasn't constipation, this was something else. Suddenly my phone starting ringing. As I answered, I was hit by another wave of pain.

'Rosie!! Are you alright? Deri's just woke me up!' Sue exclaimed with concern.

'Sue, I think something's wrong! Can you come over?' I pleaded, as another wave hit me.

Five minutes later, Sue was hammering on my door. I managed to make it down the stairs and opened the door. She took one look at me and bundled me into the car to take me to hospital. As I lay on a hard bed in an Accident and Emergency bay, the pain wasn't the only thing that gripped me. I was scared to death. A nurse came to take my blood pressure which was normal and tried to reassure me that a doctor would see me as soon as possible. I needed the toilet so badly. The pressure was building and I knew deep down, this wasn't just sluggish bowels. I was offered pain relief but I refused, not wanting to take anything that might hurt the baby. Sue looked worried sick as I tried not to cry out as the pain intensified. Soon after, an on call Gynae junior doctor came to see me. She looked about twelve with her long blonde hair in pigtails and a large shoulder bag full of books. She squeezed the cold gel onto my bump and pressed the doppler onto my skin. My baby's heartbeat was loud and strong and my heart leapt as we looked at each other.

'Your baby is fine but we need to find out what's causing your pain. We're going to take you upstairs to the Antenatal ward for further examination. Try not to worry' she said before picking up her bag and leaving to arrange my transfer.

'That's reassuring, isn't it' Sue said, sitting on the edge of my bed, gently stroking my lower leg. 'You heard how strong baby's heartbeat was. There's nothing wrong there!'

I could sense she was being upbeat just for my benefit. She was right though, my baby seemed happy enough. The pain gripped me again and I grabbed the edge of the bed. Seconds later, it subsided. Sue looked away, trying hard not to give away her suspicions. Half an hour later, I was wheeled upstairs to the Antenatal ward and put into a side room. A midwife came to take some details before leaving to pass them onto the doctor. Ten minutes later, an older lady came in with the same midwife.

'Good morning. My name is Dr. Muller, I am the consultant Obstetrician. You've come in because you're experiencing some abdominal pain yes?'

I nodded weakly. She explained that she would do an internal examination to check if everything was alright. Sue squeezed my hand as I was prepared. I lay flat on the bed with my knees up, a sheet protecting my modesty. The doctor lay her hand on my bump and as gently as she could, she examined me. I gripped Sue's hand as another wave of pain hit. The examination was quickly over, the doctor removed her latex gloves and went over to the sink and washed her hands. She dried them and then sat on the edge of the bed.

'I'm very sorry to have to tell you but you are in labour. Your cervix is almost fully dilated with your waters still intact. Unfortunately, at this stage, there isn't anything we can do to stop labour. I'm afraid you will be delivering your baby today'.

' It's too soon!' I cried 'what's going to happen to my baby, will it be alright?'

The doctor took my hand, an unusual gesture for a doctor.

'At this stage of your pregnancy, baby's lungs won't have fully developed yet. I'm so sorry but your baby won't survive outside of the womb'.

'Oh my god' Sue gasped, as she squeezed my hand tighter. I lay there for a moment, not quite understanding what was happening.

' But you can try to save my baby, can't you?', I said finally. I looked at the doctor with pleading eyes ' you will try won't you, you can put my baby into one of those resuscitation machine things surely til the lungs are strong enough!'

The doctor's face said it all.

'I am so very sorry. As hard as it is, your baby just isn't strong enough. Even if we tried, I'm afraid baby would pass away after a short time. I really am so very sorry, there isn't anything we can do.' She rose from the bed and chatted quietly to the midwife before saying goodbye to me.

The midwife came over to the bed.

'Shall we try and make you more comfortable now my lovely? I can give you some pethidine for the pain. It will mean an injection into your bottom. Would you like to try that?'

I wanted them to stop this nightmare, that's what I really wanted. I didn't want to be in labour. Every contraction was a step closer to my baby's death sentence. The door opened again and a young midwife entered the room. She looked like a trainee as her uniform was slightly different. In her arms, was a moses basket.

'Get that fucking thing out of here now!' I screamed, ' you might as well of just bought in a coffin!'

The older midwife gestured for her colleague to leave. The poor girl looked like she was going to cry. She'd only been doing what she was told.

'Rosie, Rosie, sweetheart, calm down' soothed Sue, as she put her arms around me. I looked past her, through the window. I could see a tiny sparrow on the windowsill. I watched as it hopped from one side to another. Funny the things you notice when the world is coming to an end. The older midwife came back over to the bed.

'Can you roll onto your side please my lovely, I'm going to give you a pethidine injection now'.

I rolled over the best I could, my large baby bump making it awkward to move.

'Sharp scratch'

I winced as the needle went in, the liquid was cold but burnt at the same time. Weird.

She told me I would have to stay on the bed, as once the pethidine took effect, I'd be very wobbly. I could feel my stomach begin to tighten again as another contraction started. I gripped the edge of the bed and gritted my teeth until it was over. I turned my head to Sue.

'What will my baby look like?' I whispered, as I started to feel slightly groggy.

' What do you mean my darling?' Sue asked, stroking my arm.

'Well, I'm almost 24 weeks, will it look like a proper baby or will it look horrible?'

Sue's eyes filled up. 'Your baby will be beautiful, my darling'.

She picked up my hand and kissed it. Another contraction ripped through me. The pethidine was doing nothing for the pain. The door opened and the midwife came into the room.

'We've decided you might be more comfortable in the Delivery Suite. We can only offer pethidine and morphine on the ward but once you're downstairs, they can give you gas and air. Is that ok?'

I looked at her, her head was wobbling about and changing shape but it was probably the pethidine sending me loopy. I nodded, not particularly giving a shit where I was or where they were going to take me. I closed my eyes and heard the clonk of the brakes of the bed being released. The bed jerked and I felt myself being wheeled out of the door. I opened them slightly. A mixture of florescent lights and faces around me, all blurring together in a drug fueled haze as I was taken into the lift. I drifted in and out, unsure of what was real. I suddenly felt cold as fresh air hit me. We were outside. The wheels of the bed clattered on concrete. A disembodied voice cut through the noise.

'We're just coming up to the Maternity Unit now, sorry we had to come outside, the main corridor is undergoing maintenance. Are you warm enough?'.

I felt a hand pull the blanket up towards my neck. I closed my eyes and drifted away for a few seconds until the bed jolted.

'Sorry! Kerb...' the disembodied voice apologised.

Warm air washed over me as I was taken through more doors. We stopped for a moment as the disembodied voice chatted with another. I could hear groans from behind closed doors, then faint cries of newborn babies. The disembodied voice then started to chat with someone who's voice I recognised. It was Sue.

'I'm really sorry but we think it may be less distressing for your daughter...'

' She's not my daughter, she's my friend but she's like a daughter to me'

'Oh I'm sorry, ok, we think your friend may find it less distressing if she was in a room away from the other labouring mothers. We haven't got a room as such for, I'm sorry to call it this, unhappy births. But there's a room we're currently using as a store room. We're clearing it out now. I do apologise'

So I was going to give birth to my angel in a store cupboard. The grogginess was wearing off. I watched as staff went in and out of the room taking out mops, buckets and armfuls of other equipment. My bed was eventually wheeled into the room and the headboard pushed against the wall. I glanced over to the far side of the room. There were still piles of toilet rolls, bedpans, cleaning equipment and various products. A contraction started to build again and my mind was taken off my less than comfortable surroundings. A midwife came into the room.

'Would you like to try some gas and air?' she asked.

' Can I have an epidural?' I whispered.

She shook her head. ' I'm sorry, you're almost fully dilated, we don't give epidurals at this stage of labour' she explained.

'Why am I in this room?'. I was almost back to being fully aware of things again. The midwife looked uncomfortable.

' It would be less distressing for you to be away from the other mothers.' she said quickly.

Less distressing for whom, I thought to myself. Them or me! They'd shoved me away in a store cupboard so my unhappy situation wouldn't upset all the happy births happening up the other end of the department. A contraction built up again.

'I want gas and air please!' I gasped, the pain intensifying, ripping through my back.

'Are you alright sweetheart?'.

Sue leaned over me as the pain ebbed away again.

' Am I dreaming this Sue?'. I wanted her to say yes. I wanted to wake up and find myself warm in my own bed. Sue squeezed my hand again, not knowing what to say. The midwife arrived with a very large cannister on wheels. She hooked it up to a tube with a nozzle type mouthpiece then handed it to me.

'Put this in your mouth and take deep breaths. It'll take a few seconds to take effect but it should make you feel extremely relaxed and distant from everything around you. It only works whilst you're sucking on the gas and air. Once you stop, the effects wear off. When you feel a contraction starting, keep taking in the gas until it passes'

As I felt another contraction build, I sucked on the mouthpiece as fast as I could.

'Slow your breathing down dear, slow, deep breaths in and out'.

After breathing in the gas for a few seconds, the room felt as if it was expanding. Everyone seemed so far away. My contraction was ripping through my back, downwards into my backside. But I didn't care. I was floating on a sea of nothing. I felt the tightness begin to ebb away again and as I stopped sucking on the gas, the room began to shrink and everyone was back to where they had originally been.

'Wow, can I take this home?' I muttered

'Can I check you dear?', asked the midwife. I lay back with my knees up and I could feel her as she examined me internally.

'You're fully dilated now but your waters haven't broken yet. Do you feel like you could start pushing? If your waters don't break soon, we can break them for you'.

I didn't want to push. I wanted to keep my baby safe inside me. I knew I had to push eventually, I couldn't stop the inevitable. Another midwife entered the room and gently smiled at me. She joined her colleague at the bottom of the bed. They took a leg each, supporting the weight and I pushed downwards into my bottom. They counted to ten then I lay back. Another contraction hit. I pushed as hard as I could. Suddenly there was a loud pop and the sound of water exploding like a geyser.

'What the fuck was that?!' I exclaimed in shock.

I lifted my head to see two dripping wet midwives and a wall. The midwife holding my left leg calmly said,

' That was your membranes dear'.

I started to giggle. If there was to be any funny moment in amongst the nightmare I was in, that was it. Neither midwife flinched as they stood dripping wet from my dramatically exploding amniotic sac. My contractions subsided for a while afterwards. The midwife checked me again.

'I can see your baby dear. He/she is in the breach position which explains why you're feeling your contractions in your back'.

Typical. My baby was coming into the world arse first. I suddenly felt my baby kick me hard before another contraction hit me. I pushed down as hard as I possibly could. The burning pain down below was excruciating. I felt like I was being ripped apart.

'Keep pushing, your baby's almost out' urged the midwives. I felt a final release of pressure as my baby came into the world. The midwife lifted the precious bundle and placed it on my chest.

'It's a girl', they said.

Her mouth was open as she took a tiny gasp. Her little chest rose and fell. She was breathing.

'We need to cut the cord now my dear', said the midwife gently, knowing what would happen once she did. 'Are you ready?'

I gazed at my baby girl as the cord was cut. Her tiny finger wrapped around mine. Her chest rose and fell, rose and fell then didn't rise again. My angel had fallen asleep in my arms for the first and only time.

' Can we just have her for a moment, just to clean and wrap her in a blanket. We'll give her straight back to you'.

I knew why they wanted her. It wasn't just to wash her. They needed to confirm her death. I knew she'd gone. I watched as they gently lifted her from me and took her over to the table across from the bed. I couldn't see what they were doing. Their backs shielded me from the necessary checks they had to do. Sue was quietly weeping in the chair at the side of me, trying to be as discreet as possible for my sake. She was hurting the same as I was. Within minutes, my baby had been wrapped in a white blanket. The midwife brought her back to me and gently placed her in my arms.

' Do you have a name?' she asked

I'd been thinking for weeks what I was going to call my baby. If I'd had a boy, he would've been Sam. If I'd had a girl, she would've been.

'Emily Rose' I whispered, ' her name is Emily Rose'.

'That's a beautiful name. We've weighed Emily. She weighed 1lb. We've also taken her hand and footprints. We've got a Memory pack if you'd like to have it, with her name, date of birth, weight, hand and footprints. We'll keep it for you until you're ready.'

I suddenly felt sick as pains suddenly gripped my stomach again. I let out a groan. The midwife took Emily from my arms and laid her gently in the crib next to the bed.

'We need to deliver the placenta now. You'll feel contraction pains, use the gas and air if you need to'

I looked over to my daughter as the midwives tended to the final physical stages of my ordeal. Moments later, it was over. The midwives made me comfortable and I was left to be alone with my newborn daughter.

'Can I have her please Sue?'

Sue gently lifted Emily from her crib and put her into my arms.

'Will you be alright for a minute, I need to find the loo'

I nodded and Sue kissed my head before leaving the room. I traced my finger around Emily's face. She was silent and still but perfect and beautiful. Her delicate features, her perfect little button nose, tiny rosebud lips. She was exquisite. I gently unwrapped the blanket. I picked up her tiny hand and examined her perfect little fingers with her perfect little fingernails. Her body was long and slender. She hadn't had time to become plump like a full-term baby. I continued my journey, trying to take in every tiny detail of her perfectly formed body. Her skin was pink and slightly translucent. I traced down her long slender legs then counted all her toes. Her feet seemed so big. I gently wrapped her up again and held her close, smelling her newborn smell, imprinting it to my memory. Sue came back into the room, carrying a tray of tea and sandwiches and placed them on the bed table.

'Do you think you could try to eat something my lovely?' she asked gently.

' Isn't she the most beautiful little thing you've ever seen' I whispered, gazing at my daughter. 'You should see her feet Sue, they're massive!'

I unwrapped the bottom of the blanket to show her. Sue smiled and nodded.

She put a sandwich on a plate then came and sat on the edge of the bed.

'Here, please try to eat this.'

I picked up the sandwich, took a bite then put it back onto the plate.

'I've just spoken to the midwife. The doctor will be here soon just to check you over. They said they might keep you in but if you're well enough, you can go home if you want to.'

I could hear the faint screams of other labouring women in the rooms along the corridor. I couldn't listen to that all night, knowing that at the end of their pain, they would be holding a crying, living baby. I would never get to hear my baby cry. I shook my head.

'I want to go home but not yet.'

I wanted to spend as much time with Emily as I was allowed. I had only a few precious hours to imprint every tiny detail.

The midwife who delivered Emily came back into the room. She had a camera, a tiny premature baby dress, a paper wallet and a small pink teddy in her hand.

'How are you feeling dear, any pain?' she asked

Yes, my heart hurts like hell.

'Would you like me to take some photos of Emily for you? I've brought a dress for Emily if you'd like her to wear it. It might be a bit big but I thought you'd prefer it to the blanket'

We unwrapped Emily gently and dressed her in the pink gingham dress. The midwife took several Polaroid photos, some with me holding her and some of Emily laying in her crib with the pink teddy by her head. She looked like a perfect little doll.

'What happens now?' I asked.

The midwife sat on the bed.

'Well, when you go home, we'll look after Emily in the hospital. You can either have the hospital arrange the funeral or you can arrange your own private one. We have a bereavement officer who will liaise with the funeral director of your choice, if you wish to have a private ceremony. Emily will then be collected by them and taken to the funeral home'.

I nodded quietly.

' Private I think' I replied

'I've bought you the Memory pack I mentioned earlier. We've written her details on the certificate and included her hand and foot prints. There's also leaflets in there for SANDS, the Stillbirth and Neonatal Death Society. They give support to bereaved parents and families.

It didn't seem real. I'd just had a beautiful baby but instead of making plans for a happy homecoming, I was being given information about funerals and talking to strangers from a support group.

The doctor then knocked the door. I was examined and considering what I'd just been through, I was physically well enough to go home. They didn't listen to my heart though. If they had, they would've heard all the pieces continuing to shatter. The doctor extended her condolences, adding that she wasn't sure what happened but possible causes could've been an incompetent cervix. As Emily had gotten heavier, my cervix couldn't handle it so dilated too early. That summed it up. Not only had I screwed up getting involved with a married man, even my cervix was incompetent. Medical terms really had a way of making someone feel even shittier. I spent the next few hours holding my beautiful baby, drinking in her smell, my fingers tracing her angelic face. The clock ticked away like my own personal ticking time bomb... I finally had to go home. I kissed Emily and laid her gently in the moses basket that had been brought in for her. The midwife gently picked her up and I watched as she walked down the corridor and through the double doors. My legs started to buckle under me and Sue held me as we slowly walked up the same corridor, through the same double doors but out of the hospital. What kind of mother was I? I'd left my baby all alone, with people who didn't love her. I was walking away from my baby.

CHAPTER ELEVEN

I stayed with Sue and Nick short term, at her insistence. She drafted temporary staff to oversee the running of the pub and bed and breakfast so she could look after me. The first few days after Emily was born were just a haze of condolence cards, flowers and scrambled eggs. I hated scrambled eggs but Sue was becoming desperate to get food into me. My body yearned for my baby. My breasts became engorged and painful, desperate to release their precious milk to feed a baby that wasn't there anymore. The community midwife visited me after my discharge, just to check my body was returning to normal after the birth. She advised me to bind my breasts to try to encourage my milk to dry up. I felt like I was being tortured by Mother Nature. Sue had contacted the local funeral directors and made an appointment for us to see them. It had been four days since Emily died and as I sat in the car on the way to the funeral home, the numbness still enveloped me. I caught sight of myself in the wing mirror. I was deathly pale. My eyes were vacant and empty. My life had been in high definition colour only a week ago, now it had been replaced by a sepia shade.

Sue parked in the customer car park of Williams and Sons and we sat in silence for a few moments. Finally, she reached over and squeezed my hand.

'Are you ready?' she gently asked

I nodded silently before opening the car door. I winced as I got out, my stomach still sore after the birth. Sue put her arm through mine and we slowly walked to the entrance. The reception was calm, almost tranquil, tastefully decorated in cream with a variety of flower arrangements to add warmth and colour. A middle-aged woman dressed in a pristine white blouse and black skirt sat behind a mahogany desk. She rose to greet us, her voice matched the decor, calm and quiet. For her, it was just another ordinary day. For me, it was anything but. Sue gave her our names and she directed us to a row of blue chairs whilst she phoned whoever we were going to see. I looked around the room. Leaflets with smiling faces of elderly people advertising funeral payment plans were neatly displayed on a table. Death was supposed to come after living a long life. Not one minute and forty-six seconds after being born. I stared at the grey carpet, wanting to disappear to a time when I was happy. I heard a door open from the direction of a corridor and a portly gentleman in his late fifties appeared. He gently smiled and gestured for us to follow him. He showed us into a room with another mahogany desk. The sun shone through the gaps in the blinds, bathing the room in warmth and light. It wasn't what I'd been expecting a place that dealt with death to be like.

'My name is Carwyn Williams, firstly I'd like to extend my deepest condolences for your loss'

He had a kind face and gentle voice. I felt myself relax slightly. He looked at the paperwork in front of him and carried on.

'I see from the paperwork that you'd like to arrange the funeral of Emily, is that right?'

Sue squeezed my hand as I nodded.

'She's my daughter' I whispered, blinking away the tears that were threatening to fall. I had to hold it together for as long as this was going to take.

'Today, I'll help you decide what kind of funeral you'd like to give Emily, have you thought about whether it will be a burial or cremation?'

I looked at Sue for a second, who encouraged me to reply.

'Burial I think, please. At our local church in Mynydd Eira'

He wrote on the form.

' Thank you. Today, I'll guide you through choosing a coffin, any flowers you may like to have. A funeral of a child is hard enough so here at Williams and Sons, the cost will be lower than that of an adult funeral. We won't be charging you for the coffin or our services on the day. The funeral costs will cover the burial plot, cars, flowers, any newspaper notices etc.'

Sue and I looked at each other. What a kind gesture. I wondered how many bereaved parents had previously sat in my chair. We spent the next half an hour looking through folders of coffins and flowers. I chose a tiny plain white coffin with gold plated handles and white satin trim. I began to falter. I should've been looking through catalogues full of prams and cots, not coffins. Mr. Williams kindly gave me a few moments to compose myself and rang his receptionist to ask for a cup of tea to be brought in for us. He had obviously been in the job for many years. He spoke words of encouragement and comfort without sounding patronising. It became obvious that although they dealt with death on a daily basis, arranging a child's funeral affected them too, although their professionalism ensured that it didn't show too much. After I'd composed myself, we went on to choose a beautiful pink and white wreath in the shape of a teddy bear. As we were laying Emily to rest in Mynydd Eira, we only needed one car, to bring her home. We'd walk from the pub to the church. I hoped that the plot would be close to where Bronwen was resting. Deri and Owain would be nearby on the other side of the hedge. I felt slightly better knowing she wouldn't be alone in the churchyard. My three spirits would become her guardians and keep her safe. After what seemed a lifetime, all the arrangements had been made. Mr. Williams said he would contact me once Emily was in the Chapel of Rest. I could visit her prior to the funeral if I wished. As we left, Mr. Williams gently shook our hands and assured us that Emily would be taken care of. That should've been my job.

The call came two days later. Emily was now sleeping in the Chapel of Rest and I was welcome to visit her at any time. As usual, Sue was my rock. As I picked up a carrier bag on the way out, Sue gave me a confused look. I opened the bag and she looked in. Tears started to fall down her cheeks as she nodded and lightly touched my arm.

When we arrived, Sue quietly spoke to Mr. Williams as I sat, preparing myself to see Emily. I saw him smile and nod.

'If you would like to follow me my dear, I'll take you to Emily'.

Sue stayed in reception. I needed to do this by myself.

I was shown into a small room. Candles flickered, giving off a soft, tranquil light. Emily's beautiful white coffin rested open on a stand. Mr. Williams then left me alone to be with my daughter. I slowly walked up to her, my heart banging in my chest. I was slightly afraid of what she would look like now. I gazed in and saw my beautiful girl. They'd dressed her in a tiny white satin dress with a cover of white lace draped over her body. She looked like a sleeping angel. Light flickered all around her, illuminating her delicate little face. I gently touched her soft cheek. Apart from being colder, she looked as if she'd just been born.

'Hello, my darling' I whispered, 'it's mummy. You look so beautiful my angel. I have a few things for you'

I reached into my bag.

'Here's a letter I've written to you so you'll always know that I love you so very much'

I placed the letter in her coffin.

'Here's a photo of me, so you'll never forget what I look like. I'll always be with you.'

I placed the photo alongside the letter.

I reached into the bag for the final item.

'I bought this teddy for you last month. It was going to be your first teddy bear. Do you like it? It will keep you company. You can cwtch into it, all soft and warm'

I held her teddy against my chest for a few moments then gently placed it against her tiny body.

'You may have been born too soon my beautiful girl but I will love you for a lifetime'.

Tears fell onto the satin trim as I leant over her. I kissed my finger then placed it onto her rosebud lips.

There was a soft knock on the door and Mr. Williams came into the room. He stood beside me as we gazed at my perfect little angel.

'You'll tuck her in nice and warm won't you' I whispered.

'Yes of course my dear. Have you had enough time? You can stay if you wish'.

I wanted to stay with her for always but I had to finally say goodbye. I leant over her for the last time and touched her beautiful face.

'Night night my angel. Sleep tight. Mummy loves you so much'

It took everything I had to walk away from her.

The morning of Emily's funeral arrived all too soon. As I sat up in bed, I looked over to the wardrobe and saw my clothes hanging up. Sue had washed and ironed them for me. A long black skirt, a simple cream cotton blouse and black hip length jacket. I didn't want to wear them. I didn't want to even get dressed. A gentle tap on the door was followed by Sue, bringing me a cup of tea and a plate of toast and jam.

'Morning my lovely' she said quietly as she placed them on the bedside table. She sat on the edge of the bed and looked at me. I felt five years old again.

'The vicar's just rung, asking how you are. If we can be at the church by eleven fifteen, Emily's due to arrive at eleven thirty'

I nodded silently as I stared at the flower pattern on the duvet.

'Deri, Owain and Bronwen have asked after you. They've stayed quiet as they didn't want to disturb you. You only have to call out to them you know, if you need them'

I missed them, even Owain.

'I hope they aren't upset with me' I said, as I tried to sip my tea. I felt sick.

'Of course they aren't! They of all people understand you're grieving my darling. They just didn't want you thinking they didn't care because they do'

' Maybe after the funeral, I'll be up to seeing them' I replied.

Sue nodded and looked at me with understanding eyes.

'Get showered and dressed when you're ready. We're just setting up downstairs for afterwards. I think there's going to be quite a few coming back'

She got up and left me to get ready. I pulled back the duvet and swung my legs out and sat up on the edge of the bed for a few moments. My body felt like a lead weight. Grief was a heavy burden. I got up and walked over to the window and pulled back the curtain. At least it wasn't raining. It always rained at funerals. Emily deserved sunshine.

She would've brought so much light into my life. As I looked out over the village, I imagined myself watching her growing up. Taking her first steps. Seeing her face light up as we fed sugar lumps to the horses. Being spoilt by Gwen every time we went into the shop. I put my hands onto my shrinking stomach. It was empty. I was empty. She was gone and I was alone again.

Sue held my hand as we stood outside the church gates. Nick had already gone inside. Friends and residents arrived, all expressing their deepest sympathies as they walked past and into the churchyard. I was surprised how many had taken time out of their day to pay their respects to my daughter. I looked at the red rose in my other hand. A rose for my precious girl.

Eleven thirty. The vicar had now joined us at the gate. We watched as a black Mercedes slowly drove towards the church. Sue squeezed my hand as my body stiffened.

'Deep breath my lovely, you'll be fine'.

The Mercedes drew up and gently stopped. I looked through the tinted window. Where was she? The driver got out, walked around to the passenger side and opened the door. Mr. Williams slowly rose from the car, carrying Emily's tiny coffin in his arms, as the driver bowed.

'Oh my god...'

I wobbled slightly and held onto Sue. I had to be strong. The vicar started to recite a prayer as Mr. Williams gently carried Emily through the gates, along the path and into the church. As we followed my little girl down the aisle, I saw faces of friends begin to crumple with emotion. I stared straight ahead, I couldn't bare to look. Mr. Williams placed Emily's coffin onto the stand and bowed. Sue stood back as I approached the stand. I placed the rose onto the top of the coffin and stood in silence with my hand resting against the top. It was the closest

I could get to my angel now. After giving me a moment, the vicar quietly asked if I was alright and if I was ready for him to begin. I leant over and kissed Emily's coffin before Sue led me to our pew.

We stood as the organist began to play the first Hymn. As the congregation sang 'Morning has Broken', I stared at my daughter's coffin resting in front of us. I was in a church full of people but I'd never felt so alone. After the Hymn had ended, we sat as the vicar talked about how God would love and protect Emily. There wasn't anything else he could really say. There were no stories of what she'd achieved or the kind of person she'd been during her life. She hadn't had the chance to live a life. He acknowledged me, as Emily's mother and asked that my friends support me over the coming weeks and months to come. 'Amazing Grace' and final prayers drew the funeral to its conclusion, as Mr. Williams quietly made his way down the aisle. He bowed to Emily again before gently picking her up and carrying her out of the church. Sue took my arm as we followed them to where she would be laid to rest. I watched as a startled squirrel suddenly darted up a nearby tree. I noticed a bench was by her grave and thought how I would be able to sit and talk to her. We gathered around her open grave as the vicar said his final prayers and blessed Emily. As they lowered her tiny white coffin into the ground, I felt numb. I couldn't cry, I just stared as she disappeared into the darkness.

I woke with a start. A soft glow of the street light pushed its way through a gap in the curtains. As my eyes adjusted to the darkness of the bedroom, I heard muffled crying from the bedroom across the landing. I quickly pulled back the covers, shivering as the nightly chill nipped at my bare legs. I padded my way across the carpet and listened through the door. The muffled cries started to get louder then stopped. I opened the door slightly and listened. There it was again. I opened the door wider and stepped onto the landing. I could see a glow through the gap at the bottom of the bedroom door. I hadn't noticed that room there before. Where was I? I crept closer and listened again. I could hear a music box playing from inside, its tinkling tune mixed with the crying. I nervously put my hand onto the door handle and gently opened the door. Through the yellow glow, I saw a large black rectangular box resting on a stand. The lid was open and soft crying coming from inside. The music box started to slow and fade. I walked nervously towards the box, leant over and looked inside. Darkness. The crying got louder and louder! Suddenly, a light shone from the ceiling, illuminating the inside. A pale faced porcelain doll lay inside, it's eyes shut. It looked angelic, like a sleeping child. Golden hair framed it's face, it's dress made of cream lace and satin. Suddenly it's eyes snapped open, glowing bright red as its face contorted into a grotesque mask of death. The doll screamed as I put my hands over my ears and I felt myself falling.

.

I woke up to the sound of my own screaming.

'Rosie! Are you alright!?' Sue yelled, as she burst through the bedroom door. She flicked on the light and rushed to the bed. I couldn't breathe!

' Sshh, calm down sweetheart, slow your breathing down' Sue urged as she held me in her arms. I rocked backwards and forwards, drenched in sweat. My breathing started to slow as Sue eventually brought me back from the brink of my nightmare.

'Alright now?' she asked, still holding me tight. I started to cry through shock and bewilderment. It was so real!

'Do you want to tell me about it?' she whispered gently. I shook my head. I couldn't go through that again.

'Do you want a cup of tea?'

Oh the good old teabag. The cure to all ills, alien invasions and horrific nightmares. My throat hurt from screaming. Maybe a cuppa wouldn't be a bad thing after all. I nodded as Sue got my dressing gown off the door hook and wrapped me up in the soft warmth. She led me silently down the stairs and into the kitchen.

'Are you sure you don't want to tell me about it?' Sue asked as she waited for the kettle to boil. I sat myself down at the oak dining table, wrapping myself tighter in the comfort blanket of my dressing gown.

I let out a long, weary sigh.

' I had a nightmare about Emily, except it wasn't her. When I looked into the box, it was a god awful screaming demonic doll!'

Sue made the tea then sat down beside me at the table.

'It was just a dream sweetheart. You know how beautiful Emily was so she most definitely wasn't a demonic doll!'

I put my hands around the mug and felt the warmth spread through my fingers.

'Yeah I know', I sighed, taking the packet of biscuits that Sue had thrust in my direction.

'Give it time my lovely, it's all extremely raw at the moment. You've only just laid Emily to rest. Grief doesn't follow a set path'.

'I'm sorry I woke you up', I mumbled through a mouthful of chocolate bourbon.

'Hey don't be daft, that's why you're staying here for now, so I can look after you.'

I got up, stood behind her and wrapped my arms around her shoulders, resting my head against hers.

'Thank you', I whispered. Her hair smelt of raspberries and I felt safe again.

After a cup of tea and far too many biscuits, we both went back to bed and I managed to get through the rest of the night without dreaming.

The next morning, lingering remnants of the dream were still haunting me. As I sat curled up on the sofa in my dressing gown, the grotesque face of the demonic doll kept flashing inside my mind. Sue had put Emily's photographs in the drawer of her wall unit for safe keeping. I got up from the sofa and walked over to the drawer. My shaking hand reached out towards the handle. I drew my hand back. It was too soon. My whole being ached for her but I wasn't ready to see her little face again. I did need to be with her though. I got dressed and scraped my hair back into a ponytail. I looked in the mirror. I looked like a new mother. Bags under my eyes, scraped back hair, remnants of a bump being sucked in by newly fitting jeans. But was I really a new mum? A new mum had her baby to look after. I was barely functioning looking after myself. I quickly wrote a note for Sue telling her where I was going and left it on the kitchen table. I opened the door and breathed in the fresh air. My heart started to thump and I suddenly felt scared. I quickly closed the door again and stood with my back against it. What if I bumped into someone? If I smiled and said hello, they'd think I was fine. Heartless maybe, smiling a day after burying my daughter. If I just walked past them, not saying anything at all, they'd think me rude. I had to do this. Emily would think I'd forgotten about her. I opened the door again and forced myself outside. The sun shone in my eyes, making me squint.

'Come on Rosie, one foot in front of the other, how hard is that?' I mumbled to myself. I slowly walked head down towards the church. Thankfully the village was quiet. Gwen was inside the shop, which I was grateful for. As much as I liked her, I wasn't up to conversation. I doubt she would've called me over anyway. I stopped at the church gates. Flashbacks to Emily's funeral zipped through my head. My skin prickled with painful memories as I pushed the gate open and slowly walked the path I'd followed just a short time before. I could see

Emily's flowers neatly placed on her grave, her teddy bear wreath covering most of the tiny mound of earth. The funeral director had pushed a small dark wooden cross with her name engraved into it at the head of her grave, flowers adorning its base. They'd treated my daughter with the upmost respect. I sat on the grass beside her and placed my hand onto the soil.

.

'Hello my beautiful girl', I whispered as tears bit at my eyes

'

'I'm sorry for your loss.'. The voice made me jump! I swung my head round as I quickly stood up, ready to run.

'It's alright, I'm not going to hurt you.'

Where the hell was the voice coming from?!

Then I saw him, sitting on the bench across from Emily's grave. Where the hell did he come from?! He wasn't there before. A man, dressed in a long black trench coat and black wide brimmed hat, obscuring his face from view. He slowly lifted his head up, revealing an old pale face, lined with deep wrinkles and stubble.

'I'm sorry I made you jump' he continued as I stared at him with suspicion. I'd never seen him in Mynydd Eira before.

'You lost someone recently I see' he continued.

No shit Sherlock, wonder what gave that away.

I continued to stare. My best Paddington was threatening to emerge as my hackles started rising. I was in no mood for this. I was here to spend time with my deceased daughter and he was invading my grief.

.

'I don't mean to be rude but I'm not really up for a conversation, if you don't mind'.

Polite enough, considering all I wanted was to tell the old git to bugger off. He nodded silently, his hat covering his eyes. He put his hands onto his knees, sighed then rose up from the bench. He was tall and thin. The bottom of his trench coat glanced the ground, the shine from his black shoes peeking through the bottom of black suit trousers as he moved.

'I'm sorry for disturbing you. I wish you good day', he said as he turned to leave. His face looked forlorn as he dropped his head down and began to walk down the path. Oh crap now I felt bad! Old people always had the amazing ability of making someone feel guilty!

'Hang on!' I said quickly, as he slowly walked away, ' I'm sorry, please come back. You have every right to be here. I apologise'.

He stopped and turned towards me. He lifted his head and smiled to himself as he started walking back to the bench. I left Emily's graveside and sat down at one end of the bench as he approached. He sat down at the other. A gap of silence between us. There wasn't even any bird song to fill the void. There were no birds at all, only the sound of the breeze through the trees. I looked over towards my angel's grave, desperate to be next to her.

'She was your daughter, wasn't she', he stated, breaking the quiet.

'She still is', I whispered sadly, the lump in my throat growing ever bigger. He nodded slowly.

'Indeed'

We continued to sit.

'You don't have family here do you.'

It was more of a statement than a question. I gave him a sideways glance. He sat looking straight ahead. It was a strange thing for someone to say to someone they'd just met.

'Erm, no, not blood relatives but there are people I regard as family', I replied, wondering why I was even telling him something so personal.

He continued to stare straight ahead, nodding his head slowly in acknowledgement.

I heard footsteps on the path and looked over to see who it was.

'Hey Rosie, I got your note, are you alright?'

It was Sue. I smiled as she reached the bench.

'I was just chatting to this gentleman' I replied as I looked up at her.

'Er, what gentleman Rosie?' Sue asked with a confused look. I swung my head to see an empty space where the man in the black hat had been sitting. What the fu...? How could he have moved so quickly, he was an old man!

Sue sat down beside me and put her arm around my shoulder.

'He was just here Sue! I was talking to him!' I exclaimed, overwhelmed by my own confusion.

'It's alright, it's alright', soothed Sue as she rubbed my shoulder. 'Let's get you home, shall we? I think you've had enough for today; don't you think my lovely?'

Sue stood up, took my hand and gently pulled me up off the bench. A feeling of intense fatigue suddenly washed over me as I slowly walked over to Emily's grave.

'See you tomorrow my beautiful girl' I whispered. As we walked down the path towards the gate, I turned my head towards the far side of the graveyard. Standing beside the hedge stood the man in the black hat. I was just about to tell Sue where he was but he turned and walked away through a gap in the hedge and disappeared. He was obviously a stranger to the village and maybe felt uncomfortable when he'd heard Sue walking towards us. That would explain his sudden departure from the bench. I was too tired to worry about him. I needed to sleep.

CHAPTER TWELVE

The room was dark apart from the glow of the street light. I reached over to the bedside table for my mobile to check the time. No matter how hard I tried, my mind couldn't register the numbers on the screen. I heard a noise from across the room, like a scratching sound against a wooden floor. My eyes became accustomed to the darkness and as I looked over, I saw the shadow of a figure sitting in the rocking chair.

'Sue? Is that you?" I croaked, my mouth dry from sleep. The figure kept gently rocking back and forth.

'How long have I been asleep?' God, I feel like shit. What's the time?'

Silence

I pushed myself up onto my elbows. As I stared into the corner, the rocking chair suddenly stopped. From the shadows, the figure leant forward. It wasn't Sue. I could hear the figure breathing, it's chest wheezing and rasping with each difficult breath. Then it spoke with a guttural whisper.

'Your daughter's dead. You can be with her again you know. I can help you. I can tell you how.'

It's eyes started to glow bright red, casting shadows of its black figure against the wall. Suddenly a knocking noise filled my head, getting louder and louder. A bright flash of light filled the room and I closed my eyes tight shut as it blinded me.

'Rosie...Rosie...are you awake my lovely?'

As I opened my eyes again, brightness filled the room. It was still daytime. There was a knock on the door again and then it gently opened.

'Rosie? You awake?'

Sue came into the room, a cup of steaming tea in one hand and plate of biscuits in the other. She smiled as she placed them down onto the bedside table.

'You've been out for hours. Feeling any better?'

I looked at her, my mind filled with confusion. Sue sat on the edge of the bed and looked at me with concern.

'You look shattered sweetheart. Didn't you sleep?'

I opened my mouth to speak but thought better of it. It had been just another dream. I picked up the cup of hot tea and took a sip, soothing my dry throat. Another nightmare eased by the good old teabag.

'I think I need to go back to work Sue'. Sue took a biscuit off the plate and thought for a moment.

'Well, I personally think it's too soon sweetheart but if it's what you want, why don't you ease back into it gently? Maybe do a couple of hours and see how you feel. You're still recovering physically remember as well as everything else you're contending with. I'm just worried you'll try to do too much too soon'

I raised my knees up under the duvet and hugged them.

'I need a distraction. Maybe you're right though, a couple of hours a day at first, doing the light stuff, if that's alright. I want to be in the pub again. I need to be with them'.

Sue smiled, knowing exactly who I meant.

'They're missing you, even Owain although he won't admit it of course'.

'Oh and another thing'. I added, before pausing for a second, hoping I was doing the right thing. 'You've been so wonderful Sue looking after me since Emily died but I also think I need to go home. I haven't really slept since it all happened. Maybe if I tried my own bed...you don't mind, do you?'

Sue's face clouded slightly with a look of sadness but she slowly nodded.

'You know you're welcome to stay here anytime you want, remember that. If you ever feel you need me, you come straight back here!' Her eyes misted over as she leant over and wrapped her arms around me.

'It's not as if I won't see you every day now is it' she sniffed.

'Oh don't you worry, you won't be getting rid of me that easily' I whispered.

'Oh you've decided to come back then have you'.

I chuckled to myself as I switched on the lights in the bar.

'Good to see you too Owain'.

Owain was sitting in his usual spot on the windowsill. I could feel his eyes on me as I started preparing for the day.

'Are you well Miss?' he asked. He may have sounded abrupt in his greeting but I knew he had been worrying about me.

I stopped what I was doing and looked at him.

'In all honesty Owain, I don't know. I'm just taking it one day at a time'.

I let out a long sigh as I felt the all too familiar lump in my throat begin to enlarge. Just as I was about to let my emotions win, a sudden rush of cold air whooshed by me.

'Oh Miss, Miss, you're back! I'm so happy to see you!!'

My sweet Bronwen appeared beside me, her face beaming with delight. I turned and smiled at her, forcing my raw, lingering grief back down inside for the time being. Her childlike excitement at seeing me was heartwarming as much as it was overwhelming.

She carried on beaming at me as Deri appeared behind her.

'Good morning Miss, welcome back'. He was subdued, like Owain. They had been parents themselves once, they obviously understood that although I was back, I was still fragile on the inside. Bronwen started to chatter away telling me everything that had been going on. I could feel the room begin to spin. Deri looked past Bronwen and we locked eyes for a few moments. He started to nod. He put his hand gently on Bronwen's arm and whispered something in her ear. Her excitement calmed.

'I'm sorry Miss, I need to run an errand for Deri. Are you returning home today too? If you need me, just call my name. It's so lovely to see you again Miss!'. She slowly faded, still chattering excitedly to herself.

I took a sharp intake of breath and steadied myself against the bar.

'Thank you, Deri. It's so sweet of Bronwen to be so happy to see me but....'

Owain jumped down from the windowsill and strided towards us before sitting on a chair near the fire.

'We are no stranger to tragedy Miss', Owain stated, matter of factly.

'Sadly, we saw our share of sorrow during our lives here'.

'Bronwen is young, despite her years hence. She was shielded from such things'.

He looked at me with sympathetic eyes as Deri silently nodded his head again, deep in thought. I could only imagine how harsh their lives had been. It suddenly put things into perspective. I had to suck up my grief and be strong. It wasn't that easy though. There was a storm coming, I just didn't know it yet.

As days turned into weeks, I tiptoed back into my life. Although I was grateful to Sue for looking after me in the days following Emily's death, it was good to be around my own things. The nightmares, however, continued. I tried to quiet my mind in the peace of the graveyard. Emily's grave now had a headstone and I'd made it as pretty as I was allowed with edging stones and white pea gravel. A simple toy windmill and an ornamental stone teddy bear nestled amongst the pink and white carnations that I replaced every week. It was the only thing I could buy my beautiful girl. I watched from the bench as the seasons started to change. The winds had started to blow the goldening leaves off the tree near Emily's grave, covering her like a blanket. As I knelt down to remove the deep layer of leaves, a voice broke through my thoughts.

'You're struggling aren't you. You're trying to carry on but you're just sleepwalking through each minute of every hour. Is that really how you want to be for the rest of your life?'

I slowly looked up at my familiar graveyard companion. The Man in the Black Hat had been with me from the start of my torment.

He looked straight ahead, his hat covering most of his face from view. Over the past weeks, he'd been there like a lingering shadow, a stranger with no name but somehow, he could see right into my withering soul.

'I can help you, you know that. I've been telling you that I can. Are you ready to listen to me now?'

I got up from Emily's grave and sat beside him on the bench. I listened as he leant forward and whispered into my ear. A plan of action to help me heal myself, to take the pain away, was being formed with each sentence. We then sat in silence after he'd finished. I slowly nodded to myself.

'I believe you, I believe you can help me. I want to do it, just tell me when and where.'

'Oh I'll be there with you, every step of the way, my dear. You'll be feeling better in no time'. As he sat back, I could hear him let out a satisfied sigh.

We both stared ahead at the gathering clouds in the distance. We turned towards each other and as I looked into his glowing red eyes, I felt hope for the first time since Emily left.

For my recovery to become a success, I was sworn to secrecy. He was adamant that I shared nothing about our meetings and the steps that were needed to be taken to achieve my goal towards a pain free existence. I went about my daily life the best I could, painting my smile on each morning for the benefit of normality. Inside, however, my growing feelings of hope were building. With each secret meeting, he drip fed me snippets of information, which started to make more sense as time went on. I was given tasks to perform, again, in complete secrecy. I fitted the tasks in around my shifts at the pub. He was adamant that no one suspected anything. He explained that his methods of bereavement counselling were somewhat unorthodox and if I were to tell my loved ones about them, they wouldn't understand.

The last thing I needed right now was to be talked out of the treatment plan. I'd committed myself now and there was no going back. I could sense that Sue and my spirit family were growing curious about my activities outside of work. They had grown used to the change in my character since Emily died. I was never going to be the same person that I was before she left me. How could I be? I was, however, trying to find the path to a more tranquil mind, to find a sense of peace amongst the jumbled noise that was inhabiting my head. I needed this dark cloud to lift and my alternative therapist was giving me that chance. It wouldn't be long now. I'd almost finished the tasks I'd been set. The final session was growing closer. The appointment had been made. I just needed to be patient. Timing was everything.

As the day for my last appointment approached, I wanted to spend quality time with Sue and my spirit family. I'd felt a bit guilty about neglecting them since my world caved in. They'd been so patient with me, never expecting too much from me too soon. It was time to give something back. My journey towards clarity was almost coming to its end and memories were ready to be made again. My favourite time and place was sitting around the fire in the quiet of the afternoon so I decided that's where we would spend our special time together. I'd laid out an 'Afternoon Tea' table, perhaps going slightly overboard on the chocolate cakes considering there was only going two of us who could actually eat. I wasn't entirely sure if Owain would be joining us or not, what with social pleasantries not exactly being his thing. I didn't really mind if he just lurked about or took up his favourite spot on the windowsill. I just needed to feel his presence. As I finished arranging the triangle cut sandwiches and cakes on their stand and smoothed the lace doilies I'd found shoved in the back of a drawer, I heard the familiar footsteps of Sue coming through the back door. As she came into the bar, I looked at her in anticipation. I wanted to make her happy, to show her how much I appreciated her love and support.

'Ta Da!!' I gestured cheesily, waving my hands at the table like a manic buffoon.

Sue started to laugh as she saw the calorific ally laden table.

'Are you sure you've got enough cake on there?' she smiled, lifting up the bar hatch and walking towards the fire.

'Oh shit, I've forgotten something!' I gasped, 'sit, sit! I'll be back now!'

Sue looked on with an amused smile as I rushed behind the bar and into the kitchen. A few minutes later, I hastily returned bearing a large bouquet of flowers under one arm, a chilled bottle of Prosecco under the other and two glasses in my free hand. Suddenly, an icy chill blew through the room, making the flames of the fire dance.

'You're going to drop that bottle if you're don't slow down'.

I gasped, as I turned my head and caught a glimpse of Owain on the windowsill. Sue leapt to my aid and quickly grabbed the bottle and glasses before I dropped them on the floor.

'For fuck's sake Owain, don't do that to me, you prick!' As I glared at him with my best Paddington, a slight smile of amusement and perhaps a hint of smugness came across his face.

'Ever the lady, Miss'

We stood for a second staring at each other before I started to chuckle. Deep down, that was Owain's way of showing his unspoken affection and the feeling was mutual.

Just then, another blast of icy air whooshed past me, making my slightly unkempt hair blow even more out of place.

'Hello Miss, tis good to see you', smiled Deri. Bronwen was beside me, grinning from ear to ear and looking very excited.

'Oh Miss, this is a very happy day, we're all together!!'

My beautiful Bronwen, how she made my heart melt with her youthful joy.

I finally managed to present my flowers to Sue, who looked genuinely touched.

'I just wanted to thank you Sue...well...all of you, for being there for me during recent events.'

Sue put the flowers onto the next table and opened her arms, drawing me into a warm embrace. As she held me close, like a child in her arms, she whispered,

'That's what family do, my lovely girl.'

Suddenly, a cough broke the moment as Owain, obviously feeling that there was too much emotional nonsense for his liking.

'That tea you made is going cold', he grumbled, shifting about in his favourite place. Sue and I laughed as we broke apart and sat ourselves down to enjoy our civilised afternoon tea party. Two hours of normality, laughter and memory making. Just how I wanted it, just how I'd planned it. All too soon, our afternoon had to wind down. There was the evening opening to prepare for. I went outside for some air and a cigarette before having to tidy up the aftermath of our cake extravaganza. I slowly wandered around, taking in the pub's facade, remembering the first time I ever set foot in the place. It seemed a lifetime ago. I looked over towards Gwen's shop, surprised that she wasn't outside sweeping, just as an excuse to chat with any passing local. As I surveyed the surroundings of Mynydd Eira, the field with the first friends I'd made, happily grazing unaware I was watching them, I realised that despite everything, I was happy here. Out of the corner of my eye, I saw a tall figure dressed in black watching me. He beckoned me over to where he was standing. I looked around quickly to make sure no one was watching as I really didn't need any awkward questions. We stood close enough to talk but far enough apart to not look familiar. I could hear his chest rasping through the quiet air of the village.

'I've decided to bring your final appointment forward. I believe you are ready. You have completed your tasks, there's no reason to delay'.

He gave me the location of our meeting and instructed me to bring everything he'd ask me to gather. I nodded silently in agreement then turned and slowly walked back into the pub. As I walked into the bar, I could hear Sue happily chatting away to Bronwen, both sitting by the fire. Deri and Owain stood behind them and they looked up, Deri smiling at me warmly. Our eyes met and his face slowly changed to one of confused concern. I could hear Bronwen excitedly saying

'Oh it's so good to see Miss back to her happy self! I believe that all will be well from now on!'

As Deri and I stood staring at each other, he mumbled quietly to Owain,

'Something is very wrong here, very wrong indeed'

CHAPTER THIRTEEN

The following day started as any other. I awoke to sunlight peeking through the blinds, the promise of a beautiful, crisp day ahead. I felt a serene calmness, one of which I hadn't felt in a long time, if at all. My appointment wasn't until later so there was time to organise myself without the need for anxiety. I'd packed the items I was required to take in a black backpack, which I'd left on the chair in the corner of the bedroom. After showering, I dried and styled my hair and applied my makeup with more care and attention than I normally did. I wanted to look my best. I chose my best bootcut jeans, teaming them with a deep purple cold shoulder jumper and black flat ankle boots. After fastening my favourite silver Celtic cross around my neck, I took a long look in the mirror. Today was going to be the last day of one chapter and the promise of a new, peaceful one. A rebirth of sorts. To close the door on all the pain and heartbreak of my life so far and embrace the new, happier existence. It wasn't going to be easy however. The tasks I'd been set had been relatively straightforward but I knew that at my last appointment with my alternative bereavement counsellor, the final task would possibly be the most challenging. It was down to me to make it through to completion.

He said he would be with me, every step of the way. I trusted him, The Man in the Black Hat.

Before embarking on the drive to the meeting place, I stopped at the pub and let myself in. I wasn't due in work til that evening but I needed to run a final errand before I left. I heard Sue in the kitchen but I didn't want to disturb her. I left an envelope on the bar where she'd easily find it and I quickly and quietly, slipped out of the pub. I would be relieved to end the secrecy I'd been firmly encouraged to endure. By the evening, all would normal again and we could carry on as before, only in a slightly different way. I could feel eyes upon me as I got into my car. I looked towards the bar window and saw Owain staring through the glass. As we locked our gaze, his eyes widened and he started to hammer the window with his hand. He wanted me to go back into the pub but I didn't have time, whatever he wanted would have to wait until later. I drove away, leaving the pub and Mynydd Eira in my rear-view mirror, gradually disappearing from view.

It took me twenty minutes to reach my destination as I had to negotiate narrow winding roads and lack of signposts. I parked in the far corner of the carpark and looked across towards the gate leading to Mynydd Eira Mountain. When the Man in the Black Hat first told me where our last meeting would be, I thought it was rather strange. Then I realised that from the top, you could see Mynydd Eira village in the distance. A rather spectacular view on a clear day. Being in the beautiful surroundings of a place I'd grown to love seemed rather fitting for the closure of the old part of my life into the new. It wasn't a particularly large or steep mountain by Welsh standards but it would still take a good walk to get to the top. I was just relieved it wasn't raining. I reached behind me and lifted my rucksack off the backseat. I unzipped it to make sure I had everything he asked me to bring. I'd checked it what seemed like a thousand times before leaving that morning, a habit I'd been unable to break over the years. Opening the car door and getting out, I looked around to see if everyone else had decided to make the most of a beautiful day but it was quiet and deserted. Just as well, I didn't really want anyone seeing me huffing and puffing my way to the top. I put on my jacket and zipped it up then slipped the rucksack over my shoulders. It felt heavy against my back but there wasn't anything I could've done to make it lighter. I needed everything that was in there. I locked my car and started the walk up towards the top of the mountain. My mind started to fill with the words I'd written in Sue's letter. As I walked up the grassy path which had been carved away by previous feet, I wondered if she'd read it.

'My Dearest Sue,

I want to thank you for everything you and Nick have done for me. You took a scared little girl into your home and heart when I thought no one cared. You placed your trust in a stranger to look after your business and your secrets. I will always be grateful to you all for the love and support you showed me after Emily died. I'm sorry Sue but I'm going away for a little while. I'm not sure how long for but I'm hoping it won't be for too long. I've been struggling since Emily left. I'm so tired. I've been trying to carry on the best I can but every day has taken me apart, piece by piece. So, I need to do something to renew myself. For quite a while, I've been seeing a man. He befriended me whilst I was visiting Emily. He said he was a bereavement counsellor, although not the conventional kind. He's made me think more clearly as time's gone on and has advised me to take the next step towards peace and happiness. Today is the last day I will feel the pain. Tomorrow I'll be on my journey to get Emily and bring her home. In order for me to do that, I need to give up my life as I know it now. I've left separate instructions for the arrangements that will need to be made. I'm sorry to put this onto you but there's no one else I can trust to take care of everything the way I would like. Once I've left, I'll be able to come back and rejoin you all, only in a different way. I hope you understand why I need to do this. I want to be a proper mother to Emily and my friend has said this is the only way it can be done. Please remember that I'm doing this because I don't want to leave you all forever. Owain, Deri and Bronwen are happy to exist this way. If they can be happy then so can I. I love you all, you have been like a mother to me. That means more than you will ever imagine. This isn't goodbye. I will see you very soon with my beautiful little girl.

My love now and forever

Rosie

How else could I have explained it to Sue. Before my life in Mynydd Eira, I was sceptical about the afterlife. Now I had the chance to be complete, to fulfill my motherly role the way it should've happened. I wasn't ending my life, I was going to make it better for eternity.

With each step towards the top, Mynydd Eira came closer into view. It looked so beautiful surrounded by endless countryside. I wish I'd taken the time to view it from the mountain before this, I never really took advantage of the serenity of my home. That would definitely change once I was back. I would learn to channel my energy. I would be able to spread my wings and finally fly. It didn't take too long to finally reach the top. The Man in the Black Hat was already there waiting for me. He took my hand and led me to where I would take my final breath in this life. He sat me down on the grass and instructed me to empty my rucksack. I took out a large bottle of cheap vodka, several small white pots of paracetamol, my album containing my precious photographs of my beautiful Emily, my driving licence for identification and another short letter for whoever found me, with a contact list. He told me to start drinking the vodka first. I really didn't know why I had to choose vodka. I hated the stuff! It was, apparently, the drink of choice in situations like these. I unscrewed the cap and took my first swig.

'Oh my god that's disgusting!' I spluttered, trying not to choke.

'I can't drink that, I'm sorry, I just can't! ' I put the cap back onto the bottle and tightened it before throwing it onto the ground.

The Man in the Black Hat suddenly bent down and grabbed my face in his hand. His long, discoloured talon like finger nails cut into my skin. He pulled me closer to his withering face and I could smell death on his breath.

'Do you want to be with your dead daughter or not!?'

Spittle dripped from his lips as his red glowing eyes burned into mine. He increased the pressure against my jaw and drew his face closer. I started to gag as he breathed putrid filth into my lungs.

' I told you this wasn't conventional. I found you because you wanted to be found. I heard you beg to be with the daughter you killed. She died because you didn't really want her. She was conceived because you were a slut! I watched you as you sat by the hole in the ground, consumed by guilt for making her suffer. I heard your pathetic whimpers in your sleep. You entered a contract the moment you agreed to my help. You will fulfil that contract. I will give you what you want but you must give me what I want!' he hissed

As I stared, wide eyed and petrified into his true face, I realised that my ending to this existence wasn't going to be as beautiful as he'd promised. I wanted to be with Emily so what choice did I have now.

I slowly nodded and he released his grip. He thrust the bottle back into my hand.

'Now drink!'

I unscrewed the cap again, put the bottle to my lips and started to drink. The clear liquid burned my throat but I couldn't stop. After I'd drained half of the bottle, he raised his hand.

'Now for the pills.'

I looked at the pots of paracetamol laying on the grass. My head started to spin from the vodka and every movement I made felt as if it was in slow motion. I stretched my arm out to try to pick up the first pot but I had become drunkenly uncoordinated and couldn't pick them up. I heard a low growl as the Man in the Black Hat's anger increased. Through my haze, I could see his face contorting with venomous frustration. He suddenly grabbed a pot and ripped off the plastic cap.

'Take them!' he ordered, his red eyes blazing like fire. I started to shake as tears pricked my eyes.

'I don't think I can do this anymore' I whimpered. 'Why are you being like this to me? I thought you were my friend!'

The Man in the Black Hat suddenly started to laugh, quietly at first until it built into a deafening, manic crescendo.

'Why are you being like this to me?' he mimicked cruelly.

'You really are a pathetic little bitch aren't you! You're weak! Nobody wants you! Look at you, your own mother didn't love you, much preferring your brother. You were a constant disappointment. She even told you she wished you hadn't been born! Your husband hated you so much, all he wanted you for was to be his punchbag and whore, not caring about the three unborn babies he caused you to lose. Your mother just let it happen because she didn't care about you. And then there's the man who cheated on you after you played the dutiful girlfriend and to top it off, the married man who used you like an unpaid prostitute, leaving you knocked up with a soon to be dead baby! Your life has been a continuous car crash because you, my pathetic little Rosie are a useless piece of shit!'

I stared at him as my tears fell onto the grass. As cruel as he sounded, he was right. I'd car crashed my way through life, being hurt over and over again. I'd finally crashed and burned the day Emily died. I wiped my eyes and nose with the back of my sleeve and composed myself.

'So, what's it to be?' he asked.

I slowly stretched out my arm and opened my hand. He smiled and placed the open pot of paracetamol into it. I tipped my head back and poured the tablets into my mouth, washing them down with vodka. As I curled up into a fetal like position, I waited for the final sleep to come. The Man in the Black Hat sat beside me and as I closed my eyes and started to drift, he took my hand and gently whispered

'I lied about going to Heaven you know. You're going straight to Hell, bitch'

'Rosie, Rosie, open your eyes for me!'

Was I in Heaven or was the devil trying to wake me up.

More voices

'Are these all the pills she's taken? Are the other pots unopened? '

I could feel my body being shaken. If this was Heaven, it was a shitty way to wake up in paradise.

'Rosie, my name is Rhodri, I'm a paramedic, open your eyes!'

I groaned as I felt a tightness grip my arm.

'Her BP is through the floor guys, we need to get her off this mountain NOW!'

I opened my eyes to find myself floating above my body lying on the grass, a sea of people surrounding me.

'Rosie, I'm going to put a needle into your arm, sharp scratch...'

I heard a low growl as a coldness spread through my arm. Suddenly, I hurtled towards the ground.

The familiar smell of putrid breath filled my lungs. Whispers filled my head.

'Die...they can't save you, just hurry up and fucking die...'

The whispers were broken by louder voices as I felt myself being laid onto a cold, hard surface.

'On my count...one...two...three...lift'

A woman's voice cut through the haze.

'Rosie, I'm here my lovely girl. You hang in there you hear me! Don't you dare leave us!'

Was that Sue? Why was she shouting at me? As I drifted through a haze of confusion, whispers of darkness continued to battle with the voices of light. I had no idea in which direction I was going to be led.

I could feel the sun warm my face as I opened the gate and walked into the playground. Golden leaves swayed in the gentle breeze. I slowly walked towards the swings and sat myself down. I looked to the swing next to me. A little girl in a white cotton dress swung silently back and forth, her long golden hair framed her delicate features. She slowed herself down and came to a gentle stop. She turned to me and smiled, her face radiated such angelic beauty, making me gasp.

'Hello' said the girl. Her little button nose scrunched up as she smiled.

'Hello', I replied, as I looked into the biggest brown eyes I'd ever seen.

'Are you here by yourself?' I asked, looking around the empty playground. She was far too young to be out on her own.

She giggled as she lifted her legs up and started to swing again, her hands holding onto the chains. As she leant back, her golden hair flowed behind her, shimmering in the sunlight.

'I'm not here by myself, silly', she laughed.

'So... what's your name?' I enquired gently, as I watched her going higher and higher.

'Now you really are being silly!' she giggled.

I was confused. I thought I was being rather rational. A young girl I'd never seen before, alone in a playground, what was so silly about my questions?

'Why do you think I'm being silly?' I asked, wondering if I should call someone to help.

She slowed herself down again and stopped. She jumped off the swing and stood in front of me. She was exquisitely beautiful!

To my surprise, she took my hands and held them in hers. An aura of shimmering gold light began to shine around her and I could feel a serenity I'd never felt before.

'You know my name, you gave it to me. I'm always going to be with you but you must wake up now. Wake up mummy, wake up, wake up....'

Wake up, open your eyes for me, Rosie...'

My eyes flickered as the images and sweet voice of the beautiful little girl faded, replaced by a face unknown.

'That's it, good girl'

I groaned as a bright light was shone into my eyes. A mask was firmly over my mouth, air blowing deep into my lungs. A female dressed in blue hovered around me, checking the machine that was beeping beside the bed. She looked down towards me and smiled. The beautiful angelic girl had been replaced by a kind faced nurse.

'How are you feeling? You gave us quite a scare for a while but you're doing a bit better now'.

God I felt like shit. Waves of nausea hit me and I started to gag. The nurse quickly removed the oxygen mask and turned my head to the side. She gently held my hand until I'd finished.

'There, is that better now? You're on a drip with medication to try and counteract the effects of the tablets, you'll probably feel quite sick for a while but it'll pass'.

I felt like a scared little girl as I looked at her, wide eyed. She gently sat on the bed beside me.

'My name's Jan, I'm the nurse looking after you today. Do you remember much of what happened?'

Images of the playground suddenly changed to hazy images of the mountain. Tears started to spike as feelings of shame and embarrassment washed over me.

'I'm so sorry....' I whispered.

'Hey there's nothing to be sorry for', she soothed

'Once you're feeling stronger, someone from the Mental Health team will be down to have a chat with you. There's nothing to worry about, they just want to help you'

I nodded slowly then Jan replaced the mask over my face.

'You have a visitor in the family waiting room, a lady called Sue. Are you up to a few minutes with her? She's been here since you came in.'

I sighed and closed my eyes for a second. How was I going to face her after what I'd done? I opened my eyes and nodded. Jan smiled then left my bedside to get Sue. I looked over at the beeping machine beside my bed. Wires and tubes were attached to my arm and chest. Why had I listened to 'Him'? My thoughts were broken by a familiar voice.

'Hello my lovely girl, how are you feeling?'

Sue stood at the end of the bed for a moment before walking round to gently kiss the top of my head. She sat herself in the plastic chair and looked at me with red, tired eyes.

'I'm so sorry Sue', I whispered, the words catching in my dry throat. She leant over and took my hand in hers.

'Why didn't you tell me how much you were struggling, my darling?'

Her red eyes started to glass over as a single teardrop slowly rolled down her cheek. I faltered for a moment. Where the hell did I begin?

'He told me to. He said I could be with Emily'

My voice broke as emotion threatened to take over. I signaled to Sue that I needed water. As I took sips through the blue straw, I tried to formulate the words I needed to try and explain. I nodded my thanks and she placed the glass back onto the bedside cabinet.

Sue patiently waited, knowing that I would explain in my own time.

'The man...The Man in the Black Hat...he told me I could be with Emily but I had to end my life first before I could find her. I believed him'.

I could feel my face redden with shame and regret.

'I read your letter. What else did he say to you?" she enquired softly

I let out a sigh, the realisation of how ridiculous my story was going to sound.

'He said that once I'd passed over and found her, I would come back in spirit and live in the pub, like Owain, Deri and Bronwen...'

Oh, for fuck's sake, how could I have been so stupid!

'I had second thoughts for a minute but he reminded me of how useless I was. I had no choice Sue, it was my only way out. I just wanted to be with my little girl'.

I waited for the judgement, the lecture on my utterly idiotic actions. But it never came. Sue held my hand.

'Rosie, I believe you, I really do. You've been through enough in your lifetime to floor anyone. I thought you were being too strong but I didn't want to interfere. I feel so guilty now, I should've seen the signs'

'How did you know where to find me?' I asked, as I tried to conceal the increasing feeling of nausea.

Sue smiled.

'You, my lovely girl, have three Guardian Angels....'

CHAPTER FOURTEEN

For two days and nights, I was poked, prodded and puking. The doctor in charge of me was understanding and non-judgmental. It had been a close call. Blood tests showed that any effects to my internal organs were improving and hopefully, no long-term damage. I did wonder if they'd had to scrape some internal body part off the floor beside my bed.

I was recovering slowly, physically. The next job was to try and heal my broken mind. Before I was allowed to go home, I was assessed by the psychiatrist. He was a bespectacled, middle aged, bow tie wearing eccentric. He reminded me of a 'Nutty Professor', which, under the circumstances, was rather apt. He was, however, surprisingly easy to talk to. He never raised an eyebrow when, after gentle persuasion, I spilled the gruesome tale of the shitty path of life that had finally led me up the mountain. Twenty plus years of battered self-esteem and brutal betrayals had been hiding deep inside. Locked away like my own self-imposed dirty little secret. I'd been too strong. I'd been too good at pretending I could cope with anything that life could throw at me. In the end, it had been the loss of Emily that had finally and spectacularly, broken me. The Man in the Black Hat, according to the Prof, was the epitome of my depression. I still wasn't entirely convinced he hadn't been something else entirely. Had I been possessed by a demonic presence, leaching onto my vulnerability? I concluded it possibly wasn't a good idea to divulge my own theory and decided to agree with the professionals. My cheese hadn't just slid off my cracker, it had come off the whole bloody packet! The Nutty Professor assured me that I would now get all the help I needed. He prescribed anti-depressants to help quiet my jumbled mind and referred me to a counsellor. The thought of laying on a couch in a mental hospital, wittering complete bollocks to a stranger in a white coat, didn't really appeal to me but apparently modern-day counselling wasn't like that. It would be in a calm, comfortable room with a calm, understanding person who would let me talk about my life, at my own pace. I was relieved that they weren't going to put me in a padded room wearing this season's collection of strait jackets. White never suited me and I very much doubted they came in purple. The positive thing to come from all this was that I'd fallen to my lowest point. How could walking up a mountain to throw one's mortality away prematurely be a positive thing? Well, it couldn't get any bloody worse than that! The only direction I could go now, given time, was up. I didn't have a clue how I would get there. But for the first time in my life, it was going to be a journey that I wasn't going to be taking alone.

I was discharged from hospital after four days, back into the loving care of my surrogate mum and my now, Guardian Angels. The bond between myself, Deri, Bronwen and Owain had been tightly sealed a long time ago, without me even realising it. Sue reluctantly allowed me to go home instead of staying with her and Nick, on the understanding that she would have a key and that any time I wasn't at the pub, I would text or call her at regular intervals. I did feel at first that she maybe didn't trust me not to do something drastic again. I really wasn't in a position to complain. I still felt guilty about the horrific ordeal I'd put her through. She had saved me since I arrived in Mynydd Eira, this time quite literally. I owed her my life. My three Guardians welcomed me back in their own unique ways. Bronwen had taken on her home care responsibilities to the extreme. She'd taken to giving me a good prod in the ribs to wake me first thing in the morning, just to ensure I was still breathing. I was hoping it wasn't going to be a permanent ritual. Her energy had definitely improved!

Deri welcomed me back in his usual quiet, tactful manner. I was nervous about seeing Owain again. The last time I'd seen him, he'd been frantically banging on the windows to try and stop me from leaving. Our reunion took place, quite unexpectedly, whilst I was cleaning one of the vacated bedrooms. As I busied myself with the bedding, I felt the usual chill. As I looked up to see which one of them was visiting me, I was surprised to see Owain stood quietly in the doorway. I still felt slightly nervous in his presence, even more so due to the guilt I was still feeling. I managed a weak smile before carrying on with my chores.

'May I talk with you a moment?' he asked, his voice unusually calm.

I reluctantly stopped what I was doing and invited him to sit beside me on the bed.

We sat in silence for a few moments until he broke it.

'May I ask after your wellbeing?'

I took a deep breath and slowly exhaled.

'I'm fine...thank you for asking Owain' I replied, almost whispering as if to cover up the truth.

We both sat staring at the same wall. It seemed as if he was formulating what to say next and I was silently worrying what it was going to be. The air in the room started to feel oppressive. Finally...

' May I speak freely?', he asked. It felt a pointless question as I was hardly going to be in a position to say no. I nodded then prepared myself for what was to come.

'When you arrived here, truth be told, I didn't think you were going to be the right one for us. I thought you would be too weak to take on such a responsibility. It was Deri who persuaded me to agree with the others about allowing you into our home'.

I looked at him, not entirely surprised but still slightly hurt by his bluntness. I was just about to open my mouth in protest when he raised his hand, signally his intention to carry on.

'However, I've seen many people come and go over the years. We've always had to stay in the shadows, watching life go on. It's a lonely existence, watching centuries pass and the world becoming far away from the one we knew. I didn't think you would make any difference to our plight'.

Nothing like cheering a girl up eh?

'I'd tried my best to push you away. I kept you at arm's length. You took it all in your stride. I am a proud man but I am a man who will, eventually, admit when I'm wrong. You have endured so much in your young life yet your loyalty to us has never waivered'

We continued to stare at the same wall.

'You have saved and protected us. You have given us a reason to want to exist in both our world and that of the living. We were not prepared to let demons take away someone with such a loving heart.'

I felt a slight chill go through me and looked to see Owain had put his hand on mine.

He turned towards me, his face crumpling with emotion.

' I'm a grumpy and bitter old bastard who has gone through centuries resenting the living because my life and family were taken from me. Life is a gift that should be treasured. You are a gift that we treasure'.

I cleared the lump that was forming in my throat.

' I didn't want to leave you all Owain. I wanted to be with my daughter and you. I realise now that it's not that simple. Until I can be with her again, I promise you, I will remember how lucky I am to be alive and forever grateful to the three of you. Yes, you're a grumpy old bastard, Owain Thomas but you're my grumpy old bastard. How could I let anyone else put up with you!'

Owain started to chuckle, his lined, worn face suddenly looked younger, his eyes finally had a sparkle I'd never seen before. Laughter suited him. The atmosphere in the room felt lighter now.

' Oh, by the way...I had the strangest dream whilst I was asleep. There was this beautiful little girl and...'

Before I could carry on, a look on Owain's face stopped me. A serene smile spread across his face, his eyes closing for a moment, as if in prayer. He opened them again slowly then turned to me.

'So, it was SHE that found YOU...' he whispered

'She called me mummy, Owain'.

My heart began to thump against my chest.

'And you, my lovely girl, called her Emily....'

With that, Owain slowly faded.

After Owain's revelation, my recovery was able to begin. I still wasn't sure whether to completely believe him. Even after sharing my life with them, the thought that my own deceased daughter had found me during my darkest hour and sent me back to my own world was still, somehow, hard to get my head around. However, it was something to cling to during the tough days. My jumbled mind was beginning to quieten, thanks to modern medicine. The nightmares were slowly being replaced by more peaceful, dreamless sleep. My heart still ached constantly for Emily, nothing would ever stop that. Once I felt strong enough, I reached out to SANDS. They assigned me a Befriender, a fellow bereaved parent who would be in constant contact for as long as I needed them. Although I had Sue and my Spirit family, it helped to talk to others who truly knew the pain of losing a child. Instead of bottling up my emotions, I gave in to the rollercoaster of a hopefully, temporary Jekyll and Hyde existence. Hyde's choice of release was to kick the shit out of poor innocent wheelie bins, much to the concern of Sue, as it was hers that was targeted the most. She did suggest maybe it would be safer to kick something softer during Hyde's volatile moments and after a particularly vicious attack where my foot missed the bin entirely and kicked a wall instead, I decided she was possibly right. Jekyll was having a much better time of it. The breakthrough came on a breezy afternoon. After closing the pub as usual and tidying up, I was joined by all three of my spirits. They had been staying close together during my recuperation in case their collective energies were needed to bail me out of whatever shit mood I happened to be in. Owain was having one of his usual rants about nothing in particular. The final straw came when he sent several leather-bound menus flying across the room, narrowly missing several lamps and two pot plants that I hadn't actually managed to kill off. I was, according to my beloved late Nanna, capable of killing even plastic plants. There was no way I was going to allow a toddler tantrum throwing dead person jeapodising my chances of proving her wrong.

'Owain!!' I shouted, throwing down a bar towel, 'will you just stop being a complete fucking TWAT!!'

The room hushed to complete silence. Owain and I were in standoff, each of us staring at each other, our faces in temper deadlock. Suddenly, a sweet gentle voice cut through the tension...

'What's a Twat?'

And that's when it happened...

I looked at my beloved innocent Bronwen and started to laugh. Not just any old laugh but a full eye watering, snot producing, pelvic floor destroying hysterical wail! Sue came rushing down from upstairs, fearing that I'd gone into some kind of mental seizure after finding me in a red faced, snotty, hiccupping mess, bent over a bar stool. She was just about to call 999 when she realised I was, actually, laughing.

'What the hell's going on in here?!' she yelled, as she tried to peel me off an increasingly soggy stool.

'She...hic...wanted to...hic...know...hic...what a... hic...twat was!' I yelped, trying to get my breath in between my hysterics.

Poor Bronwen stood staring at me, her face crumpling.

'Miss, have I said something wrong again, I'm just a silly girl Miss, I'm sorry!'

I managed to compose myself enough to walk over to my beloved girl.

'Oh my sweet, beautiful Bronwen! You haven't done anything wrong! On the contrary, you've brought me back! I never thought I'd ever laugh again so thank you!'

Bronwen brightened again, relieved that she hadn't been the cause of another attempted demonic possession. I looked over at Owain, his facial expression had changed from anger to one of sheepish embarrassment. Deri jabbed him in the ribs and pushed him forward. He cleared his throat.

'I apologise for my behaviour Miss Rosie, I hope you will forgive me'.

I tried to control my laughter induced hiccups as I looked him in the eyes.

'Yes, I forgive you Owain...but you're still a twat...HIC!'

He smiled, half chuckling to himself, probably amused at the severity of the previous hiccup. The situation began to calm again. Bronwen, however, still had a look of confusion. She opened her mouth to speak then thought better of it. Curiosity finally got the better of her.

'Is anyone going to tell me what a twat is then or what?' she expressed, with surprising assertiveness.

Owain stepped beside her and started to whisper in her ear.

'Owain, no don't you dare!!' I shouted

Too late.

Poor Bronwen shrieked in horror as she started to cross herself before disappearing, screaming through the wall.

And that was when, finally, my pelvic floor decided to give way....

CHAPTER FIFTEEN

From that day, I allowed myself to laugh without feeling as if I was disrespecting Emily's memory. My life as a bereaved parent was going to be two roads travelled parallel from now on. Collisions were going to be inevitable and healing wounds would be reopened but my inner strength was slowly growing again. Given time, I would be able to crash but no longer burn. That was the plan anyway.

I threw myself back into the pub. The Bed and Breakfast business was ticking along quite nicely, although I couldn't take any of the credit for that. I'd been off Planet Sanity for most of its fledgling life and thanks to Sue's unwavering hard work, the business was getting increasingly good reviews. I was getting quite efficient at being ' Chief Chambermaid', once I'd gotten over my disbelief at some people's grotty little habits. Thankfully, most of our guests were housebroken. Running a Bed and Breakfast also came with its amusing moments. I had a feeling that when Mr. and Mrs. Shadwell checked in, things were going to get interesting. An elderly couple, both in their seventies and had obviously been married forever. Mrs. Shadwell was a five foot nothing, blue haired Tyrannosaurus in a Twin Set. She obviously wore the trousers in their marriage as Mr. Shadwell just stood quietly, shuffling on the spot and pretending to admire the open fireplace.

'Oh I hope that your rooms are better than the last establishment we stayed in' she crowed, as she signed the register 'they didn't even have matching curtains and cushions, I can't abide sloppy soft furnishings...don't you agree?'

Just then, I felt a chill descend over us. Mrs. Shadwell shivered.

'Oh, there's a draught in here, I can't abide a draughty room. I do hope upstairs is warmer!'

Owain stood beside her, looking her up and down.

'What a disagreeable old boot! I could amuse myself with this one'.

'No, don't you dare, now shsshh!' I hissed through gritted teeth as I gave Owain my best Paddington.

'I beg your pardon young lady, what did you say to me!?' barked Mrs. Shadwell, oblivious to the fact that there was a centuries old grumpy arsed ghost standing right by her.

' Oh, I erm said no its just fresh air...whoosh....' as I gesticulated like an idiot...

' from the back door....be fine in a minute...aha...yep...'

Mrs. Shadwell stood there, thinking about it for a second.

'Oh...yes...quite...well I hope staff don't make a habit of leaving doors open, it's not the time of year for that'

With that, Owain suddenly blew in her hair and promptly disappeared.

Mrs. Shadwell grabbed the room keys and barked to her poor husband to take the bags up to their room. He looked at me and rolled his eyes then did as he was told. I smiled, full of sympathy for him, wondering how on earth he hadn't buried her under the patio before now.

I could hear Mrs. Shadwell complaining about the ancient staircase as she made her way upstairs and wondered why on earth she wanted to stay in such an old building if she didn't appreciate all its charming imperfections. I made a mental note to be especially diligent during their two-night stay. I really didn't want to give the old bag any more reasons to moan. The pub was practically my home and any criticism would be taken extremely personally. I sighed as I closed the guest register.

'Has the old hag gone up?'

Owain sprawled out on the windowsill and sniffed loudly, just to make the point of his disdain for the woman.

'Yep, she has. I really hope she doesn't complain about every little thing Owain. It only takes one bad review to put doubt in people's minds. You know how hard Sue's worked to get this off the ground'.

Owain jumped off his usual perch and strode across towards me and leant on the bar.

' You worry too much, young lady, you can't please every wench'.

I smiled to myself as Owain screwed his face up as he sniffed loudly again. As much as he was a pain in the arse, he was also a good judge of character and had got the measure of Mrs. Shadwell as soon as she walked in. He also had the ability to redeem himself during times of stress by actually saying the right things to make me feel better.

It was short lived. I heard footsteps coming from the stairs and Mrs. Shadwell burst through the door into the bar. Under her arms were the white bath towels that I'd taken up to their room before arrival. She threw them onto the bar.

'Feel them!' she barked

I looked at the towels then looked at her.

' Mrs. Shadwell, what seems to be the problem?' I asked as politely as I could.

'Feel them I said!' she barked, ' what did exactly did you wash them in, starch and concrete?'

I really wish I had washed them in concrete, it would've hurt more if I'd decided to smash the old bag in the face with them!

Owain looked at me and raised his eyebrows. I tried to stifle a giggle.

'And what do you find so amusing, young lady, as a paying guest, I expect that the towels are at least soft!' the old bag bellowed as she picked them up and threw them closer towards me.

I felt the towels just to show that I was at least willing to take an interest. I knew there was nothing wrong with the towels. I'd washed them myself in fabric conditioner that promised that they would be soft, fresh and oh so fluffy.

'I'm very sorry to hear that the towels don't attain your high expectations Mrs. Shadwell...'

Her face suddenly looked very smug although sarcasm was obviously lost on her.

' I shall bring up some more towels to you presently', I continued, as I scooped up the offending articles and gave her my most dazzling smile.

'Well don't be too long, I wish to bathe after such a long journey to get here, I'm beginning to wonder if it was worth it' she huffed, stuck her nose in the air and stomped her way back upstairs.

Owain and I looked at each other in disbelief. A familiar look suddenly came over him, one that I would normally shoot down in a second.

'Owain...' I sighed...' you have my permission to scare the living shit out of that old bag!'

Revenge, as it happened, was a dish best served cold. Not only for me it seemed. The rest of the day went without incident. The Shadwells enjoyed the rest of their day, made better by softer towels. Except they were the same ones, after ten minutes in the tumble dryer. The old bag's face lit up as she did the touch test and concluded that these ones were much better than the others. Their evening meal was taken, with the old boot displaying more of her whining snobbery, complaining that the napkins weren't folded the right way and that my beloved open fire was too hot. Poor Mr. Shadwell remained silent as usual. He shuffled uncomfortably in his seat as Mrs. Shadwell launched from one whining whinge to the next. He did open his mouth at one point, the room suddenly silent in high anticipation of an imminent 'shut up dear'. Sadly, he closed it again without a sound, deciding to sink into his chair and hope that no one would think he was as bad as his wife. No one thought that of him. We all fantasised about this meek little man suddenly snapping in the middle of the night and dumping his wife in the large waste bins in the carpark. Knowing my luck, however, she'd start haunting the place and we'd be stuck with the snobby old trout for all eternity. Salvation came at breakfast. I heard only one set of footsteps on the stairs. They were quieter than the usual stomps and I was surprised, yet relieved to see Mr. Shadwell was alone. He stood in the doorway and beckoned me over.

'Good morning Mr. Shadwell, did you have a pleasant night?'

He guided me to the stairs and moved closer.

'Good morning Miss. I hope you don't mind me talking to you here but it's a bit delicate you see. I don't suppose you have any rubber gloves I could possibly borrow, do you?'

Uh Oh...the old fella's done it, he's smashed her head in with the teapot and wants to clean the blood up.

'Yes of course Mr. Shadwell but may I ask what the problem is? Can I help at all?'

He coughed awkwardly whilst signature shuffling on the spot.

' Well here's the thing...Mrs. Shadwell said she had a very disturbed night. I never heard a thing, truth be told but she said she was woken several times by something poking and prodding her. I just think it was the Bread and Butter Pudding she had last night, she's always had a problem with bread and wind but she'd obviously never admit to it...ahem...anyway...she was in the bathroom this morning doing her ablutions when she said something touched her. Well I heard her screaming over the sound of the news so it must've frightened her. Well...to cut a long story short...she jumped so hard...her false teeth shot out and I'm afraid they landed...well...down the toilet'.

I put my hand over my mouth, hopefully to show shock at such a thing but I was actually trying not to laugh. I finally composed myself.

'Oh my goodness Mr. Shadwell, I do hope Mrs. Shadwell isn't too distressed! Of course you can borrow some gloves'.

Mr. Shadwell smiled appreciatively. He looked worried for a moment before adding,

' I'm also really sorry for putting you out but Mrs. Shadwell doesn't want to stay another night. Truth be told, she hasn't got a spare pair of teeth and well...you can imagine her reluctance to put her ones back in after they've been...well...where they've been. She couldn't possibly show herself in public without them so I'm afraid we'll have to go home. I'll obviously pay for our second night's stay'.

I nodded sympathetically and decided to maybe knock a little off their bill, just for him.

'May I say something Miss... I just wanted to say thank you. I haven't laughed to myself so much in the fifty years of being married to my wife than I did this morning! She'll be even more hellish to live with after this but it was worth it! I have no idea what happened in that bathroom but it'll be a very fond memory from now on.'

I smiled to myself.

' You're very welcome Mr. Shadwell. I do hope you'll consider a return visit one day. Now, let me get you those gloves'.

I only saw the back of Mrs. Shadwell an hour later as she made a hasty, head down, hand over her mouth exit out of the pub. Mr. Shadwell settled the bill and after exchanging our final pleasantries, we said a cheery farewell. I wasn't sure we'd ever see them again but I would always remember the glint in Mr. Shadwell's eyes as he left. A moment's amusement for an old man living in a world of snotty snobbery was worth having an unexpected empty room. Once they'd left, Owain appeared by the doorway.

' The old hag gone then....' he boomed with a mixture of grumpy satisfaction and slight mirth. He looked at me, as if to wait for the telling off but there wasn't going to be one.

I walked over to him and raised my hand to high five him. He suddenly moved out of my way.

' Why do you raise your hand as if to strike me, woman, I only did as you asked!'

' No, no Owain, I was high fiving...oh..shit...I forgot, you have no idea what that is...bugger...nooo Owain, I'm happy with you. It's a well done kind of gesture...oh never mind. You did well...really well!'

Owain grunted his usual grunt, nodded then disappeared through the wall. Sue came through from the kitchen to see what the shouting was.

'What's up with him?' she asked

I sighed and shrugged.

' I tried to high five him'

Sue started to laugh, shook her head and walked back into the kitchen, still chuckling to herself.

'I wasn't trying to hit you Owain' I shouted into an empty room before making my way upstairs to retrieve my rubber gloves.

Luckily, incidents with unbearable guests came very few and far between. Our reputation remained untarnished. I endeavoured to check travel review websites just in case Mrs. Shadwell decided to tell the world of her disturbing experiences, deep down however, I knew that she wouldn't really want the humiliation of reliving the tale of her false teeth going for a swim. Owain eventually came around to the fact that I wasn't trying to belt him, although the possibility of actually making contact with someone who didn't have a physical body must've escaped us both at the time. We mutually accepted that the vast Generation Gap between us wasn't going to get closer although the other two were trying harder to understand the modern world they were sharing. Owain still thought that the mobile phone was some kind of witchcraft and a communication vessel between this world and the Fires of Hell. Who was I to try and change him. I secretly enjoyed watching him recoil as I received the 'devil's messages' every time my phone pinged. Life was slowly returning to some semblance of normality for me. It was obviously a different kind of normal but normal all the same. My sparkle was dimmer but not entirely extinguished. My future was still uncertain to me but it seemed that the universe had different ideas. Fate was going to play its hand.

CHAPTER SIXTEEN

It started on a wet and windy evening around seven twenty-five. It was my night off but for some reason, I decided I needed to go back to the pub. I was walking along the footpath, trying to avoid the puddles when a dark coloured Volkwagen van sped past me, straight through a huge puddle on the road and showering me with shitty brown sludge. It screeched to a halt by the pub sign, narrowly missing it by an inch! The driver jumped out and I could hear expletives echoing through the quiet village before the van door was violently slammed shut. I ran towards the culprit of my soggy state and stood dripping wet and mad as hell.

' Oi! You inconsiderate twat! Just look at the state of me! Don't you know there's a fucking speed limit in this village!'

The driver had his back to me and after giving the front wheel a hefty kick, turned around to face me. His long blonde shoulder length hair started to cling to his head in the rain and water was starting to drip from his beard. At approximately five foot ten, he towered over me. I pulled myself up to my fullest height although it didn't make the slightest difference.

'Did you hear what I said, you moron, look at me! You could've caused an accident driving like that!'

'Whoah calm down!' the stranger yelled.

He looked a bit shell-shocked as we both stood dripping in the rain. I felt myself suddenly calm.

'Hey, are you alright?' I asked

He wiped the water off his face before clearing his throat.

Yeah, I'm really sorry about that! I put my foot on the brakes to slow down at the speed sign but there was nothing there! I had to yank the handbrake up to stop before I hit the pub sign! I dunno what's happened, the brakes were fine before I got to this place! '

I suddenly felt guilty for shouting at him as the rain suddenly got heavier.

' Hey let's get in the pub and we'll see what we can do for you, alright?' I shouted over the deluge. He nodded and quickly locked his van and followed me into the pub.

'Get yourself by the fire and I'll get some towels'. He looked confused as I hurried behind the bar.

' Where you going?' he asked, looking around as if we'd broken in.

'Oh it's ok' I reassured, ' I work here, I'm the Manager'.

On my return, I found the stranger warming himself by my beloved fire. He'd hung his jacket over the back of the chair and a puddle was forming on the floor. A few of the regulars had taken it upon themselves to sit beside him and question his predicament.

'Look at the state of you Rosie!' laughed old Idris Evans. Seventy-four years young with the mind and glint in his eye of a much younger man. A widower for fifteen years, he'd seen his fair share of unexpected things happening in the village, mostly due to sheep escaping from the fields and wandering around exploring the quiet delights of Mynydd Eira. If only he knew the invisible dramas that unfolded in the shadows whilst he was enjoying his pint. I suddenly heard a whisper in my ear.

'Who's that?'

'Not now Owain!' I whispered back, before walking towards the fire and the newest stranger to the village. I handed him a towel and he thanked me. I poured us both two small whiskies and sat in the chair opposite him. Idris politely returned to his own corner.

'So...' I asked ' apart from trying to half drown innocent pedestrians and almost killing my pub sign, is there anything else you can tell me about yourself then?'

He laughed as he raised his glass to me and downed his whisky. His blue eyes had a sparkle to them behind his metal rimmed glasses. With his long blonde wild and free hair slowly drying along with his neatly trimmed beard, he had a Viking look about him.

'Well, my name is Cadog Pendragon'

'Jeezus, what drugs were your parents on when they named you!' I exclaimed before realising how extremely rude that must've sounded!

'Shit, I'm sorry, I didn't mean to be rude' I apologised quickly.

Luckily, he saw the funny side and smiled.

'Yeah you're not the first person to say that. Tell you what, just call me Dog'

I raised my glass.

' Well Just call me Dog, you can just call me Rosie', I laughed, ' I'm pleased to meet you...even though you did half drown me!'

Dog tried to contact his breakdown provider but for some reason, he wasn't able to get through on his mobile or my landline. As we sat by the fire, I was feeling more relaxed than I had done for a long time. We chatted about anything and nothing as if we'd always known each other. Time flew by and before we knew it, it was closing time. Dog was stuck in Mynydd Eira. He said he would sleep in his van but I couldn't let him do that. Although the rain had finally stopped, it was freezing and I didn't fancy being responsible for my new friend getting double pneumonia. Luckily, the single bedroom was made up but unoccupied and as the Good Samaritan that I was, I offered it to him free of charge for the night. I grabbed the keys and some fresh towels and he followed me up the creaking staircase. I unlocked the door and showed him in.

'I'm really grateful to you for this Rosie, you're very kind' he smiled, as he looked around the cosy room. I could see genuine appreciation in his eyes.

' It's no problem at all' I replied, 'Breakfast is between seven and nine. I'll be on shift in the morning so after you've had breakfast, we can see about sorting your van. I live just down the road but any problems in the night, Sue the owner of the pub's contact details are in the information book on the dressing table. There's tea and coffee if you want it over there. If there's nothing else you need, I'll say goodnight'.

'Goodnight Rosie and thanks again'.

As I left the room and closed the door, I felt a peculiar feeling in my stomach. I shook my head and made my way downstairs, grabbed my coat and left the pub. As I passed Dog's abandoned van, I chuckled to myself. What had started as a shitty mess of an evening, had ended in a pleasant one with a new friend made.

The next morning started brighter. As I walked to work, I noticed Gwen was out sweeping away the rubbish blown by the previous night's deluge.

'Morning Rosie, what happened there then?' she shouted from across the road, pointing to Dog's abandoned van.

I just shrugged and gestured that I'd see her later. A five-minute chat with Gwen always turned into forty-five and she'd probably want to everything there was to know about Dog. There was nothing to tell as I didn't know much of anything about him.

As I walked into the pub, I could smell freshly brewed coffee wafting from behind the bar. Sue came wandering in from the kitchen, wiping her hands on a tea towel.

'I hear you brought in a waif and stray last night...' she smiled, winking at me before pouring me my first cup of the day.

'Good morning to you too! Oh he was hardly a waif and stray! Owain told you, did he? He'd be suspicious if Santa's Sleigh broke down outside...nah it was just some guy who had a bit of a problem with his van that's all.'

With a few minutes to kill, I climbed onto a bar stool as Sue placed the steaming coffee mug in front of me. I wrapped my hands around it and took a sip.

'God that's better', I sighed ' oh by the way, I put him in the single room. We didn't have any bookings for it. He was going to sleep in his van but it was bloody horrible last night so I couldn't really turf him out'.

Sue smiled and nodded as she pottered about behind the bar. I took another sip of coffee, finally feeling the caffeine hitting the spot. I shuffled on the bar stool, waiting for the right moment.

' Erm...another thing Sue. Hope you don't mind but...well under the circumstances...I said he could stay no charge. If it's a problem, I'll pay but he had no way of getting home and...'

Sue raised her hand and I stopped trying to justify my previous night's actions.

'It's fine Rosie. It was a very nice thing you did. All I ask is try not to make these good deeds a habit, my bank manager might not see helping your fellow man as an excuse for going bankrupt'.

I sheepishly grinned as she jokingly wagged her finger at me. She stopped then thought for a moment. She leant over the bar and whispered,

'I also hear he got you extremely wet last night....' she winked.

'Oh my god Sue, I can't believe you just said that, you filthy mare!!' I shrieked, almost falling off my stool.

We were still laughing and didn't hear the door open.

'Good morning...'

Sue and I sprang apart like two naughty children just being caught up to no good. My face started to burn as Dog walked towards us.

'Morning Dog, hope you slept alright' I stuttered, still feeling my cheeks burning.

'Dog, this is Sue, the owner of the pub and my 'surrogate mum'. Sue, this is the gentleman who almost killed our signpost last night' I nervously chuckled.

Dog and Sue shook hands over the bar.

' Pleased to meet you Sue. I'm Cadog Pendragon and no, before you ask, my parents weren't on drugs...well I don't think they were anyway' he laughed, winking at me.

The ice had been broken and Sue seemed quite taken with him on first meeting. I felt slightly better about my rather rash decision to not charge him for the room. After serving Dog a hearty full English breakfast, he said his goodbyes and thanks to Sue and I followed him out to his van. He decided to try his brakes before phoning his Breakdown company so he gingerly drove into the carpark. He parked up and got out, looking extremely puzzled.

'That's bloody weird, there's nothing wrong with them now!', he exclaimed, before lighting up a cigarette and offering one to me. I took a cigarette, lit it and looked up at him, shaking my head in mutual confusion.

'Wonder what was wrong then?', I pondered, 'maybe it was the weather? Can brakes go funny in the rain?'.

Dog took a long drag on his cigarette.

It's never happened before, I'll take it easy going home, its only fifteen miles so if anything happens again, I can pull over.'

I nodded as I finished my cigarette.

'I was wondering Rosie, could I have your number? I mean, your pub is lovely, erm, I know a few people who might like to come out this way...'

Dog flicked his cigarette butt onto the tarmac then looked a bit sheepish, thinking perhaps he shouldn't have done it. I dropped my finished cigarette and stood on it, just to make him feel better whilst making a mental note to sweep up later.

'Er yeah no problem, I can give you the pub's number and my mobile if you like, just in case you can't get through for any reason'.

I could feel my face beginning to glow again. I was trying not to think too much into his request. Maybe he did genuinely know people who would like the olde worlde charm of Mynydd Eira and any recommendations were obviously going to be to our advantage. I'd played my part of Good Samaritan to a stranded stranger and that was all it was. As we exchanged numbers, I could feel eyes burning into me from the window above. I could see three faces pressed against the window pane. I looked up to see Owain scowling at me whilst Deri and Bronwen had rather amused smiles. I mouthed at them to go away as discreetly as I could without drawing too much attention. The last thing I wanted was to try and come up with an excuse to cover the fact that, to Dog, I was talking to myself.

Dog and I said our goodbyes and he climbed into his van, slowly pulled out of the carpark and drove out of Mynydd Eira. I found myself watching as he disappeared from view, feeling strangely sad to see him leave. He probably only asked for my number out of politeness, feeling obligated to return the favour by hinting that he would recommend the pub to his friends. I had to shake the feelings of disappointment. I was in no emotional position for a new relationship and there had been no signs from him that he was remotely interested anyway. It had been what it had been, a chance meeting, a fleeting moment. I hadn't even noticed how blue his eyes were or how they sparkled when he laughed. I hadn't even noticed his Viking like blonde hair which he kept tucking behind his ears as he spoke. I hadn't even noticed his Richard Burton like valleys accent, soft and soothing like a warm blanket. I hadn't really noticed anything about him at all. Nothing. A storm had brought this accidental visitor to Mynydd Eira and now he was gone. I looked up at the window. Their curiosity had obviously been satisfied as they had disappeared. No doubt questions would be asked once they decided to find me again. There were no questions to answer. By tomorrow, I would've forgotten all about Cadog Pendragon. I looked at the lamppost and let out a long sigh before walking back into the pub to get on with the rest of my life.

Getting on with the rest of my life took exactly four hours and twenty-seven minutes. I was in the middle of a rather heated debate with Owain about microwave ovens. I would've thought that after all this time existing in the modern world, he'd have gotten used to things that heated food without resorting to joining a cult or a coven. He knew damn well what it was, he was just being his normal pigheaded self.

'Stop being such an arse Owain!' I screeched just as my own backside vibrated and beeped. As I reached into my back pocket to retrieve my phone, Owain made a point of poking the offending item of witchcraft only to recoil in over the top terror when it pinged. As I opened the microwave door to retrieve my mug of reheated coffee, Owain sniffed his usual sniff.

'You are going straight to hell I warn thee!' before disappearing to no doubt sulk in one of the bedrooms. I just hoped he kept his sulk to himself as there was a guest in there on a well-earned break after heart surgery. If Owain decided to share his strop, that poor person would've been through hospital food for nothing.

I finally checked why my backside had vibrated at a crucial moment in a fight I was hoping to win. My eyes widened as I opened the text message.

'Bugger me he text me!!' I exclaimed into an empty kitchen before almost dropping my phone on the floor. My hands started to shake as I read what he'd written.

'Hi Rosie it's Dog. I hope you remember me from four hours ago! LOL'

Nah…didn't remember him at all…

'Just wanted to thank you again for helping me out last night. Hope to hear from you sometime. Cheers, smiley face smiley face'

Now the dilemma. Did I place it cool and leave it for a while before texting back or should I be polite and text back saying it was my pleasure. Scrap that, too gushy. It was fine, I was just doing my job blah blah.

I decided to play it safe and just sent a polite text back then put my phone into my back pocket. Sue came into the kitchen carrying towels just as my phone started ringing. I stood there for a moment looking at her.

'Well? Aren't you going to answer your bottom then?' she laughed as she started folding.

'My bottom will stop ringing in a minute!' I flustered as I pretended to give her a hand with the towels. Finally, my phone stopped and I heard a beep signally a voicemail message. I knew it was Dog who had called me. No one apart from Sue rang my mobile anymore. She knew that.

'Are you going to check what your bottom has to say then?' Sue was obviously in a playful mood. I knew she wouldn't leave me alone unless I listened to it.

Rolling my eyes, I reached for my phone and dialed the voicemail. I tried not to smile as I listened to the message from Dog. His soothing voice took me back to the last evening sitting by the fire, talking about anything and everything. The message ended and I put my phone back into my pocket.

'Well?' enquired Sue with a smile.

I sighed, trying not to give my emotions away too much.

'Well, that was Dog.' I replied, as I eyed up the towels thinking I needed to try and look uninterested.

'And?' Sue really wasn't going to let this go.

'And nothing really' I said as I picked up a towel and started faffing about with it. Sue looked at me with raised eyebrows which I'd learnt was her silent way of telling me to get a grip and spill the beans.

'Okay, okay!! He thanked me, well us, for helping him out last night. He also said he was going to be in the area at the end of the week for work and wondered if he could pop in to see us.

Sue's eyebrows raised even further, which I didn't think was even possible.

'He wants to pop in to see US, does he?' she smirked

'Aha...that's right, to see US.'

Sue piled the towels on top of one another and scooped them up into her arms. As she left the kitchen to go upstairs, she turned to me.

'Do you want the night off?' she asked

'YES! Er...yes please, only if you can spare me' I shouted, suddenly realising how enthusiastic I sounded.

As Sue went disappearing into the bar, I heard her call out.

'Oh, I can spare you my lovely girl, most definitely!'

CHAPTER SEVENTEEN

Bronwen was sitting on the bed surrounded by the entire contents of my wardrobe.

'What do you think of this top, Bronwen?'

As I turned left and right in front of the mirror, I could see her pick up a lacy coral coloured bra with her fingers, holding it at arm's length.

'That won't go with this top Bronwen. Maybe the black one behind you might be better.'

Bronwen reached behind her to pick up a balconette bra with diamante detail and I could hear her take a sharp intake of breath.

'If you please Miss, is this really a suitable undergarment for a lady of your standing?' she enquired.

'Will you not be wearing a corset for your meeting with this gentleman?'

Now there's an idea but maybe for another night in the future if all goes well! I giggled to myself as I took off the top I was wearing to try another. It wouldn't be the kind of corset that Bronwen had in mind, bless her. Suddenly a grey cloud went across my heart. The last time I was standing in front of the mirror deciding what to wear was for my date with Emily's father. So much had happened since then. I wasn't sure if I was entirely ready to move on and potentially give my heart away again. I was lonely without actually being alone. Having Sue,

Nick and my Spirit family was an absolute blessing. I yearned for Emily every single day but the raw pain of her passing was slowly being replaced by a constant dull ache. I found that I was needing to be me again. I was always going to wear the label of a bereaved parent but I still had the rest of my life to live. I promised myself however that this time, I wasn't going to hurtle head first into something. Dog seemed completely different to the dick head of a plumber. I was in danger of tarring him with the same brush and that wasn't fair.

I finally decided on a black belted gypsy skirt and a plain deep purple cold shoulder top. Just enough shoulder to look desirable, just enough covered to not appear slutty. Bronwen looked at me with a smile and nodded.

I wasn't sure what time Dog would be arriving at the pub but he text to say he would be there early evening. He hadn't mentioned what his job was when we first met that eventful evening but with his intellect, I was sure it must've been something important and interesting. He didn't strike me as someone who would settle for the mundane. The pub had been busy and I helped out as much as I could, even though it was my night off. I wasn't able to stay still as nervous excitement was beginning to build. Every time the door opened, my heart stopped only to restart

again when it wasn't him. Finally, at eight fifteen, the door opened and in walked Dog. We stood there smiling at each other as we said our hellos.

'I'm so sorry I couldn't get here sooner' he apologised, taking his coat off and putting it on the back of a chair. His sense of style was more unusual to when I last saw him. A loose fitting turquoise blue hippy style shirt complemented his light blue linen trousers. His Viking blonde hair had been tamed into a neat ponytail. I noticed he'd trimmed his beard. I wasn't sure if this was his usual personal grooming or he'd made an effort for the evening. Either way, he looked very cool

and comfortable.

I went behind the bar and got us some drinks before settling down in my favourite spot by the fire.

'Déjà vu!' he exclaimed before taking a sip of his beer.

I nervously laughed.

'Yeah it is, except this time I'm not wet' I replied, before realising what I'd said. I sat back and took a big glug of my drink, quietly wanting the ground to open up and swallow me whole. Sensing my embarrassment, Dog broke the ice.

'Well, even if I do say so myself, I'm so sexy I even make the weather wet' he grinned

I almost choked on my drink as I started laughing and felt a lot better than a few seconds before.

'I forgot to tell you' continued Dog after the danger of my choking to death had passed. 'I had my little brother look at my van brakes, there was nothing wrong with them'.

'How weird!' I exclaimed, secretly glad that there had been a problem that night but relieved that it hadn't been more serious.

'So, your van and our lamppost are safe to see another day then' I chuckled, as the fire crackled and hissed beside us.

'Apparently so' replied Dog as he took a sip from his pint. I could see the glow of the dancing flames reflect his eyes as he looked at me through the bottom of his glass. It suddenly felt so surreal. What were the odds of something going apparently wrong with the brakes of his van as he drove past me that night. It could've happened anywhere but it just so happened in Mynydd Eira on the night I felt compelled to go to the pub even though it was pouring down with rain.

'So, what brought you to Wales?' he asked, snapping me out of my thoughts.

'Sorry, what did you say? I asked, embarrassed that I had been in a world of my own for a second.

'If you don't mind me saying, you're obviously not Welsh so how long have you lived here?' he enquired

Oh God here we go, I panicked to myself. The inevitable 'Getting to know you' questions were starting and I wasn't sure exactly how much information to divulge. We hadn't really talked about it on the night we met. It was probably best not to go into everything that happened in gory details for fear of him thinking I was a complete disaster area. I definitely wasn't going to tell him about my suicide attempt after Emily died. Some things didn't have to be relived, especially to someone I'd only just met.

'I've been in Wales quite a few years now', I started 'my marriage ended and I don't really have any family as such in England so I decided to make a fresh start elsewhere. Wales seemed the perfect place for me to do that. For some reason, I've felt more at home here than anywhere I've lived before.'

There, that was safe enough. Nothing very unusual about uprooting to another country after divorce.

'It was a good choice' he chuckled

'What about you Dog?'

My turn to see if he was going to be more honest about his life.

'Born and bred in Gwent. My mam and dad still live in the same house where I grew up. I've got a little brother, well I say 'little', he's six foot one, married with three kids. He's thirteen years younger than me so he'll always be my baby bro. I'm divorced too. There was a bit of an age gap between me and the ex which got a bit too wide after twenty-five years and we grew apart'

I nodded, appreciative that he was honest enough to tell me that he used to be married. The last thing I needed after the fiasco of the dickhead plumber was finding out there was a secret wife at home.

'Do you have kids?' I enquired, hoping that it wasn't too personal a question.

'I've got four stepsons who were only small when we got together so I brought them up as my own. I'm Bampy to eight grandkids.

My eyes widened.

'Eight?!' I exclaimed, 'you've got your hands full, haven't you?'

'Well I don't see them as much as I'd like but the boys have their own lives I suppose. What about you then Rosie, you said you've been married before, any kids?'

I started to panic slightly. I really didn't want to bring the conversation to a crashing halt but if we were going to be friends, he had the right to know at least some of my secrets. Not that Emily was a secret. Any bereaved parent faced the difficult task of reliving the pain each time children were mentioned. I slowly cleared my throat and took a sip of my drink.

'Erm, actually yes I do. I have a daughter, well, I mean, I had a daughter'

I started playing with a cardboard beer mat, tearing it into small pieces. I could feel the familiar lump growing larger in my throat as tears started to bite at my eyes. Dog looked concerned and gently leant forward, resting his arms on the table.

'Can I ask what happened Rosie' he asked gently. I could hear the dancing flames crackle as we sat in silence for what seemed like eternity.

Finally, I found my voice.

'I hadn't been in Mynydd Eira that long. I had a brief relationship with someone who turned out to be a lying cheating arsehole. Before we broke up, I discovered I was pregnant. I didn't know I could get pregnant as I'd lost three babes during my marriage. I didn't know what I was going to do but Sue and Nick had become like parents to me by then and with their support, I was going to have the baby. I didn't want the baby's father involved so I didn't tell him at first. He found out I was pregnant though when I was six months along but he was sent packing by some, er, friends'

This was going to be a tough enough story to tell without including my other 'family'.

I continued to tear the bar mat into even tinier pieces as I continued.

'When I was just over six months, I went into premature labour. The hospital couldn't stop it so I had to give birth. I had a beautiful little girl. I called her Emily Rose. She was too tiny to survive and she passed away in my arms a few minutes after she was born'

Dog reached over and took my hand. It was one of the sweetest gestures a stranger had ever done after being told such a tragic tale. So many people were afraid to talk of baby death which led to bereaved parents thinking they didn't care. It wasn't that they didn't care, it was because they didn't know what to say so they chose not to say anything at all. The life of a bereaved parent was one of mostly silence.

Dog looked at me with compassionate eyes.

'I'm really sorry Rosie for your loss' he said gently

That was all that was needed. No drama, no uncomfortable silence after a sharp intake of breath as if I'd just told him I was a mass murderer. One gentle, genuine sentence.

'Thank You' I replied, smiling as I did so. I wasn't going to add anything further to my revelation. There was no need to drag up painful, shameful memories of the aftermath. I was in a better place now and that was what I was going to concentrate on.

'Anyway', I said, keen to move on from anything else that could've proved to be a 'date killer'. Was this a date though? I wasn't entirely sure what 'this' was.

'what do you do for a living?'

Dog sat back in his chair and started to roll the sleeves of his shirt. I think he'd forgotten just how warm it got sitting by the fire.

'I'm a support manager for a company that look after naughty boys and girls.

'Oh really?' I said, watching him getting slightly irritated by one sleeve that refused to stay rolled up. He gave up on his sleeve and took another sip from his pint.

'I used to work with younger kids with severe behavioural problems in registered children's' homes but I left to join another company who look after those at the next phase. The kids are older, some nearly eighteen. They have to leave us once they reach eighteen so we try to get them prepared for the outside world. Unfortunately, we have very few success stories as sadly some, if not most, are too far gone in their behavior to change. Most of our clients have had a rough upbringing so it's understandable to a certain extent why they are like they are. Some are just spoilt brats that you just want to punch in the face but that's frowned upon apparently so I have to resist the urge'. He winked at me as he said that so I knew he was joking. He carried on telling me about his job and all the experiences he'd encountered over the years. Some of it sounded horrific but what came across the most was his passion for the job. He really wanted to help these kids even though they threw it all back in his face at times. The more I found out about him, the more I liked him. After having my heart ripped out previously by so many people, I'd been in danger of tarring everyone with the same brush, hardening my heart to anyone who dared to get close enough to try and soften it again. Dog had been the perfect gentleman. There was no hint of a hidden agenda. He seemed to possess all the qualities I admired in a person as well as a sense of humour which very much resembled my own. Also the fact that he was very pleasant on the eye was also a bonus. All I could do was see how it panned out.

As it turned out, one date turned into another then another. Before I knew it, we were a couple enjoying the first flush of a relationship. This time around however, it wasn't just the physical connection which drew us together. It was also a meeting of minds which I'd never had before with anyone else. We'd talk for hours, sometimes finishing each other's sentences or knowing what the other was thinking before we even said a word. Maybe it was what soul mates were supposed to be like but it seemed that fate had brought us together for a reason. I did wonder whether it was the romantic in me hoping that this was finally the relationship I'd been dreaming of being in my entire life. For the first time in what had seemed like years, I was finally happy and content. Even Owain seemed to tolerate him. Dog and I split our time between our two homes and the times Dog spent with me, my three ghostly companions never once tried anything to put a spanner in the works. They kept quietly in the background, watching my happiness grow with each passing week. I'd been trying to gauge Dog's thoughts into the paranormal. If I'd just launched into confessing that the pub was haunted by three spirits who were like family to me, the chances that he would probably think I'd lost the plot would be quite high and I wasn't running that risk so early into our relationship. I would have to pick my moment very carefully.

CHAPTER EIGHTEEN

That moment came three months into our relationship.

Not only was I living a life within the paranormal world, my interest in myth and legend had always been peaked. The Legend of King Arthur had always fascinated me and to meet someone with such an unusual surname as Pendragon, the opportunity to explore the myth was too good to pass up. Glastonbury was renowned to be the final resting place of King Arthur and Guinevere. History told that in 1191, Monks of Glastonbury Abbey had found the remains of a tall male skeleton with a fractured skull. Laying beside him, a female skeleton with a lock of fine hair. An inscription on the stone slab read

Hic Iacet Sepulus Inclitus Rex Arturius in Insula Avonlonia

Here Lies Buried the Renowned King Arthur in the isle of Avalon

The bones were later transferred and buried at the High Altar of the Abbey. As Arthur's father was Uther Pendragon, we thought it would be interesting to visit the alleged final resting place of the man who defended the Welsh and fell into legend.

We booked into a Bed and Breakfast which was as fascinating as Glastonbury itself. Inspired by Pagan, Myth and Magic, the entire house was filled with weird and wonderful artifacts and curios, ranging from a vampire hunting kit, ornaments of dragons and demons, everything that any self-respecting witch would possess and everything else that would probably send those of a nervous disposition running screaming that the apocalypse was imminent. Each room was 'themed'. I thought that was an amazing idea and wondered if it would work in our pub. That would be another thing that Owain would moan about and start accusing me of being the Antichrist again. Our room was 'Hern the Hunter's' room. Animal fur throws adorned the king size bed and on the floor. Wooden carvings of owls and deer filled the room. It was as if we were going to be sleeping deep in the forest. Neither of us had seen anything like it. The windows framed views of Glastonbury Tor and I wondered what spirits were living in the surrounds of the monument. Dog's reaction to our surroundings were extremely favourable. I still had to bide my time into telling him about my own amazing secret but at least I was a little more confident that he would be open to the idea of sharing my life with those who had seen countless others come and go over the centuries.

We spent our days exploring Glastonbury's quaint side streets full of gothic art and mystery. The smell of incense radiated from each shop, enveloping us in a heady mix of Dragon's Blood and Witches Curses. As we stepped into each establishment of wonders, my eyes were drawn to the psychic mediums who ran them. It felt like each one looked into my very soul, quietly acknowledging my secrets, silently vowing never to reveal them to the outside world. I watched Dog's reactions to our surroundings. Never once did he mock or scorn. There was no more need to test the waters. I decided that I was going to tell him. We were due to visit the Abbey the following day, I would wait until the time was right then reveal what I'd been hiding from him these past few months.

The hazy morning sunshine lingered over the final resting place of King Arthur like a veil. We stood there in silence for a moment, reading the plaque that marked the grave. Finally, I broke the quiet.

'Do you really think he was real then?', I asked, fumbling around in my pocket for a chewing gum.

'Dunno really', replied Dog 'I suppose the legend had to stem from somewhere. He was probably just some old King who was raised up in everyone's expectations then, like Chinese Whispers, the story was added to down the years'

'Hmm maybe' I shrugged as I looked around to find a bench. My heart was pounding as I started to build myself up for the big reveal.

'Ooh there's a bench over there, fancy a sit for five?' I asked, trying not to sound too obvious that I was beginning to get extremely nervous.

We sat on the bench and Dog reached into his pocket for his pouch of tobacco and started rolling two cigarettes. I watched as a couple wandered across to the grave site. They'd probably waited until we had walked away, wanting to stand there alone with their own interpretations of what had gone before. Dog handed me a rolled cigarette. I lit it and took a deep draw, holding the smoke in my throat before blowing it out. My heart pounded a little faster, partly due to the nicotine hit and partly due to the fact that in a moment, I was opening myself to a reaction that I didn't know which way was going to go.

'Do you believe in ghosts?' I blurted, before my nerve got the better of me.

Dog took a drag of his own cigarette then looked sideways at me through his hair.

'I don't think so in all honesty. I guess I'm open minded to a certain extent but I call myself a sceptic mostly. Why, do you think this place is haunted then?' he chuckled

I took a deep breath.

'Well, maybe it is…but I know a place that most definitely is'.

Dog took the last few drags of his cigarette.

'Where's that then?' he asked as he looked around to see what he could do with his cigarette end.

I started to look at my feet.

'The pub', I mumbled as quickly as I possible could.

'What pub?' Dog replied, looking amused at my obvious embarrassment.

'My pub... oh and my house'

That was that. It was done. I waited for a reaction.

'FUCK OFF!' laughed Dog as he took out his tobacco pouch again to make another cigarette.

It was an understandable reaction.

'Honestly! It really is! I didn't want to believe it at first but it really is. There's three of them, one teenage girl and two older men. They're called Bronwen, Deri and Owain. Another thing...I'm their guardian of sorts. I can see and talk to them'

Dog stood up and started pacing around the bench. His face was one of amusement.

'So, you talk to ghosts?' he chuckled

I looked him straight in the eye.

'Yes, I do, well them I do anyway. They've become my family'

Dog sat back down and carried on making cigarettes and putting them into his tin. He was shaking his head chuckling to himself as he did so.

'You really make me laugh Rosie. That's the best shit I've heard in a long time. You really had me going for a minute'

I started to laugh alongside him, shoulder bouncing him as I did so. He obviously wasn't going to take me seriously as I hoped so I wasn't going to push it any further whilst we were away. This was going to have to be proved to him another way.

The matter wasn't brought up again for the rest of our trip. We enjoyed our final night in our wonderfully eclectic hotel and made our way home the following morning.

We pulled up outside the pub and Dog helped me in with my bags. I didn't want to go home. I had other things I needed to do. He wasn't due in work until later that evening so I asked him into the pub to spend the last couple of hours.

As Dog sat by the fire, I went into the kitchen to make us a cup of tea. I quietly called out for my three to join me. I explained to them that I tried to tell Dog about them but he didn't believe me. I urged them to gently move things around, to stir his curiosity before they showed themselves.

Except Owain took things into his own hands before I even had time to finish.

'HOLY MOTHER OF FUCK!'

I rushed into the bar to see Dog white and shaking with his back pressed up against the wall. Owain was sat in his usual place, his eyes fixed on Dog in a steely stare.

'Owain, you dickhead! I said gently show yourself not just full on scare the living shit out of him!' I shouted.

Deri and Bronwen obviously then decided that it was too late for the gently approach so appeared at the table that Dog had just leapt up from.

I rushed over to Dog to try and calm him down.

'Hey hey, it's okay my darling! I had the same reaction the first time I met them! They won't hurt you honest!!'

Dog pushed past me and tried to open the front door, which I'd locked behind me when we arrived.

'Let me out of this fucking place right now!! You are off your nut Rosie!'

With the door in danger of being ripped off its hinges, I complied with Dog's wishes. I unlocked the door and watched as the potential love of my life jumped into his van and sped his way out of Mynydd Eira and possibly out of my life.

I slammed the door behind me, marched up to Owain who was still sat on the windowsill.

'I fucking hate you! I wish you'd just stayed dead!'

After a fractious night, I received the inevitable text message from Dog the following morning.

'I'm sorry but I don't think I can see you anymore. I think you need help'

As tears began to fall onto my mobile screen, I quietly kicked myself for spectacularly misreading the signs. He may have been open minded about all things Pagan but obviously, being faced with the reality that ghosts do exist was just a step too far. Part of me could understand why he had freaked out. I remembered my own reactions the very first time I'd met my three. How I cowered behind the bar not wanting to come out, only to be coaxed out by Sue. My initial upset quickly turned to anger however after reading the text message again. What did he mean I needed 'help'? Was he implying that I was a nutcase who had orchestrated an elaborate show to frighten him to death? I understood his reaction, that was a given. I couldn't be angry at him for that. It had taken me a long time to accept what I had gotten myself into with Owain, Deri and Bronwen. What I couldn't understand was the cold, harsh way he ended our relationship. I thought we had something meaningful and solid to nurture into a possible long-term partnership. It had only been a few months but in those few months, it was if we were one person. A deeper connection than anything a physical relationship could ever bring. Obviously not. I could feel my heart hardening again with each passing moment. I was still angry with Owain but I knew that I couldn't stay angry with him for long. I had love in my heart for them and no one could ever take that away. It was blatantly apparent that my life's choice would be them and there was no place for any other. I'd had my fleeting moment of love and now it was gone.

My world was like a constant loop in time. Déjà vu had become normality for me. Days and weeks passed without a word from Dog. My phone had become a silent slab of useless technology. There was no ringtone of excitement, no text message of belonging. I did think about throwing it down the toilet but that would've been a bit drastic as well as expensive. I avoided looking at the photos in the gallery, I deleted all the messages I'd saved. I'd lived through hurt before and I knew that in time, it would become another ache in the compartment of pain.

I'd made up with Owain after about two weeks. He lurked sheepishly around in the shadows, realising his rash decision to shock had spectacularly backfired this time. He apologised in his own way. He wasn't one to say sorry in as many words but he showed it by leaving little things around the pub. I found a flower on the sideboard in one of the bedrooms, my favourite book open on the table by the fire at a profound page. A month after my enforced solitude, I found a hand delivered letter addressed to me by the telephone in the bar. I recognised the writing but it really couldn't be from who I thought.

Or could it?

I slowly opened the envelope. The faint smell of my favourite perfume radiated from the pages within. I took it to the table by the fire and sat down to read whatever words lay inside.

'Dear Rosie

I've written this letter a thousand times. I didn't think I was going to send this one but the more time I took to write, the less time I had to try and explain my behaviour before you threw it in the bin without reading it.

Before I go on, I want to say that what I wrote, that you 'needed help' was unforgivable! It was cruel and I've kicked myself every day since I sent that text. I wanted to contact you every day since but I knew that you would understandably tell me to go fuck myself.

Rosie, you meant more to me than anyone. You touched my heart, my soul. You were my intellectual equal. You were 'the one' and I screwed it up by squealing like a girl and running away. When that 'person' just appeared from nowhere, I'm ashamed to say, I freaked out. You did try to tell me whilst in Glastonbury and I didn't believe you. I am a sceptic, Rosie but I'm prepared to be shown otherwise. That's if you find it in your heart to give me another chance. I miss you, Rosie. I never told you during our time together but I've fallen in love with you. If you choose to get back in touch, I'll be so happy to hear from you. If you choose not to, you will always stay in my heart. I wish you all the happiness in the world. I'm sure someone else will have the honour of your love and it will be my loss. You are a very special person, please never forget that.

My love now and always,

Dog

I gently put the letter on the table and sat back in my chair. He finally proclaimed his love for me and admitted that he could've handled the situation better. Part of me wanted to do exactly as he said I would. My heart, however, was telling me different. I missed him, I loved him. If I didn't give him another chance, would I regret it?

My head started to hurt as I pondered my future. Just as my head was about to explode, Owain appeared. Instead of his usual place on the windowsill, he sat beside me at the table.

'He's outside' he said gently

'Really?' I whispered as he nodded silently in reply.

'What do I do Owain?' I asked as tears started to prick.

'Follow your heart' he said as he slowly disappeared.

CHAPTER NINETEEN

As I took a deep breath, I opened the door and stepped into the unknown. I wasn't entirely sure what I would say to Dog after all these weeks. It was like I was meeting him for the first time. All the memories that we'd shared had been put into the compartment of my brain labelled 'FUBAR'D', alongside all the other 'fucked up beyond all recognition' memories I'd racked up over the years. My heart pounded as I saw his van parked by the signpost where it all began. I saw him as he reached over to open the passenger side door, a sheepish half smile on his face before he sat back over in his own seat. I climbed in, sat down and shut the door. We both stared straight ahead in silence. Gwen was outside her shop, sweeping up as usual, trying not to make it obvious that she was being nosy. It was Dog that broke the silence.

'Obviously got my letter then' he said

'Yep' I replied, slightly venomously

'I'm sorry but…'

Then the pent-up frustration and anger of the previous few weeks came flooding out in two sentences.

'Sorry but?!' I replied, trying not to raise my voice too much.

'Inside every but is an arsehole, Dog!' I hissed, before sinking back in my seat, trying not to pout too much.

I looked across and he was nodding to himself.

'Yep, I can take that one. All I ask is, don't smash my face in too much, I've only cleaned the dashboard and blood is a bitch for getting everywhere'

We looked at each other before bursting out laughing.

'You're a dick!' I laughed, still trying to sound angry but failing miserably.

'So, am I forgiven?' he asked

'Don't push it' I half joked.

I looked forward again before asking the question I needed answering.

'So…you love me then?'

He chuckled to himself

'Stop fishing' he replied. As I looked at him, I could see that he was ever so slightly blushing.

He shifted slightly in his seat to face me full on. Taking my hand in his, he leant forward and gently kissed me.

'I've been a complete dick Rosie. Will you give me another chance please?'

Sincerity filled his eyes and I knew that I couldn't pass the opportunity to be happy again.

As I looked into his hopeful eyes, I whispered

'Yes, I will…but there's one thing you need to do for me first'

'Will you stop pacing about, you're making me feel sick!'

Dog had been walking up and down the bar for ten minutes. He tried sitting down only to get back up again.

'Can't believe I'm doing this!' he sighed as another lap of the bar was completed.

'You promised Dog, remember. Anyway, it really isn't going to be that bad I promise'.

No matter how much I tried to give encouragement, Dog was still pacing.

A whisper in my ear signaled the end to the pacing as I gently told Dog to sit down by the fire and to relax.

'Are you ready? 'I asked

Dog gave me a look as if to say 'go screw yourself' but he wasn't going to get away with going back on a promise. This needed to be done and it needed doing now.

'Right, here we go then…'

Dog's posture stiffened as one by one, Owain, Deri and Bronwen manifested in front of him.

'What the actual f…' Dog whispered as his jaw slowly dropped almost to the floor.

'Dog, I would like to introduce to you my family, well, kind of. This is Deri and Bronwen and that miserable old sod is Owain who you've met before'

Dog sat dumbstruck as Bronwen beamed at him with childlike excitement.

'Ooh Mr. Dog it's so good to finally meet you!' she squealed. I chuckled to myself at how she addressed him.

'I think just Dog would be fine Bronwen' I smiled, winking at her. She nodded, still brimming with excitement.

'Pleased to meet you sir, my name is Deri. I look forward to getting to know you'. Deri extended his hand to Dog. Dog didn't know what to do and looked at me for reassurance.

'It's fine babe, go ahead. You won't feel a handshake as such but just a slight coldness. Time hasn't dulled their manners, well…not everyone's manners anyway'

I shot Owain a look and received a glare in return. Dog reached his hand out towards Deri's. I could see the reaction on Dog's face as he felt the strangest handshake he would ever accept.

'Wow that was weird but thank you' Dog sat back and he and Deri exchanged a nod in acceptance. Now it was Owain's turn. I coughed as if to clear my throat but it was an obvious signal to Owain to get a grip and be nice. He stepped forward towards the table.

'My name is Owain Thomas' he said gruffly. 'Miss Rosie has told me that you are an honourable gentleman and her special companion, so for her sake, I will extend my friendship. I speak as I find, Mr. Pendragon, I hope that won't be of offence to you. Miss Rosie's happiness is all we care about so I trust that you will respect and look after her'.

'Thank you Owain. I give you my word that I will look after Rosie to the best of my ability'

Owain grunted a response, his own way of acknowledging Dog's promise. I had a feeling that the two men would eventually come to a mutual understanding but it was going to take time, effort and possibly the occasional intervention to prevent arguments ending up in property damage. Although Dog was a patient man, Owain had the amazing ability to drive a saint to drink and if he could push my buttons, he would push Dog's even further. This was going to be an even more interesting life.

As time passed, Dog spent more time in Mynydd Eira. It was getting a bit ridiculous for him to travel between his home and mine practically everyday so the decision was made that he would rent out his house and move into my little cottage with me. Living with someone again that was actually alive took some getting used to. I soon realized that Dog had a particular way of doing things. As with all relationships, getting used to living together was going to have a few bumps along the way. Our first 'falling out' was caused by a block of cheese and a cucumber.

'Cheesegate' happened on a Wednesday evening around seven twenty-seven.

'Dog, where's my cheese?' I asked him, as he sat trawling through countless videos on the TV about people trying to sell their, apparently, sentimental valuables then getting a bit miffed when they didn't get the price they wanted. If they were so sentimental, why sell them in the first place! Back to the cheese. As I was trying to eat healthily now I actually had someone to stay healthy for, my cheese consumption had dramatically reduced. I was able to make a block of cheese last for over a week instead of just a few hours. I had carefully wrapped the last bit in a plastic food bag and placed it in the fridge. I'd been waiting until I had the perfect moment to be able to sit and enjoy my beloved cheese and marmite sandwich. I'd been looking forward to the cheese and marmite sandwich all day. Anyone who doesn't like marmite really wouldn't understand the bliss of biting into the taste sensation of the century. When I finally had my moment, I excitedly opened the fridge to retrieve the last bit of the mature cheddar. As I looked onto the empty shelf where the cheese had been, my heart sank. Where was it? It had been there this morning. The Holy Grail of sandwiches was now lost to me!

As I stood looking at Dog, I was hoping he would have an idea of where my cheese had gone.

'So, Dog. WHERE'S MY CHEESE!?'

'What, that tiny bit in the fridge?' he replied, not taking his eyes off the TV.

'I threw it out, it was past it's used by date so didn't think you'd want it now'.

Just like in the films when something shocking had happened, the walls closed in and a silent scream overwhelmed me.

'It wasn't out of date, it was perfectly fine' I replied, as calmly as I could, my hackles slowly but surely rising. Granted, I wasn't the best at keeping track of use by dates but as long as it wasn't covered in mold, it was perfectly edible.

'It was Rosie, it went out of date yesterday'

That was it, the thought of my beloved cheese and marmite sandwich being lost to me was too much!

'Dog, things don't go off at bloody midnight you know! I was saving that cheese for tonight!'

I stomped off in a spectacular strop. I couldn't even go to Gwen's shop to buy another beloved block of cheese as she had closed early to go to bloody Bingo!

'Cheesegate' lasted for twenty-four hours before I eventually stopped sulking.

Domestic bliss ensued as normal. I'd forgiven Dog for throwing out my cheese and the incident prompted several weeks of amusement for him as he continued to tease me over my spectacular over reaction. However, 'Cucumbergate' was to prove a little trickier.

We both continued to try and eat a little more healthily now we had each other to look after. Salads had become the meal of choice and each week, the fridge was full of lettuce, red peppers, spring onions and cucumbers. I was still getting used to buying food for two and my fear of running out had become a little obsessive. My lack of being able to throw anything away was getting out of hand and before I knew it, the fridge had become the place of choice for cucumbers to die.

'Cucumbergate' happened the night before the bins were due to go out. As we were determined to be the perfect domesticated couple, we tried our best to recycle everything, including food. As we were sorting out everything that needed to go out for the bin men, I suddenly remembered that I hadn't thrown out the old cucumbers for a while. They'd been left in the salad drawer of the fridge for god only knows how long. I tried getting to the fridge before Dog but I was too late.

'What the fuck is this?' he exclaimed in disgust. He held up a mushy, dripping cucumber that had obviously been forgotten for about a month.

'It looks like the Jolly Green Giant's dick with a raging case of gonorrhea!!'

I started to laugh but the look on Dog's face was not that of amusement.

'You really are a grot Rosie!' he shouted, as he poured the mushy mess into a recycling bag.

'It's only a cucumber Dog, settle down will you!', I retorted, feeling a little angry at being called a grot.

And that's when the bomb went off. I could see Bronwen appear in the corner of the kitchen before hastily disappearing just as Dog kicked the full black bin bag across the kitchen and straight through her. That caused me to start shouting and cursing and before we knew it, both of us were in a fully-fledged domestic row! I had the most annoying habit of bursting into tears whenever I was angry and unfortunately, this was no exception. I wanted to smash him in the face with a shovel and bury him under the patio by this point but all I could do was cry. Dog stormed off to bed after calling me pathetic and I decided that if he had any chance of not being smothered by a pillow during the night, I crawled into the spare bed. One mushy cucumber had caused a whirlwind of shit. The following morning, we both sheepishly said good morning to each other as I politely handed him a cup of tea.

'Do you want a cucumber with that?' I smirked

'Fuck…off…' he laughed as we both hugged each other.

'I'm sorry I let the cucumber die in the fridge'. I looked up at him with my puppydogeyes, wondering if my womanly wiles would have the desired, apologetic effect.

'Yeah I'm sorry too. I didn't mean to kick that bin bag. I did kind of over react just a bit'.

He kissed the top of my head and held me closer.

'You do realise that you kicked that bag right through poor old Bronwen!' I giggled, as I remembered the look of horror on Bronwen's face as a black bag went hurtling through her.

Apart from the normal teething problems of getting used to sharing personal space again, Dog and I went from strength to strength. I'd learnt to forgive him for leaving the toilet seat up every time he went. I learnt to always wear my slippers to the bathroom after one too many times of having wet feet due to those manly mishaps of completely missing the toilet bowl. He had learnt to forgive my obsessive compulsion to feed the five thousand even though it was just the two of us.

Six months into our relationship, we faced our first real test. I was getting ready for work when my mobile rang. Only Dog and Sue rang my mobile so I knew that something was very wrong.

'Rosie...' sobbed Sue at the other end, 'can you and Dog come quickly. I think Nick's just died'

My heart stopped for a brief second as I tried to comprehend what I'd just heard. I told Sue to call an ambulance and that we'd be right there. Luckily Dog had the day off and I jumped on the bed to rouse him from a deep sleep. As he tried to wake himself up enough to be able to listen to my mad ramblings, I was dressed and running for the front door.

As I ran to the pub, I could hear sirens in the distance getting louder and louder. The ambulance pulled up outside the pub and I directed them to Sue and Nick's cottage beyond the carpark. I let the paramedics go into the house before me so they could tend to Nick upstairs. I shouted to Sue that I was there but all I could hear was a distressed voice, begging them to help him. I sat on the stairs and waited. Dog arrived soon after and sat on the stairs beside me, trying his best to reassure me that everything was being done to help Nick.

All too soon, a paramedic appeared at the top of the stairs. He gently called me up. Outside Sue and Nick's bedroom, he told me in a kind but matter of fact manner, that Nick had suffered a massive heart attack and despite their best efforts, he had died. Dog steadied me as my legs buckled from beneath me. All I wanted to do was curl up in a ball and disappear into the abyss of my grief. I'd travelled this road before. Suddenly, visions of the Man in the Black Hat came flooding back. As he smirked and hissed, he tried to cover me in a cloak of darkness. This time however, I had an even bigger army to fight him.

'Rosie...Rosie...come on babe. We need to be strong for Sue, do you think you can do that?' I heard Dog say from what seemed a mile away. The Man in the Black Hat slowly retreated, his eyes glowed red as his face contorted into an angry, defeated sneer. He slowly disappeared as the light overtook the darkness once more. I looked into Dog's compassionate eyes. I steadied myself and took a deep breath before quietly walking into the bedroom. Sue was sat beside Nick on the bed, his hand in hers. She looked up at me, her face wet with tears. I threw my arms around her and held her as she sobbed. The paramedics had called the doctor to come and examine Nick to pronounce what we already knew. I heard voices on the landing then the doctor walked into the room. He kindly and gently helped Sue stand up from the bed and I led her downstairs in order for the doctor to do his job. As Dog made tea in the kitchen, Sue and I sat close on the settee, my arm around her shoulders. She had gone quiet now, tears still rolling down her face. I knew from experience that she was going into shock. Once the doctor had examined Nick, he came into the living room to express his condolences. I asked him if he wouldn't mind taking a look at Sue before he left. He took her blood pressure which was naturally elevated and prescribed some short- term sedatives to help her through the next few days. The doctor asked to talk to me so Dog sat with Sue and encouraged her to drink her tea. I took the doctor into the kitchen and closed the door.

'I'm so sorry for your loss. If it's any comfort, your father didn't feel any pain'.

My father.

As much as I loved my real dad, Nick had been the best father figure I could've wished for.

'Thank you', I sniffed 'Nick wasn't my dad but he was like a dad to me.'

The doctor nodded.

'I'm really sorry but because it was a sudden death, there needs to be a post mortem. I'm pretty certain that it was a cardiac arrest but until an official cause of death, I'm unable to issue a death certificate at this time. I'll arrange for a private ambulance to come and take the body to...'

'Nick' I interrupted, 'his name is…was… Nick'. A huge lump formed in my throat.

'Yes of course, I do apologise. I'll arrange for a private ambulance to come and collect Nick and take him to the hospital. Hopefully it shouldn't be too long before Nick can be released back to you and his wife in order for you to make arrangements'.

I nodded silently as he extended his hand to shake mine. He then walked back into the living room and gave his condolences to Sue again before leaving the house.

'You can go and sit with him if you want to Rosie' whispered Sue as she sat back in the sofa, her arms around a cushion. I kissed Sue on the top of the head before asking Dog if he would look after her.

As I slowly climbed the stairs, I didn't know what I was going to say to Nick. I silently opened the door, padded over to the bed and sat down beside my beloved friend. He looked so peaceful. The doctor had placed his hands on his chest. I took them in my own and kissed them.

'Thank you so much for looking after me. I know things haven't been easy but I couldn't have made it through without you. I promise I will look after Sue. You both are like parents to me. Well, more than parents…you know what I mean'

Tears rolled down my face but I didn't want to let go of Nick's hands.

'Will you do me a favour please Nick. Will you look after Emily for me when you find her'?

A loud sob caught in my throat. I rose from the bed and lent over. I kissed Nick on the cheek for one last time.

'Goodbye Daddy Nick' I whispered,

'I love you'.

I took one last lingering look at the man who reaffirmed my belief in parental love then closed the door.

CHAPTER TWENTY

It took two weeks before we were able to bring Nick home. The post mortem found that it was indeed, a massive heart attack in his sleep. It would've been quick and painless which was of some comfort to us but still never the less, hard to accept. We made the arrangements with the same funeral directors who looked after Emily. It felt strange going back to their office. The shoe was on the other foot. I was the one who was there supporting Sue in her hour of need. Mr. Williams remembered us and as well as passing on his heartfelt condolences for Sue's loss, he also enquired after my wellbeing after the loss of Emily. All I could do was just smile and thank him for his kindness in asking. All he could do was completely understand that no matter how much time had passed, the pain would never be gone.

We were able to lay Nick to rest close to Emily's grave. It was a comfort to both of us that the ones we loved the most were together. I hoped that Nick had been able to find Emily. Before meeting my three spirits, the thought of relatives being together in Heaven was just a pleasant fiction that had been passed down through the years to give the bereaved some kind of reason for carrying on.

Dog had proved his love and loyalty throughout. There were times that I had been extremely hard to live with. The Man in the Black Hat continued to try and retrieve my soul on several occasions, mostly during the hours of darkness. I'd woken up screaming, my face red with tears and my body drenched in sweat. Dog held me until I was able to fall in a thankfully dreamless sleep.

Sue remained the most remarkable woman I ever had the pleasure of knowing. She took her own grief and turned it into something positive. We all decided that we really didn't want her to live alone. She flatly refused to leave the home she had made so many happy memories with Nick so there was only really one thing left to do.

'Oh my god, look at that one!' I squealed, as Dog rolled his eyes. If he had been given a pound coin for every time I squealed that sentence, he would've been on the first flight to the Maldives for an extended holiday.

Walking around the animal shelter, Sue and I gushed almost embarrassingly at every single puppy. Suddenly, I saw him. His big chocolate brown eyes looked straight into mine. His paws looked way too large for the rest of his body, his tiny legs looked like they belonged to another dog. He was a ten-week-old, Old English sheepdog crossed with a Bearded Collie. His poor mother had been abandoned whilst pregnant and he, alongside his brothers and sisters, had been born in the shelter. He trotted up to the cage door and poked his nose through.

'Ladies and Gentleman, I think we've found him'. I whispered, as he licked my hand.

That's how Paddy came into our lives. With paws as large as his, his name was inevitable. He shared his life with all of us, staying with Sue while we were working then came to stay with us when Sue needed peace and quiet. At first, all Paddy did was eat, sleep and poo. A typical baby really. Then as he grew, he developed a habit of stealing clean knickers out of the washing basket and trotting out to show everyone how clever he was. He would want kisses every time he had a drink, his beard soaking wet and dripping everywhere. He loved to jump onto our laps and fall asleep in our arms. That was perfectly fine whilst he was a baby but true to the size of his paws, he grew…and grew. Before long he came up to the top of my legs and weighed over six stone of fluffy soppiness. We hadn't rehomed a puppy, we had rehomed a small horse in disguise. Bronwen loved him. She would play hide and seek which was quite an advantage for her considering her abilities to be able to disappear at the drop of a hat. The look on Paddy's face whenever she did so was hilarious. He would spend at least ten minutes looking everywhere for her then jump a mile when she reappeared with her arms around him. Even Owain would prove to be a surprise. During the afternoons when the pub was closed, we allowed Paddy to wander around as he pleased, once he was toilet trained of course. True to tradition, he found his favourite spot to curl up. I soon learnt that if I couldn't find him, to look under the table by the fire. Once he was fully grown however, he was easy to spot due to his tail poking out from one end of the table and his head at the other. I would stand by the doorway on many occasions, unseen and quietly watch as Owain sat by the fire, stroking Paddy's head gently and talking in a soothing, almost hypnotic tone. Animals are said to be sensitive to spirit so it wasn't unusual for Paddy to be able to see them. To him, they were just other members of the family to love and cuddle up with. It was like he had become the child of the family, bringing joy back into our lives after the loss of Emily and Nick. Paddy had brought us all back to life.

CHAPTER TWENTY-ONE

As each full moon passed and the seasons changed, my world had become unrecognizable. I was no longer the frightened little girl who had ran away yet again to try to rebuild a life that had crumbled around me. Dog and I were blissfully happy. It seemed that fate had indeed played its part that night, bringing us together when neither of us were really looking for a happy ever after. The Universe obviously had other ideas and I for one, was eternally grateful that it had. On another short break to our spiritual home of Glastonbury, Dog surprised me on our second day. We had climbed to the top of Glastonbury Tor. It was a glorious day. The sun shone through the clouds, shards of light illuminated the Tor with glistening splendour. I was rooting around my backpack trying to find my sunglasses, chastising to myself under my breath about how I could've been so stupid to have left them at the hotel. I was so busy trying to find them that I didn't notice that Dog was nervously pacing around the Tor. I looked up from the bottom of my backpack to see him fumbling around in the pocket of his jeans.

'Have you lost something my love?' I chuckled 'they were there the last time I looked'. I winked at him as he walked over to me, his hand still in his pocket.

'Oh ha bloody ha', he replied as he stood in front of me. He still had a very nervous look on his face and I began to wonder what was wrong.

'Rosie?' he asked, as I finally gave up looking for my sunglasses.

'Yep…' I replied, as I slung the backpack on the ground. I was about to sit on the grass when Dog stopped me.

'No, don't sit down yet!' he exclaimed

I looked down on the grass.

'Why? Oh, is there dog poo down there? Honestly, you would think owners would clean up their dog's crap, even up here!'

'No Rosie, there's no dog shit, well I don't think there is…anyway, shut up for a minute will you, I'm trying to say something'

Suddenly, Dog pulled his hand out from his pocket and went down on one knee.

'Rosie, will you do me the honour of becoming my wife?'

He handed me a box. I opened it to see a beautiful Amethyst and Diamond ring.

I stood there for a moment before flinging my arms around him.

'Oh my god of course I will!' I shrieked. Dog took the ring from the box and slid it onto my finger. It was perfect.

After sharing a long, lingering, blissful kiss, Dog looked deep into my eyes.

'Don't suppose you could help me up now, could you? I'm way too old for this shit, my knees are killing me!'

We married six months later, on the same spot, in a Handfasting ceremony conducted by a Pagan Officiant. As the cords were wrapped around our entwined hands, we vowed to love and protect each other for eternity. Sue looked on, her face radiant with happiness. Paddy sat quietly beside her, before trying to make a bolt for it as he caught sight of a rabbit in the distance. We dissolved into hysterics as Sue almost took flight trying to keep Paddy from disappearing off the edge of the

Tor. Dog quickly intervened, showing his previous skills on the rugby field as he ran after him and tackled our now seven stone lump of fluffiness to the ground. Our marriage started as our relationship had begun, full of laughter and surprises.

As we celebrated our special day within the grounds of the hotel, Sue pulled us to one side and handed us an envelope.

'This is our wedding gift to you both. Nick and I were going to give this to you anyway when the time was right. I think Nick would definitely agree that that time is now'.

I opened the envelope and began to read its contents, my eyes widening with each word read. I handed it to Dog, who gasped before handing the envelope and contents back to me.

I looked at Sue with huge eyes and she smiled back and nodded. I flung my arms around her.

'Are you sure?' I whispered, as I embraced the woman who had loved me like a daughter.

'I could never be surer my darling. Now go and enjoy the rest of your wedding'

We embraced for what seemed like forever before Dog gestured that it was his turn. My heart leapt as I saw the two people I loved the most, hug each other tightly before letting go with a kiss.

'I'm just going to take Paddy for a quick walk' I shouted as I disappeared through the front door of the pub.

Dog popped up from behind the bar.

'Don't be long!! They'll be here soon!'

It was too late, I was already in my car, heading for my destination. As I pulled up in the carpark, I looked up at the mountain that had almost been the last place I ever saw. It had seemed a lifetime ago that I was here, walking the same but different path to the top. As I let Paddy off the lead, he happily ran ahead, occasionally stopping to wait for me.

I finally reached the place where I had felt my life drain from me. Instead of feeling desolation, I had a feeling of complete renewal. As I stood looking at Mynydd Eira below, I made peace with the mountain and the past.

Slowly, one by one, Owain, Deri and Bronwen appeared beside me. The love that had grown between us over time had given them power and strength to go anywhere they wished to go now. They weren't confined to the place where their lives had ended. Although they were free, they chose to stay with me. As I stood with my Spirits of Mynydd Eira beside me, we watched as the sun glistened over the village that had become my haven, my forever home.

'It's time Rosie' Owain whispered in my ear. I nodded as they disappeared. I called Paddy and we scrambled down the mountain and home.

'Where have you been!?' Dog sounded exasperated as I walked through the door.

'Keep your pants on love, I wasn't long. I just had to do something that's all. They're not here yet are they?' I asked

Just then, I heard voices from the carpark. The villagers had all turned out and as we stepped outside, they greeted us with jubilation. Gwen came rushing up and threw her arms around me.

'Oh Rosie, today will be a glorious day!'

Just then, another car pulled up by the signpost. A gentleman climbed out with Sue. She came over and kissed both of us.

Dog had placed a ladder by the front door and Sue's companion greeted him, shaking him warmly by the hand. He handed Dog a black sign with white lettering. Dog carefully climbed the ladder, removed the old sign and replaced it with the new one.

Rosie and Cadog Pendragon, licensees of the Snow Mountain Inn.

Villagers cheered and clapped as Dog climbed down the ladder before taking me into his arms. Sue and Nick had given us the pub. It was now our legacy to nurture and cherish. I looked over to see Owain, Deri and Bronwen looking out of the window, a look of complete happiness on each of their faces. We were officially their Guardians, their family, for the rest of our lives. The day was filled with merriment and celebration. After the last of the villagers had left, we closed the pub and collapsed exhausted by the fire. Sue had spent her last day officially working in the pub. She was taking a well-deserved retirement. Although she was still only going to be next door, the reigns had well and truly been transferred. The air had suddenly chilled more than usual. Owain, Deri and Bronwen appeared side by side, looking over at the far wall of the pub. 'What's up? I asked I stood up and walked over to them. 'What are you looking at?' A cold wind blasted through the pub as the energy changed from its usual calm. Chairs and tables suddenly started to rattle and slide across the floor. Paddy stood with his head cocked to one side and began to whine at the wall. He suddenly darted underneath his safe haven table by the fire, his paws over his eyes as if he didn't want to see what was about to unfold. 'Oh My!' exclaimed Bronwen, as she put her hand over her mouth. Deri looked over to the wall, his eyes widened with each passing second. 'Now this is going to be interesting' said Owain 'Rosie, I think this is for you' As I looked over to the far wall, three shadows began to form, becoming clearer and clearer. Dressed in jeans and black shirts, the young men stood there, smiling. Their faces familiar, their eyes the same. 'What the hell…' I whispered. As I slowly walked towards them, they stepped forward and reached out for my hand. 'Hang on a minute, do you mind if you told me who the hell you are first!' I shouted, as the familiar feeling of wanting to hide behind the bar washed over me. I looked towards Dog for reassurance but like before, he had his back pressed against the wall. 'Don't look at me love, I'm just starting to get used to the three we've already got!' he protested, as the colour drained out from underneath his beard. I turned and looked at Owain, Deri and Bronwen. Owain just shrugged his shoulders and grunted. 'We know nothing about them I'm afraid' said Deri, who looked as confused as everyone else.

The three strangers continued to smile at me. 'Well? Are you going to tell me exactly who you are and why the hell the pub's just suddenly become Grand Central Spook Station!' 'We never meant to frighten you, Mum.' they chuckled in unison. The walls suddenly started to spin. 'Mu..mu..mum?' I stuttered, as i steadied myself on a bar stool. ' We've been sent to help you Mum. We've been sent to help our sister.' 'Sis..Sister?' My power of speech had suddenly become as useless as I was. Suddenly, the middle one of the three spoke. 'Oh, no, not Emily. She's fine, she's with Nanna Rose and Grandad Sam, she's driving them nuts by the way.' Their faces lit up even more at the mere mention of Emily's name. Was this a sick joke? 'Well if you're not here to help with Emily, then who the hell are you going on about?' I exclaimed, as my hackles began to rise. The mood suddenly darkened and the temperature dropped even further. They all approached me and i felt as each one put their hand on my stomach. 'They're coming for her Mum, He's coming…' My secret was one I could no longer hide. 'Who's coming for her? I whispered, desperation catching in my throat as my hands covered my stomach to protect my unborn child. 'Demons, mum, demons, and one in particular'.

As I tried to take in what was being said, I glanced over to the window. As the sun set, a shadow figure stood by the signpost. An all too familiar figure. As he looked back at me through the window, he took his hand and raised his black hat. His eyes glowed as he began to laugh. He placed his black hat back onto his head and slowly walked away. As he did so, I could see several pairs of glowing red eyes stare into my very soul, as the darkness finally overtook the last shards of light. He was real and he had an army. The battle was only just beginning.

35411917R00143

Printed in Poland
by Amazon Fulfillment
Poland Sp. z o.o., Wrocław